ALEX BLACKMORE

gained an LLB and LPC in law at Nottingham University and went on to practice as a finance lawyer in the City. After five years in the world of corporate finance and banking, she moved into legal and financial writing and editing before moving into freelance writing full-time. She runs a copywriting business and a fashion website championing new designers, and lives in North London with Isabella, Michael and a stubborn dachshund.

ALEX BLACKMORE

LETHAL PROFIT

TORONTO • NEW YORK • LONDON
AMSTERDAM • PARIS • SYDNEY • HAMBURG
STOCKHOLM • ATHENS • TOKYO • MILAN
MADRID • WARSAW • BUDAPEST • AUCKLAND

For Mum, Dad, Pippa, Kasra and B

Recycling programs
for this product may
not exist in your area.

ISBN-13: 978-0-373-18969-4

Lethal Profit

Copyright © 2013 by Alex Blackmore

A Worldwide Library Suspense/May 2015

First published by No Exit Press, an imprint of Oldcastle Books Ltd.

Printed in U.S.A.

LETHAL PROFIT

Acknowledgments

I would like to thank John and Vicky for everything from listening to crazy plot ideas to motivational phone calls; Kasra who underwrote my break for freedom; Pippa for the endless coffee and inspiration; friends who have listened and advised—Bea, Anna, Jacinta, Will, Katie, JP, Emily, Lizzie, Rachel, Alice, Adam; Annette who saw something in my writing and went out on a limb; everyone at No Exit for the support and guidance and taking a chance on a new writer with a stubborn streak.

ONE

THE LIGHT IN the bar was dim; the plush velvet of the seating and the garish gold leaf of the furnishings had all begun to meld into one. Eva tightened her grip around the base of her champagne glass as if it might sober her up. She looked along the small stretch of dark oak wood bar between her and the man sitting opposite her.

He met her gaze as he continued to speak. For a second Eva thought she had seen something in those deep blue pools that sent a shiver down her spine. Something predatory and cold. He blinked, his eyes cleared and the feeling left her.

I SHOULD GO back to my hotel, Eva thought to herself. But the idea of the bleak, cold room near the Gare du Nord was nowhere near as attractive as this seductive, warm hotel bar where the waiters scrambled to pop the cork on another bottle of Bollinger each time March produced his card.

She straightened up on her stool and forced herself to ask a question. March had been speaking for what seemed like hours—he always had liked the sound of his own voice. He and her brother Jackson had been friends at school before Jackson disappeared suddenly, aged 18. In the eleven years since then March—a nickname, his surname was 'Marchment'—had stopped dressing like his father and punctuating all his sentences with 'like', and apparently developed quite a thing for a Tom Ford suit.

'You look tired,' he was saying as Eva felt herself sway slightly on the bar stool. She stared at his expensive jacket as something metallic on his breast pocket caught her eye. Looking closer she saw it was a small acorn. She looked away when she realised he was waiting for a response.

'Yeah, it's been a long, unproductive day.'

'Have you been able to speak to any of Jackson's friends?'

'No.' She sighed. 'I've been in Paris a week now and all I've really managed to do is track down someone Jackson apparently spent five minutes with before he dropped off the radar.'

'What's his name?'

'Shaun Thompson.'

'It's a start.'

'I'm trying to look at it that way but I can't imagine he's going to be much help. He shared a cigarette with Jackson just before he disappeared but I don't think they even exchanged names.'

'Did the police not tell you much about Jackson's death?'

'They did and they didn't. I've seen a summary police report but it's not exactly detailed—it could be about anyone.'

'Non-specific?'

'Puzzlingly so. I know that Jackson and I weren't that close any more—after he went missing at school we all thought he was dead. I spent an entire decade believing that. It was…' She hesitated. '…difficult when he suddenly appeared again.' Eva forced the words out. She didn't find it easy to talk about.

'But in that year after he was suddenly there again, I felt like he was happy here in Paris. He was working for that aid agency, he had friends, a pretty girlfriend, lots to live for. Why would he…' Eva's voice trailed away.

As she was discovering, grief tended to sweep over her in sudden waves that completely took her legs away. Although she had already grieved once for Jackson when the family was told he had died in a car accident all those years ago, and then soon after for her mother, for some reason this time it had hit her much harder. She looked helplessly at March, tears filling her eyes. She felt her mouth open and close several times before she was able to whisper '…why would he kill himself…?' March nodded in that comfortingly well-bred way which indicated enough had been said and she could stop being emotional. 'Want some water?' Eva shook her head and took a big gulp of her drink. She forced herself to calm down.

'What about the girlfriend?' said March, giving her just enough time to pull herself together.

'I've got her number but she's screening my calls.'

'If I'd have known he was living here I would have got in touch. I can't believe we were in the same city for three years without knowing it.'

'None of us knew he was here.'

'He must have had other friends in Paris?' Eva had now succeeded in righting herself.

'Same thing. Either the French are a bloody rude race, or these particular people don't want to speak to me,' she joked, trying to pretend she hadn't just peeled the walls of her chest open and shown him how much she was hurting inside.

He smiled. 'I've lived here five years and I can tell you now, it's a combination of both. You'll get there.' Eva drained her glass. 'I know you're right.' She was grateful for the support. Most people thought she was crazy for coming over here on a hunch. If the police said Jackson had shot himself, then he had shot himself.

'I'd probably better get back,' she said as she felt another wave of emotion threatening.

'I'll walk you home.' As they stepped out of the bar into the cold November air, Eva began to feel herself sobering up. The sky above them was a dark, velvety black with an orange glow and there were stars twinkling everywhere she looked. She let March direct their steps; he lived in Paris after all so he was less likely to lead them in the wrong direction. However, after a while Eva realised that she was recognising some of the sights around them and they seemed to be walking away from her hotel, not towards it.

'March, are we going in the right direction?' He looked around. 'Think so.' They carried on walking in silence for several minutes until Eva stopped. She laughed as she spoke. 'Look, I'm not being funny but I think my hotel is the other way!' March smiled but said nothing. The hair began to stand up on the back of Eva's neck. There was that same look she'd seen in the bar. He looked like a wolf.

She took an involuntary step backwards, but he anticipated her movement and lunged for her, grabbing hold of the front of her coat, pulling her off her feet, then dragging her with him as he stepped quickly from the quiet street they had been walking down into an alleyway lined with enormous refuse bins. Eva opened her mouth to scream but, as March shoved her upright against one of the bins, he knocked all the breath out of her. She struggled to breathe as she felt him tearing at her coat. Disbelief screamed in her head at what was apparently unfolding but she felt paralysed by the shock. She glanced at the street but it was completely empty, not even a single light on in any of the homes. Suddenly her breath returned and her senses roared into action.

'Stop! What are you doing!' He punched her in the face, hard. She stumbled sideways, reaching out for something to hold her up but she was seeing stars and her hands flailed uselessly at nothing. She landed hard on the ground and immediately he was on top of her. He went to hit her again but she managed to block him groggily with her forearm; the pain of the blow made her scream out loud. He grabbed both her wrists, wrapped one hand around them and pulled them back over her head. His grip was like iron, she couldn't rip her hands apart. She screamed as loud as she could and he slapped her with his free hand. 'Shut up,' he spat at her. 'Just shut up. You can go when I've finished with you.' He started unbuttoning his trousers.

Eva looked him straight in the eye. 'Daniel, you were Jackson's friend,' she said, calling him by his real name, 'you were once my friend. Why are you doing this?' She realised she was crying.

'I'm not your friend. You have no friends here.' Having already ripped open her coat he was now tearing at her jeans, cursing as he realised how tight they were. Suddenly he swore and stopped. He let her go, moved to a crouch and paused. Eva held her breath. Was it over?

Slowly, March pulled out a flick knife from one beautifully-tailored pocket and opened the blade.

'Take them off.' Eva's pulse went through the roof at the sight of the knife. She glanced past him at the end of the alley only metres away but even if someone did walk past there were no lights where they were.

'Please don't.' She whispered.

'Do it now or I'll fucking cut you.' She opened her mouth to speak again but he jabbed the blade in her direction. Eva felt anger ripple over the back of her scalp. Had this been his intention all along? She had met him because she had felt so lonely…so confused about Jackson… Stupid girl. Her tears began to dry up. She slowly undid the patent belt and slid it from the belt loops and then she began to unbutton her jeans. She tried to pull them off but they were too skinny. 'I need to stand up. I can't get them off lying down.'

'Hurry up,' he roared at her. For the first time that night she realised his eyes were unfocused. Whether it was lust, power, or control she didn't know, but March was drunk on it. She hesitated for a split second and then flicked her leg up and kicked him hard in the face. March, surprised, fell back, dropped the knife, but managed to steady himself on one hand and lunged for it as it skittered towards a bin. As he dived left, Eva ran right, grabbing her bag from where it had fallen behind them and running as fast as she could out of the alleyway. She heard him curse and start running after her but she had already reached the end of the alley and as she threw herself around the corner she thought she could hear his footsteps slow. But she did not slow. Eva ran every day—seven miles, come hell or high water—and she finished every run with a sprint. That's what she did now, in four-inch heels, down a dark and empty road in the wrong part of Paris. She ran.

As Eva examined her face in the bathroom mirror the next day she felt pretty low. Overnight, the black eye that March had kindly given her had developed into a large purplish splat, with black bruising in the eye socket. When she had got back to the hotel she had spent several hours sitting bolt upright on the bed watching the chair she had propped up against the door. The sudden assault had shocked and shaken her; she had remained for a long time just sitting, staring at the door, catching each one of her thoughts when it came too close to out of control. She tried to work out what had happened; she briefly wondered whether she had done something to make it happen, but she quickly stifled those trains of thought as pointless and dangerous. Finally, her pulse had stopped thudding, her mind had stopped racing and she had passed out, exhausted, fully clothed in all her make-up. Now she looked like a police mug shot. Gently, she began to clean away mascara and eye-liner from the edges of her eyes. The make-up-removing wipes stung her black eye and she winced with each stroke. She stopped and looked at herself—dishevelled long dark hair, low fringe swept awkwardly to one side, face just a bit too thin.

'What the hell are you doing?' she said out loud to herself. But there was no reply.

As she turned on the shower and stepped into the hot clouds of steam she wondered again what the hell she was doing. Three months ago her life had been relatively normal. She edited other people's words for a living—a dream job—she lived in London with her house-mate Isabella and she spent most of her time going from gig, to party, to shopping, to long lazy weekends. Her only real faults were an addiction to running and an inability to put the cap on the toothpaste. Then Jackson killed himself.

She heard her phone ringing as she stepped out of the shower but she let it ring, slowly dried herself and then sat down on the bed. She had just begun to get to know Jackson again—after ten years of thinking he had died in a car crash when she was sixteen. He'd promised to tell her exactly what had happened and where he had been all that time but after a year he still hadn't and Eva felt his presence in her life was too fragile to risk pushing him to open up. Now he never would. Eva sighed and pulled the small handset over to her and watched as the phone notified her of a missed call two minutes ago. She navigated her way through her phone records. And then she stopped. Suddenly she felt as if she had been punched in the stomach. There on the screen was the identity of the caller: 'Jackson.' As she continued to stare at the white display, suddenly the phone jumped into life and the name was large, filling the whole screen. 'Jackson calling.' Eva dropped the phone and pushed herself away from it, as if she had been stung. What the… He's alive.

Just before the ringing stopped, she made a grab for the phone.

'Hello.' Her voice was tense and hard.

There was a crackle on the other end of the line. Eva had absolutely no idea what to do. 'Jackson?' It sounded crazy just saying his name. He was dead. But he was calling her…'Jackson…' Her voice was now almost a whisper. She pressed the phone closer to her ear listening for signs of anything on the other end and then she heard it. A breath. An exhalation. There was someone there.

'Jackson, is that you?' The connection cut and once

again Eva dropped the phone. She stared at it. For one delirious moment she allowed herself to believe that the whole horrible nightmare of the past three months was just another bad dream. But every logical cell in her body told her that it couldn't be.

JACKSON'S DEATH HAD been reported to the family by the French police. It had a stamp of official authenticity on it which meant that no matter how much Eva wanted to believe it had been a mistake, that it was someone else who had taken his own life in a squalid flat in a Parisian suburb, it was there in black and white that it was Jackson. The police said they had found him surrounded by the paraphernalia of a serious heroin session. There were puncture wounds in his skin. The area was notorious for drugs and violence, and drugs and violence were notorious for triggering depression and suicide.

They suggested he had got himself in so deep there was no other way out. They intimated he was a coward whose life had become out of control and that he had just given up. But Eva had lived with him for sixteen years and even though he had badly let her down, she knew he had never given up on anything.

TWO

Wʜᴇɴ sʜᴇ ʜᴀᴅ recovered her composure Eva suddenly knew that there was something very wrong with the situation she found herself in. From the evasive answers she and her father had been given by the French police three months ago, to the phone call she had just received, every one of the circumstances surrounding Jackson's death made her seriously uneasy. Her skin was still tingling with adrenaline after seeing Jackson's name appear on her phone like that; she was naturally sceptical as to whether or not it was really him, but who else would it be? Even if it wasn't him, it was someone who had his phone.

Briefly, she remembered the horrible encounter with March the night before. When she had awoken that morning her mind had once again begun to turn over everything that had happened but she had quickly decided not to think about it anymore. March had the problem, not her, and she needed to be clear-headed. Still, she wondered if he had any involvement in what had happened to Jackson. As he himself had said, he had been in Paris the whole time Jackson had lived here and he had attacked her so savagely the night before for no apparent reason. But realistically, what motive did he have for murder? It was more likely that he was just a serial opportunist.

Still sitting on the bed with the phone beside her, wet

hair dripping onto her shoulders, Eva realised she had a clear choice.

Either she took the advice of the friends who kept worriedly messaging her from home, headed back to London and tried to carry on with her life; or she followed her hunch that Jackson had not taken his own life and struck out on her own: Eva Scott, vigilante. She smiled resignedly to herself. In reality she knew that there was no choice for her. She was just a regular person who had taken a few self-defence classes—she was hardly prepared for even mild peril—but she couldn't live with the knowledge that she had done nothing to find out what happened to Jackson. That wouldn't be right. Especially after that, she thought, looking at her phone.

She pulled on a pair of tight, black jeans, a wide-necked, cable-knit jumper and some leather ankle boots and combed out her long dark hair. Then she walked over to the curtains, drawing them back and letting the weak, milky light filter into the room. She threw open the window and was met with a bracing gust of Parisian air—coffee-edged with a slight hint of drains.

Coffee. She needed coffee.

EVA WAS ETERNALLY grateful for the fact that Paris was a city of pavement cafés and bars serving a universally high standard of coffee. She sat in the corner of a small establishment near her hotel, hunched over an English newspaper she'd bought on the way. In front of her, a black coffee, a glass of water, an untouched croissant and a small red plastic bowl containing a printed receipt. She added another sachet of sugar to the thick, dark liquid, stirred it slowly with a spoon and then placed the spoon carefully on the side of the saucer. She turned the page of the paper and took a slow sip of the strong coffee.

In front of her, the world's current affairs were laid out like a depressing comic. Pictures of politicians showing off their veneers, footballers in thousands of pounds worth of designer clothes cheating on their wives, and financiers striking deals that would benefit only the 1 per cent. This was the first recession she had really experienced and she had never imagined how much it would change the country she had lived in all her life. In the past few months the news had seemed even more unbelievable—banks manipulating exchange rates for their own profits, political figures making decisions against public interests motivated by big business and the destruction of seemingly permanent institutions like the National Health Service. It shocked and surprised her that—on the whole—whilst all this damage was being done to their society most Britons did nothing. But then neither did she. At the tender age of twenty-eight she had become utterly apathetic; too concerned with her own survival to put time and effort into holding anyone else to account. Jackson had left her money—an unexpectedly large amount of money—and that gave her the luxury of inaction. Without that her life right now would be very difficult.

EVA FINISHED HER coffee and signalled to the waiter for another.

She took an unenthusiastic bite of her croissant. Jackson. All her thoughts came back to Jackson. Even now there was another memory, waiting at the edge of her consciousness to be let in. This was one of the fights they'd had as teenagers, often about politics—she blinkeredly left-wing and he already a staunch capitalist. Their father, a journalist for a big daily, had encouraged them to debate and question from an early age, to speak out when they felt they saw injustice. Of course, that had massively backfired on him when his affair had been uncovered. She had no doubt he had wished then that he had raised his kids to be seen and not heard.

Jackson, especially, had been unable even to look his father in the eye when that happened. At eighteen he still looked up to Paul Scott with childishly adoring eyes, but his father's affair with Irene Hunt—cheating on their mother after twenty years of marriage—enraged Jackson. When he crashed his car several weeks later he simply walked away, leaving the family to believe he had died. In recent months Eva had realised that she never really grieved for Jackson in the ten years that followed. Not like she was now. Perhaps somewhere deep down she had known he wasn't actually dead. She checked the display on her phone and saw she had been sitting there for half an hour. Throwing a note and a few coins into the red plastic bowl, she zipped up her leather jacket, jammed a Russian hat down over her ears and headed for the door.

THE TRAIN TO the suburb where Shaun Thompson lived took less than half an hour, but getting off at the station was like stepping into another world. Whilst Eva was used to the dirty, occasionally mean streets of London, by comparison Shaun lived in a very rough suburb. The area was populated with low, square blocks of flats up to four storeys high, either dirtily whitewashed or preserved in their original grey concrete. Other than the flats and the graffiti that decorated them, the area didn't seem to have much else to offer. Gangs of kids of all origins hung around, hands in pockets, kicking balls at passers-by or listening to music pumping out from the tinny speakers on their phones.

Eva felt the heaviness of being a fish out of water. She wondered why Shaun, as a foreigner, and therefore presumably a natural outsider, had made his home somewhere like this. She pulled the Post-it note she had written his address on out of her bag and looked at it again: 134 Rue des Villiers. According to the very old map she had managed to acquire from her hotel—the only one they had that went out as far as this suburb—the flat was on the same road as the station.

When she reached it, she found that Shaun's block of flats was one of the nicest on the street, although that wasn't saying much. Running to four storeys, the white-wash had retained a little of its gleam and someone had planted flowerbeds either side of the path leading from the road to the front door. There was a small, white-haired man standing outside with a brush, repeatedly sweeping the same spot of concrete.

'Hello.' Eva smiled directly at him, choosing to speak English to try and discover straight away whether she could avoid having a whole conversation in painful broken French. The man continued to sweep his spot and totally ignored her.

'Hello?' As she leaned in a little closer, Eva noticed he was singing to himself and smelled quite badly of urine.

'Oh, I'm sorry, don't mind my father.' She jumped as a younger woman appeared from the ground floor flat and placed her hands around the old man's shoulders. He stopped rocking and looked at her.

'Can I help at all?'

'You speak English.' Eva smiled, unable to contain her relief.

'Yes, I learned from my father, he used to be very good at it.' She stopped and gazed at the vacant old man.

'I'm sorry,' said Eva awkwardly.

'It will happen to us all someday!' the woman said cheerfully and rearranged her long, dark hair into a tortoiseshell comb that sat just above her left ear. 'Did you want something?'

'Yes, I'm looking for someone called Shaun Thompson. Apparently he lives here.'

'Shawan...?' The woman frowned.

'Thompson.' The woman thought for a second. 'You know, I know everyone in this block—there are only sixteen flats—and there is no one by that name.'

'I was given this as his address.' Eva handed over the Post-it note.

'Well, this is the same address. Are you sure they have the right person?'

'Yes, I think so. He's English?'

'But, of course, that's Shoon!' Eva stared at the woman nonplussed, wondering if she was as mad as her father.

'Yes, he's the only English person for miles around. Yes, Shoon,' she said again, saying the name so that it sounded nothing like Eva's pronunciation—the English pronunciation.

'He lives at number nine—third floor, second door on the right. You'll have to take the stairs, I'm afraid, as the lift is broken.' She smiled apologetically and put her hands back on the old man's shoulders, gently drawing him back to the flat.

'Nice to meet you.'

'Thanks very much.' Eva followed the couple in through the front door and then started up the first set of concrete stairs that, like all stairwells, seemed to smell of smoke and urine. When she reached the third floor, she followed the woman's instructions and went to Shaun's door. His name was scrawled neatly in a small plastic box on the right but there didn't appear to be a bell. She took her hat off and shoved it into her bag, knocked quickly at the scuffed surface of the wooden door and waited. No answer. She waited a couple of minutes and then knocked again but there was still no response. Glancing around to make sure no one was looking she pressed her left ear up against the door to try and detect signs of movement. The door creaked open. Eva stepped back. She looked around again to see if any of the other residents in the housing block had noticed her, but there didn't seem to be anyone around. Gently, she pushed the door so that it was fully open and took several steps inside.

'Hello?…er…Shaun?' No answer.

Eva walked further into the flat then paused and looked back at the open doorway. Still no sound came from the hallway. If anyone had noticed, they were keeping themselves to themselves. She took a deep breath. Was she really going to do this? She wanted to find Shaun himself, not go searching through his flat. And why was his front door open? Realising she was probably wasting her time, she turned back towards the door, about to leave. Suddenly she stopped.

In the corner of the door leading through to what looked like the living room was a bare foot, sole up. The foot was completely still. Eva stepped closer, her heart almost stopping as she held her breath, knowing there was only going to be one outcome to this regrettable burst of curiosity.

She walked quickly into the living room, came to a sudden halt and rocked backwards on her heels, a scream stuck somewhere in the back of her throat. Oh my God.

A MAN—PRESUMABLY Shaun—stared back at her from the floor, eyes wide and bulging. His mouth was open and gaping and his body was lying twisted at an unnatural angle, his lower half facing down and his upper torso twisted so that from the waist up he was lying on his side, almost on his back. A wave of nausea overwhelmed Eva and she turned out of the living room door and retched. When she managed to compose herself she looked again at the corpse; his eyes were wide open, desperate, almost surprised, his naked body so white against the faux wood flooring. She took several steps towards him, slowly bent down and felt for a pulse, just in case. Nothing. She stepped back again. She had never seen a corpse before; the complete stillness was unnerving. There were red marks around Shaun's wrists but other than that she couldn't see anything on the flaxen white skin that could explain his sudden demise. There was no blood, no knife wound, no ligature marks around the neck. She took a tentative step forward and leaned in closer, fighting her imagination that was convinced he would rear up and suddenly grab at her like a character from a cheap horror film.

THEN SHE NOTICED an angry red dot on the back of his right thigh. It was tiny and wouldn't have attracted her attention except that it was so red and his body so white. She bent down and looked at the mark, aware of her

breath coming in short, measured bursts. It was a small
red welt, like a small version of the mark she'd been left
with after a Hepatitis B injection before a holiday several
years ago. It was the mark left by a needle. I have to get
out of here, she thought suddenly as a flight reflex kicked
in. She started towards the door but something held her
back. Shouldn't she look around? If someone had come
here based on the same information she had, then maybe
she was on to something. Shaun's death could be completely unrelated but maybe it wasn't; maybe there was
something here that might give her some clue about what
had happened to Jackson.

VERY SLOWLY, HER heart hammering, Eva walked back
to the front door of the flat and pushed it closed. She returned to the living room, trying to ignore the growing
sense of unease creeping up her spine. The living room
was tiny, dark and a total mess but empty of hidden at-
tackers. Although all the curtains were drawn, all the
windows in the flat were open, which was probably why
the smell of the corpse had not reached her at the door
or drawn the attention of the neighbours. In the middle
of the room was a tiny TV perched on a stack of books,
an old battered orange armchair and a low metal coffee
table littered with cigarette butts.

THERE WAS NO obvious place to look for anything—no letters, no bag, no wallet, no mobile phone, nothing—even
if she had known what she was looking for. She noticed a
lone birthday card embossed with 'Happy Birthday Son'
perched on top of a grubby mantelpiece. She quickly
looked away. Another family would have to go through
what hers had. Eva tried to focus. If she were Shaun,
where would she keep her important documents? She

looked around again. It didn't look like Shaun had any important documents, there didn't seem to be anything of value in the whole flat.

THEN SHE HEARD an electronic beep. Muffled at first, but when she heard it again she realised it was coming from the orange armchair. She ran over and threw off the cushion and there, underneath, was a mobile phone, singing out at regular intervals to indicate its battery was low. That would do. She grabbed the phone, stuffed it in her bag and turned back towards the door. As she was walking out of the living room, she heard footsteps coming up the stairs towards the flat and she stopped and stood still. A woman's voice was speaking in French she could just about understand, telling someone 'she went in there.'

EVA SCANNED THE room and noticed a fire escape ladder through one of the open windows on the other side of the fluttering curtains. She ran over and threw herself out, clinging to the rusted railings, wincing in pain as small slices of paint cut up underneath her nails. She forced herself down the ladder as fast as she could go and jumped the last two rungs, accidentally ripping a small part off the inside of her coat as she became airborne. She grabbed the material off the ladder and picked up a small black button that had fallen at the same time, determined to leave no trace. Eva glanced up to see if anyone was looking out of the window at her but she hadn't been spotted.

Suddenly there was a terrified scream from the flat upstairs.

Obviously whoever was up there had discovered Shaun's body.

EVA GOT AS far as the bottom of the fire escape before she had to check her pace. Outside Shaun's apartment block at the front, two police cars idled at the kerb. From her position behind a large bin, Eva could see two policemen, one in each of the cars, which presumably left a maximum of two other policemen inside. She tried to calm her frantic heartbeat. Think. Had the woman downstairs called the police? They had arrived very quickly if she had. But why would she do that? Eva's skin chilled. There was no reason for the woman downstairs to have called the police so someone else must have done it—someone who knew exactly where Eva was. From what she had heard from inside the flat—'she's in there'—the police seemed to have been looking specifically for her, which should have been impossible as no one knew she was here. But it looked like someone did know.

EVA TRIED TO remember whether she had touched anything in the flat. While it was unlikely that the rough material of the orange armchair would provide a good surface for fingerprints, the door she had pushed open certainly would. Was she being set up? She felt the heaviness of Shaun's phone in her bag and realised it would not look good if she was caught sneaking out of the flat of a dead man with his phone, no matter how innocent she might be. She needed to get out of there. Suddenly there was movement out front and both policemen in both cars got out and walked towards the front door of the flats. At the same time Eva noticed a figure appear at the top of the fire escape she had jumped down. She had to move. Now.

AS SOON AS the two policemen at the front disappeared through the door Eva left the protection of the bins.

Veering left out of the flats she crossed the road that led back to the station and, unable to walk in front of the flats and risk being seen, went deeper into the housing development opposite to try and find her way around. Here, the flats were in a far worse state than Shaun's. At every step Eva took she could feel her presence attracting attention. She walked quickly past a stairwell occupied by six young men, all wearing loose, dark clothing and staring at her with a mix of suspicion and anticipation. She quickened her pace. By the time she was at the edge of the estate she thought she could feel a presence behind her. Unable to turn around, Eva pressed forward and tried to ignore the scenarios playing out in her head. Instinctively, she veered right again and hoped she was walking back towards the station.

ALMOST AS SOON as she rounded the corner, Eva felt an urgency push all her senses into overdrive. She turned slightly, reacting to movement to the left of her field of vision and thought she saw one of the men from the stairwell running towards her, steel glinting in his hand in the weak wintery sunshine. A knife. Immediately she took off in the opposite direction, pumping her hands to force her body forward, despite the cold grip of panic that had taken hold of her throat and lungs. She rounded another corner in the maze of narrow passageways that ran between the mid-height tower blocks of the housing complex and skidded, almost colliding with an old woman in a printed scarf who shouted something unintelligible at her, but she had no time for apologies. Running down an uneven path, Eva was aware that at every step she could stumble or trip, giving her pursuer the opportunity to close the tiny gap between them. She

considered stopping and challenging whoever was behind her but instinctively she felt that would not end well.
Keep going. Ducking under a line of fresh washing Eva
ran on, risked a quick glance behind her and then hearing footsteps just behind the wall of laundry, pushed her
body to move faster, get further away.

Suddenly, around another corner a wall rose up in
front of her. The way ahead was blocked.

STOPPING MOMENTARILY, Eva made a quick calculation, ran
to the wall, pulled herself up onto a plastic bin and then
tried to pull her body up onto the top of the wall. Her
flailing feet kicked the bin over and it spilled its stinking contents all over the floor. She fought desperately
to pull herself up to the peak of the wall but her arms
were too weak and the rough surface was already strip-
ping the skin from her fingers. Eva tried one more time
to heave herself up over the wall but it was too high and,
horrified, she realised she was slipping. As she lost her
grip she landed in the rubbish, slipped backwards, struggled to find her footing and then turned herself around
so that she was facing whoever was following her. For
what seemed like minutes, the path behind her remained
empty. Then very slowly, a small group of men, those
she had seen at the stairwell, rounded the end of the narrow passageway. When they were just paces away they
stopped and looked at her; they must have been all of
fifteen but they were working hard at being menacing.

EVA REALISED SHE had made a big mistake coming into
what was essentially their turf and then reacting like
a spooked deer. There had been no trained assassin
following her. Obviously they had nothing to do with

Shaun. She had allowed her imagination—and maybe the residual fear after being attacked by March the night before—to get the better of her. She took a deep breath. Slowly, she walked towards them. As she reached the group of five, she smiled at the first boy, a tracksuit-clad figure, taller than her, his eyes rimmed with dark circles and his dark hair shorn close to his skull.

'TON MOBILE.' HER smiled quickly faded. Eva ignored him and took a step to the right, trying to walk around the group but they fanned out, completely blocking her path.

'Your mo-bile,' the boy repeated, this time in halting English, and then held out his hand. Eva hesitated. What choice did she have? She reached into her bag and handed over her phone then, in a split second, wished she had given them the device she had taken from Shaun's flat instead. Too late now, she thought, trying to meet the boy's eye with a steady gaze.

'And cash.' His English was appropriated from gangster films, and as if to illustrate his point, he lifted two fingers and rubbed them together in the air, causing the four boys standing behind him to laugh menacingly. She handed over a small leather purse and the boy opened it and peered inside.

'Carte?' She shook her head and opened her palms. 'I don't carry them.' It was a lie but she hid her cards separately for this very reason and she wasn't about to just hand them over to this child.

A flash of anger crossed the boy's features and he glared at her, bristling at the reply. Clearly a stolen credit card was worth much more than a foreign phone or such a small amount of cash. He continued to glare at her, apparently waiting for her to flinch but Eva stared him

down and the boy seemed to have no wish to search her
or take possession of her bag. After several heart-stop-
ping minutes, he made a clicking sound in his throat,
nodded briefly at her and then ambled off, his crew following behind. Eva stood motionless in the alleyway,
her heart thundering in her chest. Never in her life had
so much happened to her in 48 hours. Suddenly she felt
a vibration against her hip. She opened up her bag to see
that Shaun's phone had sprung to life.

THERE ON THE stark white screen were two words: 'Jackson calling.'

THREE

EVA LOOKED AT the clock display on Shaun's phone: 7.30 p.m. Since the phone call from 'Jackson' earlier she had checked the phone constantly, afraid to see Jackson's name jump up again, but somehow also afraid that it wouldn't. She had bought a universal charger on the way back to her hotel, just to make sure the phone didn't die. Sinister as it was that whoever had called her own phone had now also called Shaun's, it was also her only possible link to…well to what? Did she really believe Jackson was still alive? She felt exhausted.

SHE HADN'T EATEN since the croissant she had forced down with her coffee that morning before travelling to Shaun's flat. She was starving. She got up and walked over to her laptop on the other side of the room and pressed the refresh button; no new emails. She considered going for a run—she hadn't been since she arrived in Paris and she could feel her body aching for the release—but March had made her wary of adventuring through streets she didn't know in the darkness. She looked around the dingy hotel room for another excuse not to go outside and when she could find none, cursed her choice of a hotel without room service. It was raining as Eva stepped down from the chipped double stairs at the entrance to her hotel and into the street. She flipped up an umbrella and felt the cheap device bend as a gust of wind almost turned it inside out. She stood still for several seconds in the light of the hotel reception and looked around. The street was still; cars gleamed in the moonlight and there was a smell of wood smoke in the air.

Nothing moved. She realised her heart was hammering in her chest. The rain drove into the fabric of her jeans.

SHE STARTED OUT at a slow pace, turning left at the end of the road and walking in the direction of a restaurant she knew was four streets away. She felt uncharacteristically nervous, but that was unsurprising after the events of the last 48 hours. Although she had dismissed March's attack on her as a random event by a sick individual, when stacked up with the mugging, finding Shaun earlier that day and two strange phone calls, it left her feeling pretty unsettled. To say the least.

BAD THINGS ALWAYS come in threes, I've had my quota, she told herself moving quickly along the quiet, wet streets, a lithe figure almost disappearing into the shadows between each pool of street lamp. As she walked she tried to talk herself back to her usual state of calm. March was unlikely to try the same thing twice, people like that were sick opportunists and he had too much to lose to track her down just for revenge. The mugging could simply be a case of the wrong place at the wrong time. The only event she really couldn't dismiss was finding Shaun's body and the police turning up whilst she was there—that was troubling. Either she was having the worst luck of her life and it really was another random event, or someone had set that up. Someone who had potentially sought him out for the same reason she had—because he had spent Jackson's last five minutes with him and could possibly offer some kind of insight into what had really happened next. If that was the case, presumably Shaun had known something that someone out there wanted to hide; something so serious that it justified permanently silencing him.

Eva was aware that she didn't really know what had happened to Shaun, or what kind of person he was. There was a chance that his death was completely unconnected to his contact with Jackson—maybe he'd got himself into trouble with a local gang, or been the victim of a random burglar… Who took nothing and apparently killed Shaun with some kind of poison… It wasn't outside the realms of possibility for that to have happened, but it seemed unlikely. Eva had no idea where to look for answers next—Shaun had been her only lead.

As she reached the door of the restaurant, she snapped her umbrella shut and shook it before walking inside. There were a few customers enjoying a late night meal and no one really took any notice of her. Inside, the restaurant was dated, the waiters decked out like penguins and the tables covered with white tablecloths that had seen better days. Eva let the waiter guide her to a seat in the corner, dropped her umbrella on the floor and shrugged off her leather jacket. She looked down at the menu and decided to order a prix fixe meal of carrot salad and a tomato omelette. The waiter brought her a Diet Coke in a shapely bottle with a straw, which she finished in five minutes before ordering a large glass of thick, warming red wine. She looked across the room at the steamed-up restaurant window. Opposite her, an extra place setting and an empty chair stared back at her. She took a large gulp of the red wine and tasted the tartness on the roof of her mouth.

IT STRUCK HER that perhaps she should feel sad about being in such a romantic city alone. Paris was well known as a destination for proposals and honeymoons and there were plenty of couples in the streets glued together at the palms of their hands. Why didn't she feel sad about that? Eva couldn't remember the last serious relationship she'd had. She tended to treat men as distractions, entertainment, or a release, but never anything more permanent. She rarely planned for the future but when she did it wasn't with a wedding in mind. Not that she was immune to the pressures of someone her age. For several years now friends had been pairing off and her summers had been filled with weddings. Some followed a familiar, stiff formula and others were spirited and fun, but to Eva it was always just a party. A shrink would pin this to her father's affair, maybe even Jackson's disappearance, she thought, consuming more of her wine. Presumably the theory would be that she was afraid to trust a man because all the men in her life let her down. Was it really that simple? Maybe she just wasn't the marrying kind.

EVA REALISED SHE had finished her wine and ordered another as the food arrived. She ate slowly, deliberately, chewing each mouthful, tasting the creaminess of the eggs in the omelette and the fragrant tomatoes. Her meal came with a basket of soft, white sliced baguette and a small salad with a vinaigrette dressing and by the time she had finished the whole plate, and her second glass of wine, she was feeling distinctly sleepy. She ordered a cognac and a noisette coffee and settled back in her seat. For a moment, the post-food heaviness made her feel calm and satisfied, almost content. But as the coffee kicked in, her current situation seemed to come back into focus.

SHE THOUGHT ONCE again about Shaun, forcing herself to go back over every detail of his flat to try and recall any possible clues about who had been there and why. She already knew that he was simply a delivery courier and his 'meeting' with Jackson had been accidental. They had shared a cigarette outside the front of her brother's office moments before he seemed to have disappeared, Jackson providing the nicotine in exchange for Shaun's lighter. A friendly gesture, an amicable moment between complete strangers. But then why was Shaun dead? Eva pulled his phone out of her bag and began scrolling through the records. On the missed calls screen she saw the name 'Jackson' at the time that she had received the earlier call. Seeing his name made her heart start to beat faster. Who was making those calls? She looked further down the list but his name didn't appear again. It seemed that the first time 'Jackson' had called Shaun was when she'd had the phone in her hands. The two men didn't know each other so how was Jackson's name in his phone and how had the phone call even come about? At the back of her mind, Eva acknowledged the possibility that 'Jackson' was not in fact Jackson but someone else. Someone with motives she didn't even want to think about; and someone who through this phone and her own appeared to be trying to make contact with her. Perhaps the phone had even been left there for her to find. She had a sudden sense that she was outside of normal life, as if the moment she had stepped inside Shaun's flat today had changed everything. Unsettled, she looked up from the phone and glanced around. Her waiter was rearranging glasses on a shelf; on the other side of the room two pensioners sat in companionable silence looking through the condensation on the glass window. The room was warm, quiet and smelled of coffee and steak. Nothing out of the ordinary. Eva dropped her gaze back to the phone and navigated back through all Shaun's call records, his text messages, his internet history and even his apps. She didn't recognise any of the names and she found nothing to indicate that he had been anything more than a parcel courier in the wrong place at the wrong time. In fact, Shaun had virtually nothing on his phone at all.

THE NEXT MORNING, Eva was up and out of her hotel by 9. She had found a local café, steamy and rich with the smell of freshly ground coffee, and breakfasted on a buttery croissant and several *tartines* of light and fluffy French bread with butter and apricot jam. Buoyed up by a huge black coffee, she had then set out to find Jackson's old office. The long, leisurely walk allowed her the time and space to take in her surroundings and she found herself wandering along the streets, gazing at the ornate buildings, the wide, clean boulevards and the pretty Métro signs and street lamps. Paris really was incredibly beautiful, especially on a day like today when the sun was shining brightly and the air was crisp.

SHE WALKED TO the huge interchange of Châtelet where she took a Ligne 1 train going west. She couldn't help noticing how the Métro train was clean and spacious without the crowds or the discomfort of the London Underground. At Concorde she left the train and climbed up the exit stairs to find herself in the huge, traffic-laden square of Place de la Concorde, the Eiffel Tower dominating the view to the left and ahead the Arc de Triomphe far away at the top of the Champs-Elysées. Following several hair-raising attempts at crossing the cobbled square, Eva finally reached the other side and, after consulting her map, headed west past cinemas and designer showrooms, luxury glass-fronted shops and restaurants that charged 15 Euros for a soft drink. Halfway up the Champs-Elysées she took a side road to escape the hordes of stampeding tourists and then suddenly she was standing opposite Jackson's old office, the exact spot where he had last been seen alive. The aid organisation where Jackson had worked was in a small, nondescript building nestled between residential flats and a small travel agency with dusty brown windows. Eva crossed a treacherously busy road and peered briefly through the window, before pushing open the glass door. Inside, it felt more like a dentist's waiting room, complete with dated, brown carpets, faux pine furniture and large, dusty, dark green Yucca plants in woven pots. Eva looked over to the receptionist's window but there was no one there. She frowned. She was sure she had seen a silhouette there when she had been crossing the road. She walked over and looked inside but the desk behind was empty except for a small, elegant leather bag with a red silk scarf draped carelessly over it. That's surely a robbery waiting to happen, thought Eva, looking at the silver mould of a purse clasp peeking through the top of the bag. Somewhere out at the back of the reception she heard a door slam.

'Hello?' The place seemed deserted. Behind the receptionist's desk there were four doors and a fire escape, separated by a staff sitting area with two old, brown sofas and a kitchenette. There was a shiny metal bell on the reception window and Eva rang it. When no one had appeared she rang it again until a small man, wearing glasses so huge he looked like an inquisitive owl, stuck his head out of one of the nearest doors. He looked around the reception area as if expecting to see someone, gave a short sigh and then walked towards Eva smiling.

'Oui?' Eva tried to form the correct French words in her head and then decided that he must surely speak English. This was an international organisation after all. 'Hello. I'm Eva Scott, Jackson's sister.' The man stopped as he reached the reception window and immediately his smile changed to an expression of sorrow.

'Hello, Eva.' He reached for her hand. 'I am so sorry for what happened to your brother.' The genuine emotion on the man's face almost brought tears to her eyes. She fought them back.

'Thank you. Monsieur…?'

'Huillet. Michel Huillet.' Jackson's boss.

They shook hands awkwardly through the window.

'Come in, come through to my office.' M. Huillet indicated a door to the left of the reception window. 'You have come for Jackson's bag?'

Eva hesitated and then nodded, slightly nonplussed. She hadn't been aware that there was any bag. Nevertheless… 'Yes, I have.'

M. Huillet nodded and hustled her into the reception area. He led her back through the first door to a small, sunlit space with a large, wooden desk, two ancient-looking grey metal chairs and several enormous book-shelves that made the room feel much more cramped than it actually was. Eva noted the copious number of green plants and the distinct lack of a computer. M. Huillet indicated a seat and she sat down. There was an un-comfortable silence.

'Are you here for long?'

'No. I've just come to tie up a few of the loose ends Jackson left behind,' she lied.

M. Huillet nodded. 'Of course. Of course.' He leaned behind his desk and hauled a large kit bag over his right shoulder, dropping it with a loud thud onto the leather-covered desktop. 'These are the belongings that he kept at the office. We have not opened it.' The bag was enor-mous. No wonder they had kept it rather than pay the postage that would presumably have been involved in sending it back to England.

'I do apologise for not being able to afford to post this,' said M. Huillet, as if reading her mind. 'We had thought Valerie would be able to liaise with your fam-ily to arrange sending it but she…well…' M. Huillet faltered as if considering his words carefully. 'She de-cided she did not want to deal with it. Perhaps it was the grief.' Eva felt a little pang of resentment. Valerie had been Jackson's girlfriend of eighteen months when he died and receptionist at the agency, where they had met. Eva had not met her but had been surprised at her complete refusal to interact with the Scotts, or to help out in any way, after Jackson's death. M. Huillet shifted uncomfortably in his seat and Eva sensed he did not care much for Valerie.

'Is she here?'

'Valerie?'

'Yes. I was hoping I might be able to speak with her.'
M. Huillet looked puzzled. 'She should be here, she was
here this morning. Perhaps she has taken an early lunch.'
Without her belongings, thought Eva, suddenly remembering the bag on the reception desk.

'Monsieur Huillet, could you tell me a bit about what
Jackson was doing before he died? He never really spoke
much about it.' The Director looked mildly surprised.

'Of course. One of the things we do here is to monitor the countries that receive our aid. Jackson was allocated to the Sudan. By the time he died…well…he was
promoted and promoted and in the end he was Head of
his monitoring group.'

Eva nodded. 'So what did that involve?'

'Well, unfortunately we are, and always have been,
quite underfunded and understaffed here so Jackson was
juggling on his own the schedule of communication with
the recipients of our aid, keeping in touch with our contacts in the country, monitoring, fund-raising, meeting
with Sudanese living in Paris and collecting all our cor-
respondence.'

'And did that include trips to the Sudan?'

'When the funds allowed—I think the last one he
went on was over a year ago. We had a terrible row
because he refused the injections he was supposed to
have—a fear of needles? He had an enormously stubborn
streak—I expect you knew that.' He smiled at her, shar-
ing the memory. 'Jackson was very good at extracting
money from sponsors though, he certainly managed to
get out to that part of the world more than anyone else.'
Eva nodded.

'He would have gone far, he was so very bright and he had such a desire to do good.' M. Huillet smiled at her, obviously wanting to convey once again his condolences. Eva remembered when she had met up with Jackson for the first time after finding out he was still alive. He had seemed overjoyed to see her, but very reserved, and by the end of the conversation she realised, almost consumed by guilt. Perhaps that was why he had taken a job so focused on helping others and 'doing good'. Eva could understand that he felt terrible about lying to his family for more than ten years, but there was something else in his eyes that spoke of a deeper pain. He'd had a pleading, slightly wild, look that she hadn't understood when she saw it—it was that look which had made her believe the story of his suicide at first. She'd thought perhaps he just couldn't take any more.

'Did you notice anything strange about him just before he died?' she asked.

M. Huillet frowned. 'Strange?'

'Yes, issues with Valerie or turning up late to the office. Did his work suffer at all, was he rude or difficult to be around?'

M. Huillet shook his head. 'No, nothing like that. If anything, the opposite—he was working late all the time and he seemed especially committed to his work.'

'Do you know exactly what he was working on?'

'No, I'm afraid not. Unfortunately, his computer was destroyed on the day he disappeared and we don't have much in the way of resources for IT support,' he said, apologetically.

'His computer was destroyed?'

'Yes, it just suddenly stopped working and we couldn't turn it on again.'

'Odd.'

'Yes. But the machines we use here are hardly state-of-the-art—almost everything is donated or second-hand, it does tend to happen rather a lot.' He smiled again, apologetically.

Eva wondered whether she believed the coincidence. She looked at the little man in front of her, but she sensed he had nothing to hide.

'Eva—do you mind if I call you Eva, Miss Scott?'

'No, please do.'

'I get the sense that there's something unsettled in your mind about the way Jackson died. Perhaps you're not here just to tie up loose ends.' He looked at her steadily, his bright eyes piercing.

'I don't feel comfortable with what happened to him, no. It's really nothing more than an instinct,' Eva replied honestly.

For a second M. Huillet looked like he wanted to say something. She waited to allow him to speak but he seemed to hesitate.

Finally, he said, 'Sometimes our instincts are the most accurate tools we have.' The two sat in silence for several seconds. Eva sensed he wasn't going to say anything more.

'OK. Well, I had better take this then.' Eva pulled the bag towards her. It was heavy. Getting it back to the hotel would be difficult.

M. Huillet stood up. 'Shall I call you a taxi?'

'No, really, I'll be fine.' The old man looked doubtfully at her struggling with the huge bag.

'Eva?' Eva stopped and looked at him.

'Jackson really was a lovely young man. He was kind and helpful and a wonderful campaigner. We miss him.'

'Thank you.' She coughed to rid her voice of the wavering.

'I miss him, too.' With a mammoth effort, she picked up the handles of the rough canvas holdall and hoisted it up onto her shoulder before making her way to the door.

FOUR

THE POLICE STATION was not dissimilar to an English police station on the outside, a fairly nondescript building with a number of marked police cars parked in front. With few other sources of information available to her, Eva had decided that her next stop should be the police report on Jackson's death. Valerie, not the family, had identified Jackson's body after his death and thanks to the physical distance and the grief, Eva and her father had challenged very little. Maybe, just maybe, the report might reveal something that would give some foundation to what she thought might have happened—possibly even provide a new lead.

STEELING HERSELF FOR a conversation in French, Eva clutched at the soft leather of her bag, feeling for the shape of the dictionary inside. She hauled Jackson's enormous holdall up onto her shoulders once again and pressed forward. It was late afternoon in Paris now and the rain had cleared, allowing the sun to cast pink and orange rays across the clear blue expanse of sky with the last of its light. Once inside the police station, Eva had trouble getting anyone's attention. There was no desk sergeant but instead the entrance door seemed to open onto a series of unmarked corridors. Eventually, she came across a reception area, or at least a room with chairs. There was a slightly open door to one side, behind which a heated argument was taking place in fast-paced French. Eva dropped the huge bag and took a seat on one of the old fabric-covered chairs. She sat and watched a spider attempting to bind a pot plant in its silvery web.

AFTER SEVERAL MINUTES, an elderly man in a highly starched uniform flew out of the open door at an unfeasibly fast pace and marched past Eva without a second glance. The door slammed behind him. Eva looked at the floor and tried not to anticipate the painful situation that was bound to ensue if she was going to be forced, as appeared to be the case, to knock on the door and explain herself in French. Taking a deep breath, she stood up, smoothed a non-existent set of creases out of her already skin-tight jeans and walked slowly towards the door, leaving the bag by the chair in reception. She knocked gingerly at the dark wood.

'*OUI!*' roared the occupant.

Eva considered coming back later.

'*OUI??*' The door flew open and she found herself facing a large man with a red face and a huge moustache, who was looking at her as if he would like to run her through with the knife he held in his left hand. The knife had a knob of butter attached to it.

The man grunted quietly as his face collapsed from rage to irritation and the butter-knife fell to his side.

'*Qu'est ce que vous voulez?*'

'*Um, je voudrais...* In English if you prefer.' He ushered Eva into the room and casually indicated a chair positioned in front of a huge mahogany desk.

Thank God, thought Eva, taking a seat and gratefully putting away the dictionary.

'My name is Eva Scott. My brother, Jackson, died in

Paris just over three months ago.' Eva hesitated; it still felt like such an odd thing to say out loud. She waited for a reaction from the man opposite but saw only an almost imperceptible twitch in his right eye. She pressed on. 'My family and I never saw all the documents relating to his death, my father just spoke to someone on the phone and I think there was some kind of summary report—a single page. I was hoping I would be able to see the full report into his death, just so that we can lay ghosts to rest. If you know what I mean.' If he did know what she meant, the rotund man in the uniform opposite showed no sign of it. Nor did he show any sympathy or even any interest as he carried on slowly buttering a hard piece of baguette.

'There is nothing for you to see.' His response took Eva quite by surprise. She had expected that at the very least there would be some sort of procedure to follow, details to be taken, more questions asked, a file to be located.

'I'm sorry?'

'There is nothing for you to see,' he repeated, tossing the buttered baguette end into his mouth and crunching loudly on it as little crumbs launched themselves through his fleshy, parted lips.

'But there must be.'

'Nothing.'

'Don't you need to check a database or something?'

'I am sure.' Eva felt herself getting riled. The man was not even looking at her as he spoke; he appeared to think he was addressing the coat hook on the back of his door.

'Look, I just want to see the documents, that's all. I'm not here to make trouble.' Suddenly the man's eyes moved so that they were fixed firmly on hers. 'For what are you asking these questions? This matter has been closed.'

'There are still unanswered questions.'

'There are not.'

'There are.'

'What—*exactement*?'

'My brother was not a drug addict.' The man snorted and folded his arms across his rotund gut with a disdainful expression on his face.

'I worked on your brother's case, Mademoiselle Scott, and I can assure you your brother had quite a history with drug use.'

'Yes, but that's just it—he had a history with it, it was history.' Jackson had spent a year before he arrived in France in a well-known rehab centre in Hampshire. He had been reluctant to tell her why but eventually had admitted addiction to an assortment of mind-numbing substances, from Class As to painkillers.

'My brother was clean for two years before he died.'

'How do you know that? I was aware of his family circumstances and you were rarely in Paris with him.'

'He told me. I believed him. Besides, he didn't behave in a way that would have led any of us to believe he was still having issues.'

'He was an addict and that caused him to kill himself.'

'He was not.'

'Calm down, Mademoiselle Scott.' His tone was utterly emotionless and completely cold. Eva realised the volume of her voice had been rising. She decided to try another approach.

'Inspector…?'

'Gascon. Inspecteur Gascon.' He leaned back in his

chair and rested a pair of badly groomed hands on the
top of his fat stomach, his small black eyes looking at
her challengingly, almost as if he were enjoying her discomfort.

'Inspecteur Gascon. I've come a very long way to see
you. Jackson was the only brother I had, my only sib-
ling. I can see that now the file is closed it would not be
particularly…convenient…to open it again but I would
be incredibly grateful if you would allow me to deal
with some of my unanswered questions. So that I can
let Jackson rest in peace.' She looked steadily at Gascon.

The fat man sighed, stretched, leaned forward and
rested his arms on his desk, unaware that his left elbow
was now heavily greased with pale yellow butter. He
took a slow draught from a large tumbler of water on
his desk and then carefully replaced it on a coaster. Eva
wanted to throw it in his face.

'Mademoiselle Scott.' His beady black eyes rested on
her, almost pinpricks beneath the fat folds of his eyelids
and the dark, saggy skin pulling down his lower lid. 'I
don't know if it is because you are just a stubborn En-
glishwoman or just because you do not understand. There
is no reason to start hunting around for these documents,
or to re-open this issue and I will…not…do…so.' He sat
back in his chair, looking haughtily content.

EVA FELT UTTERLY depressed as she slowly made her way
back to her hotel after the encounter with the policeman.
Another avenue firmly closed off. And still she really
had nothing to go on but instinct. It was dark now and
she could feel how exhausted she was. She forced herself
to take steady, firm paces, properly supporting Jackson's

bag so that she didn't damage her back, but she felt like hurling it on the floor and collapsing on top of it.

She looked up and realised she was almost back at the hotel.

She needed to get some supplies as she didn't feel like another night of dining alone. She changed direction and walked towards a supermarket several streets from her hotel. Her back was aching from carrying the bag. She tightened her stomach muscles and forced herself to stand up straight until she was in front of the supermarket, its bright strip-lighting spilling out onto the wet pavements. Inside she picked up a two-litre bottle of water, a bag of apples, a pack of madeleines and a premade cheese and ham baguette. On a whim she added a large bar of salted almond chocolate and a packet of menthol Vogue cigarettes to her basket. She hadn't smoked for three years but she couldn't think of a better time to take it up again.

The cashier was surly and threw her purchases back at her, peering out from under a greasy fringe with tiny dark eyes like a sullen pig. Eva was too tired to be annoyed and meekly packed her things into a flimsy carrier bag, hoping it would hold the weight of the water until she got back to the hotel. Then she set off again, lugging the enormous holdall. What was inside it? It wasn't until she was two blocks away that she heard footsteps on the street behind her. They were quiet—too quiet—as if someone was trying very hard not to be heard. She tried to turn her head to look but the enormous bag on her shoulder was blocking her view. She picked up her pace and behind her the footsteps quickened too. She was walking down dark, wet, deserted roads, at least five minutes jog from the nearest busy Parisian street. She had chosen this area because it was cheap. Safety had never been a major concern—this was only supposed to be a fact-finding trip. Eva pushed energy through her muscles as she forced her body to move faster. She kept moving, driving herself forward, not daring to look behind in case she lost the advantage and found herself staring straight into the face of her pursuer. Suddenly she was one street from the hotel, one empty road to cross. The footsteps behind her quickened to a run. Eva's senses suddenly went into overdrive and, despite everything she was carrying, she began running too. She could see the hotel right in front of her. She jumped off the pavement and, too late, noticed the car coming at speed to her left. She felt the car clip her painfully on the leg, sending her sprawling to the floor. She saw her bag of shopping and Jackson's holdall fly through the air as she fell, landing heavily against the curb. There was a burning pain across the back of her skull and then nothing.

'I CANNOT KILL the English girl.' Wiraj Hasan turned slowly from his position at the window of the grubby hotel room in the 18th arrondissement of Paris where he was leisurely smoking a cigarette.

'You are joking of course, Nijam,' he said slowly to his brother.

A tense silence filled the room as the two men stared at each other while their roommates ignored them and continued to play a slow and unabsorbing game of cards. The brothers always fought, both here and at home, it was just how it was with siblings.

'No, I am not joking.' Nijam's stocky frame moved

swiftly over to where his brother remained by the window. He had the large, open face of a child, the body of a heavyweight boxer and the hands of a professional strangler. 'I told you, I have found God now and I do not think this killing to order we are doing fits with His plan.'

Wiraj laughed scornfully. 'Your God is a white man's God. He has no time for you.'

'He has time for everyone, Wiraj. All those who follow the path.'

'Like sheep.'

'We are his flock and he will guide us.'

Wiraj stared at his brother then suddenly threw his cigarette to the stained wooden floor and ground it down with his heel. 'You have become weak, my brother,' he growled, with such an intensity that the three men at the table glanced over.

Nijam was immediately placatory. 'I know that we are here for good reason but, Wiraj, can't we achieve the purpose peacefully?' He stepped closer to his brother and laid a conciliatory hand on him. 'After all, what kind of purpose must it be if we need to kill to achieve it?' Immediately Wiraj cast off his brother's arm.

'What purpose?' he spat. 'You stand there and ask me what purpose?' He pushed his brother backwards with the flat of his hand, destabilising Nijam, whose face was etched with surprise. As suddenly he remembered they were not alone, Wiraj glanced warily over at the table where the other men sat; they continued to play cards but he could see they were listening. Roughly, he grabbed Nijam's shoulder and hustled him over to the window, before continuing in a hushed voice. 'Their purpose is unimportant, it is for our own ends that we are forced to do this. You forget, my brother, what we have lived through,' continued Wiraj, stroking the thick scar running down his left cheek. 'The poverty, the violence, the sanctions imposed on our broken nation by those that should have stepped in and helped. Instead they branded us terrorists, left us at the mercy of our corrupt government. These super powers, these rich nations. They will only help themselves.'

'But, Wiraj, now we have…'

'Now we have nothing, Nijam, only an opportunity.' Nijam was silent now, his brother's anger and the truth of his words hitting home with double-edged accuracy.

'We have nothing without this opportunity,' repeated Wiraj at length. 'Do you want to go back to Sudan a failure? Is that what you want?' Nijam quickly shook his head.

'If you had morals you should have left them back home.' He turned to Nijam and seeing the compliance on his brother's face, Wiraj began to cool down. 'Do you understand, my brother?' he said, taking a step towards Nijam and cradling his left cheek with his hand.

'Yes?' Nijam nodded, any religious fervour roundly trounced from him.

'Yes, Wiraj,' he said quietly, 'I do.'

EVA OPENED HER EYES. Nothing. She shut her eyes and opened them again but it made no difference. The darkness was complete. She blinked into the gloom then sat up and felt around for the light on the bedside table at the hotel. Her outstretched arm knocked over a glass and it fell to the floor with a loud crash. This was not her room at the hotel. Further exploring with the palms of her hands, Eva found that she was sitting on a single bed with a coarse covering that seemed to be wedged in the corner of a room papered with uneven wallpaper. There was a wall behind her head and also to her right; the air smelled of cigarettes and aftershave.

For a second, Eva wondered whether she was dreaming. Since Jackson's death she'd had almost no dreams but she had no idea where she was or how she had got here, which made a dream the only plausible explanation. But her left leg was aching horribly and her head was thumping. That pain was very real. As she felt herself starting to panic, she heard heavy footsteps coming closer to the vague outline of a door she could see across the room. Suddenly the door was thrown open, filling the room with light.

Eva raised her hand to shield her eyes as her pupils adjusted to the brightness. As soon as she was able to see again she dropped her arm. She squinted at the shadowed form in front of her. A man stepped fully into the room; he had broad and well-muscled shoulders that looked enormous, like a cartoon action hero. Eva tried to control her racing pulse. This was not a good situation. The man flicked on a bare light bulb above the bed and stared at her for several seconds. She stared back, counting each breath in and out for three to make sure they remained even and calm.

'My name is Leon,' said the man in English with a French accent, walking over towards her and holding out his hand. He had dark hair and dark eyes and he wore a pair of black jeans and a navy cargo sweater. Eva nodded at him. Was she supposed to shake his hand?

'You're probably wondering where you are.'

'Yes.' Eva realised her throat was painfully dry.

'You had a car accident—well, you ran out in front

of my car—and you passed out.' Suddenly Eva remembered running across the road away from the stranger she had thought was following her. She recalled the pain of being clipped by the car—that explained the leg at least.

But why was she not in hospital?

'Why am I...'

'I brought you here because you were injured.'

'I see. Well...thank you.' She made a move to get up. 'I should go...'

'Eva...' She stopped and stared straight at him. The hairs began to stand up on the back of her neck.

'You know my name.' He nodded. A silence descended on the room. The man looked at the floor. Eva tried to force herself to move but she seemed to be paralysed from the neck down.

'I knew your brother,' he said suddenly. 'Jackson.' Eva felt her blood drain southwards.

'You knew Jackson?'

'Yes.'

'How well did you know him?'

'We were close.' Eva had never heard Jackson mention someone called Leon.

'I can see you don't believe me.' She said nothing in response. She was starting to feel very uncomfortable. What this man had done—bringing her to his flat—was not a normal thing to do. In fact, it was almost kidnapping.

'Wait...let me show you something...' Leon started for the door.

Instantly, Eva was on her feet. As Leon turned right out of the door, she silently followed him to the edge of the room. She looked carefully around the door-frame, just in time to see him disappear through a door at the end of the corridor. She heard the click of a key turning in a lock in the room Leon had entered. The corridor was shabby, with a dated but clean carpet and old, well-preserved light fittings. On the opposite wall there was a photo of a family standing in front of a farmhouse. Leading off the corridor were two other rooms and then to her left…bingo…a front door.

A quick appraisal of the door revealed a Chubb lock system and a manual key below that. She glanced once more towards the kitchen and then began to tiptoe across the thin carpet, her heart hammering in her ears. She flicked up the notch on the Chubb mechanism and quickly turned the key in the lower lock. Both movements were soundless. She heard a cupboard door close again at the end of the corridor and quickly she twisted the Chubb handle and smoothly pulled open the door in front of her.

OUTSIDE WAS AN unexpectedly twee doormat with a picture of kissing bees and beyond that a dark and cavernous unfurnished hallway decorated with graffiti and, from the smell that hung in the air, urine. Eva pulled the door closed behind her and then started to run. She ran across the concrete landing and down a stairwell, taking the stairs two at a time. She had no idea where she was and no idea where she was going to go when she reached the end of the stairs, but she trusted her own instincts more than she trusted this person. She would find a road, there had to be a road somewhere, and she would flag someone down. But the stairs just kept coming.

'Eva!'

Eva gasped out loud as she heard her name. 'Shit,' she muttered and tried to pick up her pace. She heard the ominous thundering of footsteps on the stairs above her and tried to remember how many flights she had put between the flat and where she was now. There had been at least four, surely he couldn't catch her.

'Eva, wait! You don't understand!' Leon's voice echoed down the stairwell.

Suddenly Eva pulled up short—she was at the bottom of the last flight of stairs and there were no more steps. And no door. Eva stopped, her heart thumping, and then realised she had come down a flight of stairs too far and was in a utility space with no exit. She was going to have to go back up towards him to get out. Panic singing in her ears, Eva started up the stairs two at a time, holding her breath and expecting at any minute to see those dark features appear around the corner. At the next break in the stairs she looked around her and after several seconds of rising anxiety realised she was standing right next to an emergency exit door. She threw herself against it and suddenly she was outside in the bitter night air, shivering. She looked over her shoulder but there was no sign of Leon. The door slammed behind her and she looked back again and took in the enormous tower block she had been inside. Then she turned, started to run and cried out as she hit what felt like a brick wall. Hard fingers gripped her, flipping her over onto her front, pushing her to the floor and a bag was whisked over her head. She tried to scream but the bag was pulled tight over her mouth as she felt someone trying to fasten her wrists together behind her back.

She struggled hard and heard swearing as she succeeded in freeing one of her wrists.

'Merde!' Then a huge hand grabbed both her wrists behind her back and held them together as hard plastic

was wrapped around them and pulled tight. Before the plastic was fastened suddenly there was a noise like a basketball thudding against a wall, followed by the sound of splintering bone and a grunt in her ear as the weight of the person lifted from her. She lay on the ground trying to figure out what was going on as noises of a scuffle filtered through the bag. When she realised she was no longer the centre of attention, Eva tried to free her wrists from the unfastened plastic handcuffs, pulling and tugging as she felt them gradually become loose. Then a gunshot rang out. She lay face down, rigid, blindfolded, confused and disorientated.

'Eva.' Leon's voice. The bag was pulled off her head and Eva looked around her. Leon was behind her, pulling the last of the plastic handcuffs off her. He threw them away and then came to stand in front of her. In his right hand was the dark shape of a gun. Eva looked past him and saw a lump form on the ground behind the back tyre of a burned out car.

FIVE

WITH SOME HESITATION, a shaky Eva allowed Leon to shepherd her back into the tower block and up to the sixth floor where he poured her a shot of cognac. She lowered herself unsteadily onto a patched, brown suede sofa in a room that reeked of 1980s décor.

'Do you understand what just happened?' she asked, looking at him with large, round eyes.

Leon nodded, screwed the top back on the cognac bottle and stowed it into a drinks cabinet with only one other bottle in it.

'This is difficult to explain.' His voice was gravelly and accented, he sounded like he never got much sleep.

'Try.' Leon looked at Eva as he heard the hostile tone in her voice.

'Wait there.' He walked out of the room, glancing back at her as he went as if he was afraid that she might once again make a bolt for the door. Several seconds later he came back into the room carrying a brown paper file. He laid it down on the sofa beside her, moved over to the window and lit a cigarette.

'Read it.' Eva put her empty glass down on the floor and picked up the file. She could feel Leon's eyes watching every move she made. Inside the thin file were some photos. In one, Jackson and the flame-haired girl Eva recognised as his girlfriend Valerie, and in another

Jackson with a short-haired blonde whom Eva had never seen before.

'I don't understand…'

'There's more.' Eva turned over the two photos to reveal two more. This time Valerie was being photographed from a position across the street. Eva recognised the outside of Jackson's office building. Valerie was standing several metres down the street from the entrance to Jackson's office, pulled back into a doorway. She was on the phone but her attention was elsewhere. Eva looked at the focus of her gaze and recognised Shaun the bike courier standing next to Jackson smoking a cigarette.

Eva tried to make sense of the picture. It was obviously taken moments before Jackson disappeared, but it changed nothing.

'Who took this?'

'I did.'

'So you saw what really happened to Jackson?' Leon shook his head. 'I left almost as soon as I took the photo.'

'I must be missing something. I don't understand what you think this means, or how it's relevant to what just happened.' Leon shook his head, frustrated, and stubbed his cigarette out in a Moroccan ashtray.

'That guy in the photo—the bike courier,' he said, moving over to where Eva sat and jabbing his finger in the direction of the photo.

'What about him?'

'He's dead.'

Eva put the photo back in the file. 'I know.'

'I didn't take this photo because of him. I took it because of Valerie.'

'Jackson's girlfriend?'

Leon nodded.

'Why?'

Leon began to pace the floor. He lit another cigarette and scratched distractedly at his hair.

Suddenly he was still. 'She's involved.'

'Involved in what?'

'In what happened to Jackson. She has something to do with it.'

'How do you know that?'

'I just do!' Leon seemed anxious, almost manic. This is really not a good situation, Eva thought to herself once again.

'What did you find at Shaun's flat?' Eva almost answered and then stopped short. 'The only way you could know that I went to his flat is if you followed me.'

'I followed you.'

Eva stood up. 'Okay, I think I'd like to leave now.'

'You can't!' said Leon, jittery and overexcited. 'Didn't you see what just happened outside?' Eva recalled the bag over her head, the prone man lying shot on the floor. He had certainly not been a rescuer. She sat down again, focusing hard on keeping her heartbeat below danger level.

'OK, Leon, explain to me what happened outside and I will tell you what I found in Shaun's flat.' Leon nodded. Clearly he liked the idea of a bargain.

'He was one of them.'

Eva sighed. 'You're going to have to be more specific than that.'

'The Africans.'

'The Africans,' Eva repeated.

'They appeared on the scene six months ago. They killed Jackson, I know they did.' Was this man completely crazy? He certainly looked pretty crazy. And yet he seemed to be the only person who thought Jackson had been killed like she did. What that said about her, she didn't know.

'You don't believe Jackson committed suicide?'

'Ha!' Leon laughed. 'I knew your brother for four years. He was happy, he was clean. Besides the police claimed it was heroin he was taking. Jackson didn't do heroin.'

'He didn't.' Eva's voice was expressionless.

'No. Coke, pills, weed, acid yes. Heroin, no. He hated needles.' God, thought Eva to herself, he's right. She remembered what Jackson's boss had told her—that he had even risked a work trip to the Sudan without his shots because he was so afraid of needles.

'You can smoke heroin, can't you?'

Leon looked at her and laughed. 'Of course. But didn't you see the police "report"? Needle marks in his arms they said. Impossible!' Eva nodded slowly. She remembered reading that in the one page summary they had been sent. In fact, that part of the report had made her particularly sad. Heroin seemed such a sad drug to get addicted to, a drug people craved so much they would inject it into anywhere they could.

'Why include that in the report you saw?' Leon continued.

'They fucked up there!'

'Can I have one of your cigarettes?' Leon thumbed open his pack of blue Gauloises and Eva took a white tab. She rolled it momentarily between two fingers and then took Leon's proffered lighter and lit the cigarette.

'How did you meet my brother?' she said as she exhaled. Leon's eyes sparkled.

'Rehab.'

'What were you there for?'

'The same as him. I have trouble with drink though, too. The only alcohol I can't drink more than three glasses of is cognac.' He gestured at her empty glass. 'Anything else and I get through a bottle in an hour.' It was hard to know what to say to that.

'Did you know him in Paris?'

'Yes. We left the UK together after rehab. He came to my parents' farm and spent a year with me getting back on track. Then we moved to Paris together.'

'Did you live together?'

'No. That wouldn't have been a good idea. I need my space. There's little enough space in the city as it is.'

'Look.' Leon suddenly got up. He walked quickly over to a bookcase and returned with a handset in his left hand. 'I got your phone.' He handed it over to Eva who looked at it in amazement.

'But those kids…'

'Estate scum.' She took the phone.

'What exactly is it you do?'

'If I told you that I'd have to kill you.' He smiled at her but Eva had the chilling feeling that he was serious. She pressed the On button on her phone, entered her pass code and began going through the phone. Among spam emails, a large number of text messages from worried friends and several missed calls from her father she found a text from Valerie. After hesitating for a second, she showed it to Leon.

'She wants to meet me on the 20th. That's tomorrow.'

'You have to go.'

That wasn't the response she had expected. 'After everything you said?'

'She's the key to this, trust me.'

'Right.'

'Suggest that you meet at the Tuileries Gardens at 1pm. I'll be there too.'

'Right.' Eva replied to the text. She felt uneasy about the idea of being shadowed by Leon.

He picked up on it immediately. 'It's better than the alternative.'

'Which is?'

'More like him,' he said and indicated towards the ground outside where they both knew the body lay. After several seconds of silence, Eva got up.

'Don't you think we should search him? Try and find out who he is—was?' Leon produced a small black wallet from his back pocket and tossed it to her. Inside she found a book of carnet travel tickets and forty Euros in cash.

'Clean. Just like all the others,' said Leon.

'The others?'

'Like I said, he's not the only one.'

'But who are they?'

'I'm not sure.'

'Are they something to do with his work?'

'I don't know.'

'Right.'

AN HOUR LATER and Eva was sitting in her hotel room. Leon had driven her back in a small, rickety Citroen and had seemed surprisingly willing to let her leave once he had returned her phone.

Eva felt nervy. But she reasoned with herself that whoever it was that had been outside Leon's tower block, they had not been there for her. She half-believed that.

SHE CLOSED AND locked her hotel door and then, after some hesitation, dragged the night stand over and pushed it up against the door frame. It took some effort as the table had a heavy metal base. But at least it would be more use than a chair for keeping intruders out. After a stiff drink from the bottle of Calvados she had bought from the supermarket on the day she arrived, she settled down on the bed with the sandwich she had bought before the accident and opened her laptop. Her left leg still ached mightily after the crash, but she was still walking and the pain had at least not spread to her back, which was her usual weak spot. She thought about the events of the last few hours as the heat of the Calvados dripped down her throat. She had absolutely no idea what she had stumbled across but she felt she had taken a step closer towards the truth. Leon's revelation about the needle marks was important and she felt like this confirmed her fears that Jackson had indeed been murdered. By who and why, though, remained a total mystery.

SHE STILL HAD Shaun's phone and had not fulfilled her side of the bargain and told Leon about it during the encounter at his flat. In the end he seemed to have forgotten that he had asked her what she had found and she felt there was no need to share too much with him. It would be great to think she now had some kind of ally in Leon but he had also tailed her and possibly knocked her down with his car, and his jittery, manic behaviour didn't encourage her to trust him.

OUT OF HABIT, she navigated to Facebook and looked at
her own page. Her profile picture was a shot taken on a
night out. She had used a camera app with a flattering
filter and she was sitting in the middle of two of her best
friends, each of them brandishing a huge curved bowl
of a cocktail glass filled with a red liquid. The snap had
been taken way before Jackson's death and looking at it
made her feel sad. She scrolled down the page and on
the left saw that Jackson was still listed as her brother.
She clicked on his smiling face and opened the page.
His 'wall' was full of messages in French that she didn't
understand. She recognised the sad face emoticons and
realised the page had probably been turned into some
kind of tribute. She looked at all the faces of his French
friends, her mouse scrolling over each face in turn. Over
one face she stopped. A short-haired woman with a nervous smile looking directly at the camera. She had seen
her before. Eva opened up the woman's main page and
saw immediately that it was the woman from the photo
Leon had shown her earlier that night. Her name was
Sophie Vincent. The rest of her profile was restricted.
Eva took out her Moleskine notebook and printed the
name in black letters.

SIX

THE NEXT DAY, Eva made her way slowly along the crowded Parisian streets. She was finally on her way to meet with Jackson's girlfriend Valerie for the first time, but she felt foggy and unfocused and her mouth was dry. Arriving at Exit 5 of the Tuileries Métro station precisely at 1pm, Eva scanned her immediate vicinity. No sign of Valerie. Whilst the two women had never met, Valerie's flame-red hair and model-like poses had featured frequently on Jackson's Facebook pages in the year before he died, and Eva felt familiar enough with that face to pick it out in a crowd. When she realised she had a few minutes to herself, she moved out of the flow of pedestrians to the back edge of the pavement. At her back a sandy stone wall topped with rusted black railings, behind which stretched the beautifully manicured grounds of the Tuileries Gardens. In front of her, a busy Parisian road bustling with cars, bikes and mopeds, bumpers glinting in the morning sun. Eva found a railing to lean against and rested the back of her head against the cold metal as her gaze drifted up towards the sky. She closed her eyes.

'Eva.' Eva jumped, knocking her head against the railing. Valerie was standing directly in front of Eva, her auburn hair glinting in the winter sun. They shook hands awkwardly.

'How are you?'

Valerie hesitated before answering. 'I am fine. You?'

'Quite hungry. Shall we get lunch?'

Valerie looked taken aback. 'I had thought we were to have just coffee.' She held up a take-away coffee cup.

'I'm going to have to eat, or there's a serious possibility I might pass out.'

Valerie didn't laugh at the joke. 'OK.' They set off in silence at a brisk pace away from the gardens, through a covered walkway carved with arches and lined with shops selling postcards and painfully expensive coffee. As they walked, Eva looked for signs of Leon but as far as she could tell he was nowhere to be seen. But then that was probably exactly as he wanted it. They had made no arrangements before he dropped her at the hotel the night before, and as Eva had been keen to get back to an environment in which he wasn't in control, she hadn't pushed the issue. However, she did wonder what the next steps should be after what had happened that night— and deep down she knew the encounter had unnerved her more than she was willing to admit. The fact that she seemed suddenly to have become his target made her feel unsure of her own ability to protect herself, something she had never considered before. He had seemed unstable, paranoid, and volatile, a combination she would usually swiftly distance herself from—but his conspiracy theories had somewhat chimed with her own. She would just have to wait to see what it was he really wanted from her and hope her nerves could stand it.

Valerie led the way to a modern-looking local establishment with large windows and red velvet curtains. It was warm inside and there was a smell of toasted cheese. The waiter greeted them and put the menus down. Valerie immediately pushed hers away.

'Why did you want so desperately to see me?' Eva looked up from the menu, surprised at all pleasantries being so swiftly dispensed with.

'There are a few things I wanted to ask you.'

'Well...' began Valerie but stopped as the waiter had arrived to take their order. After he left, an awkward silence persisted until the drinks were set down on the dark wood table. Valerie took a short sip of a thick black coffee and squared her narrow shoulders. 'What are your questions?'

'I think Jackson was murdered.'

'What?' Valerie's hand flew to her rosebud mouth; her long-lashed eyes widened around each startling green iris.

'No.' Her voice was surprisingly firm. 'He killed himself. Because of drugs, Eva. Why would you say that?'

Eva was a little surprised by the ferocity of Valerie's reaction. She decided to tread carefully. 'Because I don't believe that's how he died. You identified the body?'

'Yes. But he was disfigured, Eva. Beyond recognition. In the end they had to use dental records. He shot himself in the head.' Across from their table, Eva felt the gazes of a young couple and a dark-skinned man in a black suede coat fall on them.

'Doesn't it seem strange to you that he did what he did?' she continued in a lower tone, moving away from the emotive topic. 'I thought he was finally happy.' Valerie stared at her in silence, her gaze steady, and then looked away as the waiter arrived and set the plate of food down in the middle of the table. Eva started to eat, reluctant to allow Valerie time to think but keen to satisfy her hunger.

'I didn't know him.' Valerie's voice was so quiet Eva

almost didn't hear her. She looked directly into those big green eyes, tearing up slightly at the corners, and then took another bite of the cheese sandwich. 'I did not want what happened to him,' she continued, 'but your brother was not all he seemed.'

'What do you mean?'

Valerie visibly swallowed hard and fiddled with an ashtray in the shape of the Eiffel Tower. 'He was…he was…unpredictable.'

'How?'

'He changed. In the last month. He became…ugly.'

'What does that mean?'

'I'm sorry, I don't know all the English. My English is not that good.' Valerie pushed the ashtray away in apparent frustration.

'What kind of ugly?'

'Mentally ugly. In his mind.'

'Violent?'

'Yes.' Eva felt the colour slowly drain from her face as Valerie quietly finished her coffee.

'Did he hurt you?' Valerie looked at Eva for a second and dropped her eyes.

'No.' Well, at least that was something.

'But I thought he might.'

'When did he start to change?'

'Maybe three weeks before he killed himself.'

'Right.' Suddenly Eva had lost her appetite. She pushed away the remainder of her food.

'I did care for him, Eva.' They stared at each other and then Valerie looked away. Eva followed her gaze to the street outside and suddenly realised that, around the two women caught up in this tragedy, life just carried on. No one else felt the aching bruise of the loss, and no one cared. They all had their own problems.

Suddenly Valerie began to speak again. 'Just before he disappeared we had a lot of fights. I thought he had gone that day because of the fighting.'

'What, just walked out?'

'Yes.'

'Why?'

'I searched his mobile phone a couple of times.' Valerie looked down at the table. 'I know it's not…the right thing to do…but I was desperate. I had heard him on the telephone in our flat—we had two handsets and, when I picked the other up, it was always a woman's voice. Each time I listened he would suddenly hang up as if he knew I was there. So I looked at his mobile.'

'So he was cheating on you too?' Eva remembered the photo Leon had shown her that seemed to show Valerie spying on Jackson. This could well explain her suspicious behaviour. She considered mentioning it but thought better of it.

'I think he was. He wouldn't tell me who it was on the phone. He said that I would have to trust him.' Eva raised an eyebrow. It still all sounded a bit cloak and dagger for Jackson.

'I have seen men do this, Eva.' Valerie's voice suddenly became hard, her face almost flint-like. 'When they cheat, they lie. They don't care what the lie is that they tell, they just lie to save themselves. It has happened before. I can read the signs.' The waiter came and cleared the table and Eva watched Valerie who seemed to be unable to look her in the eye. She keenly remembered her own family's shame when her father's affair with Irene Hunt had been revealed. It was all a sixteen-year-old

Eva could do to stop her mother hurling him down the stairs. She had never seen anger like that which she had witnessed in her mother's bright blue eyes during that time. After that the light had gone out of them altogether.

'Did you confront him?'

'Yes. He told me he wished I would just trust him and that I was making his life more difficult by asking so many questions. I tried to ignore it, but it was always there.'

'So, what happened?'

'I looked through his phone numbers and texts and found a message from a French number—"Sophie". No surname.'

'What did the message say?'

'3pm. Sacré Coeur. As usual.'

'Did you go there?'

'No.'

'Didn't you want to find out what was going on?'

'No,' Valerie repeated determinedly.

Eva stared at her, nonplussed. Her mother had wanted to know everything about her father's affair. Even though each word seemed to wound more, she wouldn't let her father stop until she knew where, how long and why. Although he had never been able to answer the last question.

'Do you know anything about Sophie?' asked Valerie suddenly.

Eva looked up, surprised, as Valerie asked the question.

'No,' she responded, puzzled. Was Valerie still looking for this woman? 'Why do you ask?'

'I want to know what she looks like. Whether she

was…' Valerie hesitated, as if trying to think of something to say.

'Whether she was more beautiful than me.' Eva gazed at Valerie's perfectly structured face; the high, strong cheekbones, the blazing green eyes, the full lips. Could anyone so attractive really be that insecure?

'I…' Eva opened her mouth to respond but Valerie didn't let her finish.

'I must go,' she said as she got up and threw some coins onto the table. 'I hope you have got what you need from me now.' Without another word, she picked up her coat and walked out.

The kissing couple opposite briefly observed Eva as she followed Valerie's retreating figure with her eyes. When the waiter finally arrived with their bill they separated for just long enough to deposit a twenty Euro note and put on their coats to face the autumn cold before their lips locked again. The dark-skinned man had paid his bill and left before Valerie. He waited outside the café, lighting a sweet-smelling cigarette and pulling his cheap overcoat tightly around his thick torso. As Valerie left the café he watched her walk determinedly across the small square on which the café stood. When she took the first right turning down a typically narrow Parisian street, away from the Métro and the hordes of tourists, he pulled the collar of his coat up high, stepped off the pavement and followed her.

EVA PAID THE remainder of the bill and wondered why she had bothered trying to communicate with Valerie. Leon must have completely the wrong end of the stick to imagine that she was at the centre of it all. She was simply a vulnerable young woman who had been hurt.

Jackson had been a passionate man who did nothing in moderation and this had been especially true when it came to Valerie. From what Eva could gather, Valerie had arrived in her brother's life with a history of abusive relationships. A tragic, secretive beauty who needed to be saved. Of course, Jackson had saved her. Other than a weakness for beautiful women his downfall had always been that he wanted to be a hero; after what he had done as a teenager he had told Eva helping others fleetingly made him feel like a decent man. He had asked Valerie to move in with him just a month after they had met at the aid agency and then he had supported her with his modest wage, whilst she apparently spent her own on shoes and handbags. Eva had found the idea of their relationship uncomfortable. It had happened too quickly and it seemed just too reckless—too much too soon. But when it came to having any authority on relationships, Eva was on shaky ground.

WALKING BACK TO the hotel, she gazed around at the beautiful city, with its wide boulevards, elegant vistas and cosy cafés. She felt unable to enjoy her surroundings, or really see what was around her; inside something just felt numb. Since Jackson's second death, everything had fallen apart, she thought sadly. Or had she destroyed it? It was difficult to tell. As she approached the glass-fronted door of her hotel close to the Gare du Nord, Eva felt the vibration of her phone that Leon had returned to her. She stopped outside, pulled open the zip on her bag and leaned against the peeling orange-painted wall to read the text. As the screen came to life, revealing the sender beneath her fingertips, shock flooded through her body, inflaming every one of her nerve endings. Jackson.

She opened the text, her fingers fumbling over the buttons to the point where she almost dropped the phone. The message contained a series of incomprehensible letters, numbers and symbols. She read it several times but it made no sense at all. Eva's skin chilled. She had no idea what was going on, none at all. The powerlessness made her feel uncharacteristically panicky and out of control in a way she had not allowed herself to feel for many years. She thought about March. She wondered if he was playing games with her but how on earth could he have gotten hold of Jackson's phone? She had thought again about their encounter—how he had called her to set it up; how he seemed already to know where she was staying. But these texts didn't seem to match his bull-dozer style. Other than March, Leon and Valerie she knew no one in this vast city. But then the texts could be coming from anywhere.

SEVEN

TERRY DOWLER SAID goodbye to Sophie and climbed into the waiting taxi. He was a journalist who loved a good sensation. There had been a time in his life when he had wanted desperately to be a critical, intellectual success, to be able to produce highbrow, wordy pieces on politics, art and culture, but the opportunities had always passed him by. His parents owned a fish shop in Essex, he hadn't been to a redbrick university and he'd never even had a whiff of the old boys' network, let alone joined it. Although he'd certainly seen it in action—the upstarts fresh from their Oxbridge quads waltzing into the newspaper, bypassing the open-plan 'pit' where he and the other drones sat, ferreting out stories for a byline above a two-paragraph feature on one of the lost pages between the sport and the classifieds. If Terry and his ilk ever found a story really worth writing it was taken away from them and given to one of the office occupiers. Terry had grown more resentful as the years had gone by and he'd taken every opportunity to stick one to the posh boys and the intellectuals. When the offer of a move to a red top had come in, he'd jumped at the chance but it hadn't eased the bitterness he felt at being kept so low by his old employers. Now he spent his days using his web of contacts to get him the latest dirt on footballers' affairs, pop stars' breakdowns and politicians' dirty little secrets. And he'd made himself a good name. For a tabloid hack.

That morning one of his sources had come to him with a story so unbelievable he'd told them to stop wasting his time.

That was before they produced an eye-witness source of their own—a French woman named Sophie, who had a conspiracy theory about the death of a kid called Jackson Scott. Terry had jumped straight on a train to Paris and spent the afternoon getting the full story, including an interview with the woman in question. Not a bad-looking blonde as it happened, so it had been a pretty pleasant way to spend a couple of hours. Now, equipped with the sound recording on his iPhone as well as the photos he'd taken, he was on his way back to the Eurostar terminal to get everything to his editor to write up for the next day's paper.

'Geoff, it's Terry.'

'Where the hell are you, Terry? We've got two Premiership boys playing away from home again and we need someone on the story before the lawyers get an injunction.'

'I'm in Paris.'

'Paris? What the fuck are you doing there?'

'I've got something, Geoff. It's big. Really big. I've been doing an interview, I've got everything we need. No other paper has this story, we'll be the first to break it.' Terry could hear the hesitation on the other end of the line. Geoff was clearly angry that he'd inexplicably disappeared abroad on the company's time and expense account, but the temptation of the story was winning him over.

'What have you got?'

'I can't say,' Terry replied quickly into his phone as he climbed out of a taxi in front of the Gare du Nord. 'I don't know who might be listening. Honestly, Geoff, this is massive. It's front page broadsheet, but these people don't trust anyone they don't know. I got this through a friend of a friend, so we'll be the ones to break it first.' Like Terry, Geoff had always had aspirations above red top status that had been thwarted at an early point in his career because he didn't have the right accent or well-connected parents. Terry could hear the anticipation in his boss's voice as he told him to get back to the office with the story and fill him in right away. As he hung up his phone and shoved it into the pocket of his shiny suit, Terry Dowler's jowled face was set in smug anticipation of the glory and recognition waiting for him back home. Finally, his time had come.

WHEN THE SMART but unremarkable dark-skinned man carrying a small leather briefcase hit him hard on the shoulder, spinning him so that their bodies met almost like lovers, he opened his mouth to spit a retaliatory curse but was distracted by a small stabbing pain in his right thigh. He dropped his bag in shock, bent down over his thigh and, by the time he looked up again, the man had disappeared. He rubbed his leg with his palm as the pain subsided and picked up his bag. It had felt as if the man had pinched him but it must just have been a muscle twinge from the impact—he was getting more of that as the years went on. Terry pulled himself together, cursing the rudeness of the damned Frogs and then treated himself to a Eurostar upgrade as a reward for the day's efforts. On the train he noticed his iPhone was missing and realised the man at the station must have been a thief.

Once again he cursed the damned Frogs and anyone else he could think of. When he calmed down he decided he'd report it the minute he arrived in London. He could claim it on insurance, get a knock off one from his brother then sell the new one on eBay for a tidy profit. The theft of the phone might mean he had lost the sound recording, but he had Sophie's number so he would just call her back and explain what had happened, maybe get her to email a quotable statement or something. Anyway, it wasn't like he was going to forget the story in a hurry. He sat back in his seat with a beer and looked forward to getting back to London and breaking this thing wide open.

By the time the Eurostar pulled into the terminal at St Pancras International Terry Dowler was dead.

Pushing open the glass doors to her hotel, Eva greeted the sour-faced receptionist. She felt his eyes on her as she walked away from reception and noticed the hairs on the back of her neck stand up with unease. She stood waiting for the tiny lift to make its rickety way back down to ground level and then leaned against the mirrored interior as it took her up to the first floor. Finally, she opened the door to her room and threw her bag on the bed. She walked towards the bathroom.

And then she stopped. On the floor next to the battered old wardrobe was her hairbrush. Eva looked around the room. Had she left it there? She thought back. No. The hairbrush had definitely not been there when she had left that morning. She walked into the bathroom and checked for clean towels. The towels were hanging over the door in exactly the same position that she had left them, one was still damp. The maid had not come.

EVA IMMEDIATELY RUSHED to the bed and pulled back her mattress. She dragged out her laptop and sighed with relief. Thank God. At least she hadn't been robbed. But when she opened the laptop she realised it was off. She had charged it overnight, which meant it had full power, and from the standby state she had left it in that morning would have had to be physically shut down in order for it to be turned off. She sat down on the bed with the laptop in her hands. A chill trickled down her spine. Someone had been in her room.

As she looked around it become obvious that, although not much was out of place, things had been moved. The wardrobe door was slightly ajar even though she had shut it firmly that morning. The two books on the night stand were not lined up as she had left them. The chair was not exactly parallel to the small, scratched dressing table. Eva suffered from a mild obsessive compulsive disorder, which required straight lines, clear surfaces and shut doors—she would not have left the room like this. She turned on the laptop and searched for anything that might have incriminated her. But incriminating for what? And to whom? There was nothing on there other than a few old articles for the magazine and some drafts of boring emails about bills or rent. If someone had been through her things, who were they and what were they looking for?

AFTER SEVERAL MINUTES of sitting on the bed, Eva began to move again. Methodically, she checked the latch on the one window in her room—locked—and on the small frosted glass opening in the bathroom—large and openable but barred from the outside. Gently she opened the door to her room and ran her fingers over the lock as she glanced down the shadowy hotel corridor. The metal felt smooth and unscarred. She looked more closely at the metal mechanism and gently moved the handle up and down. As she leaned in, she realised there were tiny, almost invisible scratches on the moveable part of the lock; the logical assumption would be that it had been forced. She closed the door again, locked it and took a long drink from a plastic bottle of water. There was a strong possibility that this was Leon's handiwork. He had known she would be out with Valerie today and she hadn't seen him at any point during the time she had spent with Jackson's old flame. But there was no logical reason for him to break in here when he had already made contact. Years of watching conspiracy films made Eva stand up and begin running her hands over and under surfaces for bugs or listening devices of any sort. But of course she didn't even know what she was looking for, and if that was the reason her room had been broken into then she doubted whoever had done it would make them so easy to find that an amateur could do it. This was a worrying development and one that made her feel even more vulnerable, as if she didn't feel that enough already. She needed to do something.

EVA FLICKED ON the light on the bed side table and immediately her eyes fell on the sports bag that she had picked up from Jackson's old place of work the day before. She hauled it up on the bed and pulled open the zip. Inside was a mass of papers. Eva sat back in surprise. She had not expected that. Presumably, whoever had broken into her room had already had a good old rifle through these documents, but it still might be worth her having a look.

She started pulling out pages of documents, some photo-copies, some heavily redacted and some made up purely of graphs and tables. They made very little sense to her at first glance, particularly because they seemed to be in no particular order and the subject matter different in almost every case. Frustrating. She paused for sev-eral seconds and then picked up the bag by one end and tipped the whole mass of papers out onto the bed. Then she began the time consuming process of sorting each paper into a relevant pile.

It was 2:00 a.m. before Eva finished her mam-moth sorting exercise. Now she was sitting on the bed thoughtfully, eating a strip of chocolate and staring at the achievement on the floor at her feet—twenty-five neat piles of paper. She finished the chocolate, wiped her fin-gers, picked up the pile nearest to her and began to sift through the papers once again. The theme for this pile had been 'the Sudan'. All the documents related to that country, in particular an apparently fairly remote area in the vicinity of a town called Torit. There were ordnance survey maps, aerial photographs, a report entitled Spate Irrigation For Rural Growth and Poverty Alleviation by UNESCO, and several long, apparently unpublished, ar-ticles that looked at the health of the local population. The document that had really interested her was pro-duced by the organisation Doctors Without Borders and reported in 2010 on one of the worst disease outbreaks in the region for eight years. The outbreak was described as a humanitarian crisis, one that had been made worse by a lack of basic sanitation or access to proper medical care. Eva tried to think back but she didn't remember seeing anything on the news about it. The disease was thought to be a strain of Kala-azar—fatal in almost 100 percent of cases—but there were parts of the report that questioned whether it wasn't some kind of new epidemic. The report interested Eva because it didn't seem able to make up its mind about the disease and yet it had still been published.

OTHER THAN THE Sudan pile, Eva had tidied piles on 'Paris' (more maps, photos and directions to places in the French capital), 'Photos' (a collection of mug and action shots of people who she assumed could be Sudanese, mostly taken in Paris from what she could tell), 'Paraguay' (more maps and aerial shots of some remote location between Brazil and Paraguay), 'PX 3' (a pile of scientific formulas that she didn't grasp at all), 'meetings' (a list of times and dates with apparent code names such as 'Mr C' listed alongside them), 'phone calls' (reams of print-outs of telephone conversations that she hadn't read all of but that seemed harmless enough) and 'ACORN', the biggest pile which seemed to be made up of almost completely useless documents about a company called ACORN that, as far as she could tell, was an all-purpose shelf company. Eva felt as if she had read and absorbed a hell of a lot of information but was still none the wiser as to what she had found. The only link with anything that had happened to her was Leon's reference to 'the Africans', but he hadn't explained it so she couldn't re-alistically connect it to anything here. The heaviness of tiredness began to pull her downwards so she turned away from the papers, curled up on the bed with her mobile phone clutched in one hand and went to sleep.

EIGHT

THE NEXT MORNING Eva awoke with a start. Sophie. The name Sophie was running through her head and suddenly, as clear as a bell, she started to make connections. The face she had seen in Jackson's 'friends' on Facebook and also in the picture Leon had shown her whilst at his flat; the name Valerie had mentioned as the suspected person with whom Jackson had been having an affair and now...she rolled over, bent down and rifled through one of the piles of paper on the floor. There...Sophie Vincent. The name was written in stark, black type along the bottom of one of the sheets of paper she had been sorting through the night before. Sophie Vincent had printed out these documents. Eva propped herself up on one elbow and stared at the name on the bottom of the sheet of paper as she realised that she had seen it on a huge number of the documents she had leafed through the night before. She threw back the bed sheet, slid off the bed into a crouch on the floor by all the piles of paper and started sorting through them again, this time looking for that name. Within thirty minutes more than half the papers previously divided into neat stacks were on the 'Sophie' pile.

'WE CAN'T FIND HER.' It was obvious to Nijam that his brother was not happy even before Wiraj had turned his narrow features to face his brother's broad face.

'We must find her.'

'She is impossible to find.'

'I thought we had a tail on her.'

'We did. And we found the man she spoke to yesterday—a journalist, Terry Dowler. But she slipped away and has not come into work today, Wiraj.'

'She cannot have just disappeared in the middle of the night.'

'It seems that she has.'

'And what about her apartment?'

'There is no-one there.'

'Have you been inside?'

'Yes. We have turned the place inside out but we had to do it at speed, Wiraj.'

'Dammit, we should have acted sooner, why didn't we act sooner?' Silence filled the room and Wiraj glanced slowly at each of the faces of the three men he had brought with him to fulfil this delicate series of steps. Delicate because with their dark skin and borrowed winter clothes they stood out so obviously in the areas of Paris they had so far had to operate in. And delicate because there was only so much room for failure before they would find themselves losing more than just the fee for the job.

JOSEPH SMITH'S BONY FACE, with its dark hollow eyes and square-set jaw, filled Wiraj's mind. Back in the Sudan, Smith held an exalted position, having left at an early age for Europe and returned with money, power and influence that only a foreign business connection could buy. No one knew exactly what he did or who he worked for, but he had come back to his home town and begun recruiting former friends and acquaintances, offering

the kind of money that no one could ig̶
he gave with one hand, he took with anot̶
he had arrived in the village there had bee̶
explained disappearances. Several of Wira̶
had gone to work for Smith and never returne̶. As the
oldest in his family, their father already passed, Wiraj
had accepted Smith's offer of work for him, his brother
and three of their friends, in spite of the risk, but had
never foreseen it would bring them here, to Paris. He
still had no idea who stood behind Joseph Smith, or
why they were being asked to carry out the bizarre list
of tasks they had been given. But Joseph Smith was not
the kind of man that many people dared to question. If
he wanted them to rub out every trace of a life that was
what they would do. Wiraj glanced around at the faces
in the room. They seemed anxious, deflated and lack-
ing in fight. If they were going to get out of this situation with their money and their lives then he needed to
be a better leader.

'Come,' he said, taking a step towards the group. 'We
are not defeated yet, are we? Sophie Vincent will re-
surface, she must, she is just a common secretary, she
doesn't have the resources to disappear.'

'Yes,' said his brother, his face visibly brightening.

'And in the meantime we know the location of the
British girl.'

'We know her hotel.'

'And we have her mobile telephone.'

'Not yet.'

Another burst of irritation pricked Wiraj's skin. 'We
don't have it?' he repeated, making sure he kept his voice
as calm as possible.

'No. But we will—we just need to collect it.'

ᴇVA SPENT FIFTEEN minutes staring at the bundle of papers in front of her before she finally got up and decided to take a shower. She had checked each one of the—now creased—documents and they all had the same tag-line at the bottom. Sophie had printed all of them out over the period two months before Jackson disappeared, at regular weekly intervals and almost at the same hour of the day each time. Most had been printed out at 6am but the last batch—the largest one—was time-stamped between 11pm and 1am. In the 'Sophie' pile were all the documents that Eva understood the least. The aerial photographs and ordnance survey maps were in this pile, along with documents filled with what looked like mathematical calculations, a set of passwords and the strings of email conversations. Eva had read these several times but could see nothing more than a casual discussion about unimportant matters. She had found it impossible to draw together a common thread from everything in front of her—the only thing all these documents had in common was Sophie's name on the bottom.

Aꜱ ꜱʜᴇ ᴄʟɪᴍʙᴇᴅ out of the shower and dried herself, Eva tried to imagine what it was that was connecting Jackson to any of the documents in the bag. Some of the materials related to Sudan and there the connection was obvious as that was where his work had been focused, but few of the papers dealt with anything related to the distribution of aid that had been his job. Perhaps the sports bag was simply a dumping ground for peripheral information that he meant to read later or wanted to take home with him and she was looking for meaning where there was none. At the back of her mind was the constant niggling thought that someone had been in her room the day before. She couldn't start getting too deep into that kind of paranoia, but if she was right, no doubt whoever it was would have searched the sports bag and if there had been anything in there of interest it was probably now gone.

KNOTTING THE THREADBARE towel around her chest, Eva began drying her hair, brushing it through and following the slow brush stroke with the hotel's unenthusiastic hair dryer. She was going to have to contact Sophie Vincent and hope that was a good move. Leon had been in touch several times the day before trying to arrange another meeting and Eva was unnerved by the fact that he had programmed his number into her phone before he had given it back to her. It made her wonder what else he had done to it or taken off it. She hadn't forgotten their encounter several nights before and nor could she settle on whether or not she trusted him. However, the man he had shot outside his flat—the man who had put a bag over her head—gave her pause for reflection when she thought about trying to disappear from him. Perhaps she needed Leon in the sidelines—as long as she was in control—but the question of whether or not it was possible to remain in control of a situation that involved someone like Leon weighed heavy on her mind. Either way, he could not be her only option for moving forward. She couldn't solely rely on his conspiracy theories, she needed ammunition of her own. She would message Sophie Vincent through Facebook and hope she checked her messages. Leon would never know.

NINE

'WE THINK IT'S a gang execution.' Inspector Legrand of the Préfecture de Police frowned as his sergeant delivered this piece of news.

'Really?' he said, glancing down at the spot on the floor where the British victim had been found.

'You think that was an execution?'

'This estate is a notorious area for the Apaches, sir. This man was not local, he lived alone and, by all accounts, he was not particularly respected in this area. His neighbour said he was often on the receiving end of taunts and bullying.'

'That's still not a motivation for murder.'

'Sometimes the fact that someone is an outsider is all they need.' Legrand looked at Gagnere.

'I grew up around here, sir,' the junior policeman said in response to the look. 'I was myself almost a victim of their violence as a teenager. If you find a corpse within several miles of these estates you can guarantee they are responsible.' Legrand digested this less than impartial information.

He looked around the shabby flat where the dead man had been found. What a way to live. 'Nevertheless I'm not sure we should write this case off as a simple execution until we know for sure.' Gagnere nodded and then watched as Legrand walked over to the other side of the room and plucked a lone birthday card from the mantelpiece. 'Happy Birthday Son.' He carefully replaced the card and turned to face Gagnere.

'I wouldn't have thought suffocation was the Apaches' style, Gagnere. If that is indeed how that man died.' The smaller policeman shifted on his feet.

'Well, it's not—usually. But, like I said, murder and these gangs, they go together. I can start flicking through the profiles we have for possible suspects, sir—to make sure we get a head start on them.' Legrand could see he had already charged and convicted someone in his head. But maybe he had a point. He decided to allow Gagnere to run with his theory—within reason.

'Fine. But don't make contact with anyone until you have my say-so. And get forensics to take a good look at this place. There must be fingerprints here somewhere, a boot-print on the carpet, a hair on the floor. Most people cannot murder in cold blood, no matter how schooled they have been. It's an emotional business taking a life. And emotion makes people careless.'

'Yes sir.'

'When are we likely to see the preliminary autopsy report?'

'Some time this afternoon.'

'I want to know the minute it's ready.'

As soon as Eva had sent the message to Sophie she immediately felt better. Just taking some action—any action—was enough to shift that feeling of not being in control. She had taken care to compose a message that gave nothing away but would (hopefully) not cause Sophie to feel threatened. Once she had pressed 'send' Eva shut her laptop. This time, she didn't hide it but left it resting on top of the bed. Carefully, she pulled out one of her own long, dark hairs and wrapped it over the front opening of the laptop. She tucked one end under the laptop between the machine and the bed and placed a book on top of the laptop with the hair underneath it so that it was stretched over the opening. The hair was completely invisible against the black laptop case and she would know immediately when she returned if it had been opened, even if the book was replaced on top. Checking the hair was still in place as she moved, Eva stood and walked over to the wardrobe. She selected a light-coloured blouse with a small round collar and a cheerful blue anchor print, put it on and buttoned it right to the neck, before tucking it into a pair of black jeans. The weather outside seemed bright, the sky blue, so she opted for a warm woollen military-style coat with bright gold buttons, rather than something more waterproof. Once she was ready to leave, Eva did one last sweep of the room, straightening corners and shutting doors. Then she picked up three of the papers she had selected from the 'Sophie' pile and shoved them into her bag before heading out of the door.

SEVERAL STREETS OVER from her hotel Eva stopped for breakfast at one of the many tiny cafés in the area. From the outside these establishments seemed to be the French equivalent of a greasy spoon—watery coffee and tasteless food—but she was always pleasantly surprised to find that inside she could consume hypertension-strong, sweet coffee and the butteriest, flakiest of croissants for just small change. As she sat down at a small metal table, she felt the waistband of her jeans press slightly into the slight curve of her stomach and wondered whether she should lay off the croissants for

a while, before concluding that now wasn't the time for
dieting. As she drank her coffee in slow, short sips, Eva
looked at the documents she had brought with her. Next
to all the information that ran along the bottom displaying Sophie's name and the dates and times that she had
printed the documents was the name of the company that
Sophie presumably worked for—Bioavancement S.a.r.l.
Eva had spent at least an hour searching the internet but
had found no trace of this mysterious organisation. There
was no company website, no hits on business networking pages, no news stories, no directories recording its
address. Eva had searched UK Companies House website but Bioavancement S.a.r.l. had no UK subsidiary
and she didn't know the French equivalent of Companies
House. This in itself was puzzling to her. Everyone used
the internet now—it was the primary source of marketing for many businesses and almost impossible for any
company to escape even a mention of its name on a website or chatroom posted there by someone else. The only
organisations that didn't have a public web face were
those that didn't want the public to know they existed.

HOWEVER, WHILST THE internet had proved to be barren
ground for information on Bioavancement S.a.r.l., the
papers in the sports bag had not and she had discovered
that one of the printed-out Google maps showed a Paris
location with the word 'Bioavancement S.a.r.l.' scrawled
next to it in black pen. The writing was Jackson's, without a doubt, and his unintelligible scrawl made it virtually illegible to anyone other than another person with
an identical style of terrible handwriting. Once she had
finished her breakfast, Eva packed the papers away deep
in her bag, other than the map, which she stowed in the

pocket of her jeans. She asked for a glass of water, which she finished in one go, and then she paid her bill and left. Outside, the sky was still a brilliant blue and the streets were quietening down as the post-rush-hour buzz began to fade away. Eva took her phone from her pocket and opened the maps app in which she had managed to find the Bioavancement S.a.r.l. address, thanks to a Métro stop and road names on the paper copy. The app showed that she was less than a mile away, just north of the location. She memorised the next three turnings she would have to take, pocketed the map and then set off south.

WHEN WIRAJ HAD heard nothing from the boys he had recruited to rob the young English woman of her phone, he had taken Tahir, Muhammad and Nijam and gone to look for them. The estate where the children hung around was across the road from the flat where they knew the dead Englishman had lived. When the four men went back there after a wintry darkness fell that afternoon, there was a police cordon around the flat where the execution had been carried out. Wiraj was acutely aware that he was breaking every rule in the book by coming back here. They could be identified at any minute by a neighbour or the crazy old man they had passed at the front door, but Wiraj had to find that phone. He hoped that under the cover of darkness, with their hoods and low-slung jeans making them look like all the other shadows moving stealthily around the dark housing estates, he and the others would not be identified. The four men took a side road away from the cordoned-off area and traversed the estate opposite looking for the kids. At the back of a long-abandoned children's playground, they saw the shadows of a group of five people smoking and taking long gasps of air from black plastic sacks. The men approached the group silently, so that they all jumped when Wiraj stepped out of the darkness and spoke.

'You were supposed to contact me.' The tallest boy turned in his seat on the asphalt and looked up at him steadily, meeting his gaze with darkly ringed eyes.

'There was no point.'

'I paid you to get me the phone.'

'We did get it.'

'I want it.'

'We don't have it any more.' Wiraj took a step forward. 'Who did you sell it to?'

'We didn't.'

'Then where is it?' The boy rose to his feet. He was as tall as Wiraj, although skinnier and not as broad.

'I told you, we don't have it,' he said, aggression leaking into his voice.

'Then give me my money back.'

'No.' Silence fell between the two.

Wiraj regarded his opponents. These were not children, he thought steadily, forcing himself not to overreact. They had the angry, unpredictable air of damaged adults. Before he could complete his train of thought he realised that the boy opposite him was now holding a knife. It had a curved, serrated blade that caught the light as he moved it subtly from hand to hand. He looked at the boy who met his gaze blankly, continuing to move the knife just below Wiraj's eyeline. The two stood opposite each other; nobody moved. Neither party could anticipate the reaction of the other; both were on the defensive. After several minutes, there was a slight movement behind Wiraj and, as he turned, he saw that a gun had been drawn by one of the other kids, a small handgun that looked like a very old model Glock. The balance of power had shifted.

WIRAJ FELT MUHAMMAD tense up behind him. The enormous rhino of a man could probably rip these children in two with his bare hands—unless they shot him first. He willed him to stay calm. They needed to get information. The boy in front of him took a step towards Wiraj. There was a narcotic glaze over his eyes. 'We don't have your phone.'

'Then give me back my money.'

'Are you threatening me?' The kid swiped the knife at Wiraj, who recognised it as a feint and stayed absolutely still.

'Give me my money back or give me the phone,' he repeated.

Suddenly the boy began to laugh and all the others joined in, creating a high-pitched, maniacal sound like a pack of hyenas. In the almost complete darkness, with the only light from a small fire on the ground where they were burning newspapers, it was an eerie scene. The boy with the gun moved so that he was standing next to Tahir and put the gun up against his right temple, apparently without any fear of reprisal. Tahir looked at Wiraj, who looked away. Once he had finished laughing, the first boy leaned in to Wiraj so that their faces were only a hand-breadth apart, the knife flashing in his hands only inches away from Wiraj's waist. He paused before he spoke, drawing out the tension of the situation.

'You have an enemy, my friend.' Drops of spittle flecked Wiraj's face.

'And he's way ahead of you.' He smiled a yellow-toothed, leering smile.

'He came and took that phone; he knew exactly what he wanted. We told him all about you.' He smiled.

'You're next,' he said, lifting two fingers of his free hand into the air to simulate the firing of a gun. As he did so Wiraj, with a skill and speed acquired from spending his life defending himself on the streets and slums of Khartoum, snatched the fingers wrapped around the knife and disembowelled the boy by his own hand. He moved quickly out of the way as the body fell forward, a stunned look on the boy's face as he briefly saw his entrails falling through his tracksuit in front of him to the floor. A split second later, Tahir brought a fist up into the face of the boy holding a gun and heard the satisfying crunch of a broken nose. The boy's gun hand flew up in reaction and Tahir punched him hard in the ribs and swiftly disarmed him before pushing him to the ground and stamping down hard on his head with the heavy sole of his thick boots. The boy didn't move. The other three boys recovered quickly and began to run, disappearing like wraiths into the shadows without a sound. Wiraj held his hand up to stop any pursuit. He pulled a small case from the inside of his coat and flicked it open, letting the shell drop to the floor as he withdrew a small syringe from inside. Then, calmly, he walked back over to the prone child that Tahir had felled and injected him in the thigh.

TEN

IN AN AREA in the far west of London, a new development had been fascinating the locals. The temporary structure had appeared on the site of a disused waterworks, a series of enormous plastic tents the size of several football pitches, underneath which there seemed to be some kind of construction taking place. Local residents had noticed lights and activity over three nights and had seen JCB diggers and workmen arriving during the day. There was a buzz about whether this was lottery money—a new project for the local community. Close to the muddy banks of the Thames in a forgotten area of old waterworks and abandoned land, they desperately needed some kind of regeneration. Those who thought about it realised they hadn't seen any planning permission notices, but it had only been three days and they assumed there would be an article in the paper by the weekend. The lorries that had been making deliveries were unmarked, other than a small acorn image on the back door, and the security around the site was tight. The residents had busy lives; three days went by in a blur of offices, school runs and evening meals. No one did anything.

Inside one of the tents, engineer Rob Gorben surveyed the results of the last three nights' work. Six large raceway ponds, so named because of their similarity to a racetrack, were set out before him. Each one was 1000

metres square, 35 centimetres deep, lined with cement
and fitted with a motorised paddle at one end. The raceways were the most typical design for uncovered algae
growing and he and his team had managed to set these
six up in just three days, which was a record even for
his efficient group. It had helped that they were starting
on the site of an old waterworks but they had still had to
demolish much of the existing structure and start again.
They had been working through the night through the
whole 72 hours and they had hit their incredibly tight
schedule bang on time, which meant they'd be in for
a sizeable bonus. All that was left now was to fill the
ponds and implant the algae. Gorben shut down everything other than the security lights and went home to
his family.

LATER THAT EVENING, Eva returned to her hotel, none
the wiser about the identity of Bioavancement S.a.r.l.,
or what the company's business was. She had easily located the building after just a half an hour's walk, only to
find it as impenetrable as Fort Knox. There was a small,
rectangular metal plate marking the spot as belonging to
Bioavancement S.a.r.l. but the building appeared to be
empty as no lights showed at any of the windows, and
not a single person had gone near the building for at least
an hour. Eva had taken up a position in a café across the
street, determined to watch the comings and goings, but
no one had come and no one had gone. The office was
not located on a particularly busy street but nevertheless there were people going in and out of the apartment
block on one side of the Bioavancement S.a.r.l. office,
and the florist's shop on the other. After she had consumed three strong coffees, she had decided to go over

and try to get into the building herself on some pretext or other, but the reception bell had gone unanswered and the door—when she tried it—was locked. At this point, Eva had become frustrated and she had turned back towards the hotel. That was when she had spotted Leon.

AT FIRST SHE wasn't sure that it was definitely him, but there was something about the well-built man in the dark baseball cap that reminded her of that moment she had seen Leon for the first time silhouetted against the light from the door in his flat. Over the past few days Eva had done her best to forget about the violence of that incident. Whilst she couldn't dismiss Leon from her mind and had felt almost constantly on edge, she had been so caught up in the documents in the sports bag that she had managed successfully to sideline the shooting. Rather than dwell on the startling events of that night she had chosen to push it to one side and look instead for positive steps forward. Deep down, she knew that if she thought about it too much she would most probably lose her nerve with this whole situation. Right now, what had happened that night—someone getting shot—had seemed almost like a dream. In fact, if it wasn't for the enormous bruise on her leg where he had clipped her with the car then she might even have been able to write it off as just that. But here he was again. On foot this time, but very definitely there.

AS EVA MADE her way back to the hotel she spotted him twice, once in the curved surface of a parking mirror and then again in the reflection of the glass doors as she entered her hotel. She considered stopping and speaking to him. That he felt the need to shadow her incognito when he could just call her was faintly ridiculous, but the fact that he was still doing it made her think twice.

There had been someone outside Leon's block of flats who had attacked her. Had Leon set that up? Had that been a genuine attack? She still didn't know. But for some reason she found Leon's shadowing comforting rather than threatening and so—despite her better judgement—she just let him do it.

'WE MUST GET that fucking phone.'

'Wiraj we have no idea where it is.' Nijam was almost pleading with his brother as they sat once again in their shabby hotel room, the bare electric light bulb flickering weakly overhead.

'We are not psychic, I don't understand how you expect us to find it, Wiraj.'

'I don't care!' came the roared reply.

There was silence for several seconds and each man in the room found something on his hands, or a spot on the floor, to occupy him. None of them dared to look at Wiraj. The incident with the estate kids had been a disaster and Wiraj was ashamed that he had so quickly lost control and reacted with violence. They were supposed to leave no trace and yet they had two more deaths on their hands now, as well as witnesses. Whilst he seriously doubted that those kids ever went near the police, they could still identify Wiraj and his crew to other interested parties who might want to seek some kind of retribution for the deaths in the community. Suddenly, Wiraj's own mobile phone buzzed to life with the only number it contained, 'Joseph Smith'. He jumped violently and then ended the call. He could not speak to Smith now. He needed time to think. As he put the phone back on the table he saw the look on his brother's face as he noticed the name of the caller whose call had been so rudely ended. Nijam was afraid. That enormous killer of a man was afraid. They were in too deep now.

'KILL HER.'

'Who?'

'The British woman. I have had enough. We cannot waste any further time. Kill her and search her room for the phone, or for any other trace of those messages.'

'Wiraj is there no...'

'Nijam,' Wiraj spoke wearily. The flat tone of his voice surprised his brother. 'We have no other choice. If you want to live, we have no other choice.'

'This must surely be a gang execution, sir.' Gagnere looked almost triumphant as they stood above the bodies of two teenage boys, both known to Legrand, one of whom had been savagely stabbed.

Legrand stared down at the carnage on the tarmac, the abandoned bags of solvents, the glassy eyes of the dead child at his feet. He briefly wondered what the point of a life was that was so wasted like this. He felt Gagnere staring at him and looked up.

'I'm still not convinced. There's no consistency here—one stabbed and the other, what, suffocated like the Englishman? Beaten to death?' Gagnere frowned.

'But these kids are gang kids. You know that sir, we've dealt with them before.'

'I know. Does that mean they cannot be victims themselves?' Gagnere was silent, reprimanded. Around the two men, the Parisian police force was moving silently, setting up spotlights, donning forensic suits, preparing to work through the night in an area that most of them would not have wanted to be in during daylight hours.

'It just doesn't feel right, Gagnere. This is not the way these gangs normally carry out their executions. There is no mutilating mark, there is no motivation. These estates have been quiet for two months now. Why should a killing like this suddenly happen?'

'I don't know sir.'

'Have we managed to corral any witnesses?' Gagnere shook his head.

'No, of course we haven't,' said Legrand wearily. 'No-one around here sees anything.'

ELEVEN

JOHN MANSFIELD WAS not a man who liked to be kept waiting. He particularly did not like to be kept waiting when he had gone out of his way to attend a meeting that was taking place in the dead of night—a fact that would create intense suspicion if it made it into the papers—and that could effectively end his entire political career if his presence there was made public. He looked around the mahogany-lined room at the other participants also waiting for the Bioavancement S.a.r.l. CEO to arrive. Thankfully, these were members of some of the most media-shy organisations in the world, or he would never have agreed to be physically present for the meeting, no matter how important the CEO thought it was. Around the room everyone was waiting, constantly checking Rolex or Cartier time-pieces, watching as the solid gold hands made their inevitable progress towards the hour after the meeting was supposed to have started. Finally, a small door at the back of the room opened and the CEO emerged, padding across the dark fields of the Persian Tabriz rug-lined floor to a red, stuffed leather chair. He gazed around the now silent room, coolly taking in every feature of the nine faces gathered around the table. Between them they represented three of the biggest and richest pharmaceutical conglomerates on the planet. And their lawyers.

'Gentlemen, thank you for coming.' When he spoke

it was with the cut-glass confidence of the highest echelons of British education. There were nods from around the table and John Mansfield nervously downed the remainder of his creamy coffee from the delicate bone-china Worcester cup.

'Today is something of a momentous day for us,' the CEO announced, his smooth tone and open gestures intended to set at ease those around the table who might be having any last minute doubts.

'Thanks to the excellent groundwork of our board member,' he gestured at Mansfield, who nodded at the assembled heads that immediately turned his way, 'we have our approval.' There was a wave of recognition around the room.

'As of this moment, the Medicines and Healthcare Products Regulatory Agency has certified us free and clear to go ahead with the manufacture and sale of PX 3.' The CEO paused for several seconds to let the implications sink in and the financial rewards be calculated.

'We have already begun building the algae pools in locations around the UK and the first set-ups are complete. In just a few days the plants themselves will follow from our storage facility in Africa.'

'When will it be ready for sale?'

'As you know, thanks to the genetically modified design of the algae, they bloom on contact with oxygen. The bloom will yield algae in triple quantities in around a fifth of the time it would normally take to grow. Once the ponds are established, we can trigger the bloom, harvest the plants and begin the manufacturing process.'

'How long from harvest to delivery?'

'Roughly two months.' There were nods around the table.

'We are almost ready to sell the people of the UK their youth back. Your investment is about to pay off, gentlemen.' Mansfield could almost hear the collective exhalation of relief around the room. To many of these industry heavyweights, their connection with Bioavancement S.a.r.l. may have created a sense of unease, in spite of the fact that it was always a somewhat rocky road that pharmaceutical companies trod when it came to launching new supplements. The PX 3 was by no means the first supplement to claim to preserve, or engineer, youthfulness in those who took it, but because it was made from a genetically engineered plant, there was an extra hurdle of distrust to overcome. Nevertheless, they had invested heavily in its development, predominantly because, with the right marketing, it had enormous mass market appeal, and the potential to generate billions in profit.

FEW OF THOSE around this table had believed at the beginning that the company could ever obtain approval for the product without palms being greased somewhere along the line but somehow, although the CEO had never mentioned any inside connections, he had still managed to convince each one of them that their investment would yield results that were worth the risk to their businesses and their reputations. No doubt the enormous profits had been a fairly substantial carrot; and the fact that Bioavancement S.a.r.l. held all the patents on the groundbreaking genetically engineered plant was probably a pretty big stick. Mansfield had always had the impression that many of those present felt rather swept away by the force of the CEO's charm and, afterwards, had perhaps regretted both the capital outlay and the association with the company. Now, however, they were about to receive the ultimate reward for the investor in risky ventures: an enormously high return.

MANSFIELD WATCHED AS the CEO closed the meeting and then made his way around the room, oiling the wheels of his investments, congratulating, flattering and exciting all those in the room. He really was quite a piece of work. When he came to Mansfield, his smile was bright.

'Minister. Congratulations. I really can't tell you how happy I am that you have been of such great assistance.'

'As am I.'

'Is anyone aware of your involvement with us?'

'No,' the MP replied confidently. 'And I would like to keep it that way.' He laughed nervously and the CEO smiled.

'Of course,' he said, locking Mansfield's hands in his own cold grip. 'Well, I hope we make it worth your while at the very least.' He released Mansfield's hand, bade him goodbye and walked away.

EVA WAS JOLTED out of her sleep by the sound of a new email arriving on her laptop. She sat up stiffly and checked the time on the small travel clock by her head. It was 9:00 p.m.; she had been asleep for several hours. Rubbing her eyes and stretching her limbs, she tried to get the blood flowing into her sleepy body. She felt terrible. She hated sleeping during the day, it always made her feel grumpy and irritable. She realised she must have fallen asleep searching for information on Bioavancement S.a.r.l.; another wasted hour spent fruitlessly tapping in different combinations of words into search engines. She didn't understand why there was no information at all on the company. It was almost as if it didn't exist. She reached into her bag for her phone and checked for new messages, but there was nothing, not even from Leon. Unwilling to drag her heavy limbs off the comfortable bed just yet, Eva turned her attention to her computer. Her email inbox told her a new Facebook message had arrived. Quickly she navigated to the website, glancing over a news feed full of gurgling babies, tropical beaches and drunken revellers and opened her messages folder. It was Sophie. At first, the message she was reading made no sense to Eva. It seemed almost as if it had been written in code.

'It is never safe. You must understand. Soon.' As she read it again Eva tried to put it in context. Sophie could well have written this in a rush from a location in which she didn't feel safe and where she wasn't confident that she wasn't being overlooked. That would explain the short sentences and the urgency of the message: 'It is never safe.' However, whilst the fact that she had replied at all was positive, as was the fact that she seemed to want to meet, it wasn't the kind of response Eva had hoped for. Sophie hadn't named a time or place, or even a method of communication so, once again, Eva could do nothing but wait.

She flipped her laptop shut in frustration, leaned back against the bed and ran a hand through her long hair. For some reason her skin was tingling with adrenaline. Sophie's message had made her nervous. Every step Eva took seemed to fall short of getting her any closer to what was really going on. And yet here she was, 'never safe', as Sophie had phrased it. She stood up and pushed her laptop aside, paused at the edge of the bed, then stalked around the room for several minutes. Finally she drew the curtains shut, threw off her T-shirt and headed for the shower.

OUTSIDE EVA'S HOTEL, Tahir watched as the light flicked on in the room he knew was her bathroom and then he waited until he saw clouds of steam starting to rise through the extractor fan. He regretted volunteering for this kill, but he was well aware that Wiraj felt he had not yet proved himself. During the execution of the British man in the suburbs he had taken up a position by the door, his back to Joseph Smith as he did his devil's work. Wiraj had been visibly unamused by Tahir's apparent cowardice, ashamed almost. Tahir had tried to ignore the sense of shame it created but Wiraj had a way of making one see one's own faults so clearly.

Sometimes the fervour in Wiraj's eyes frightened Tahir. Back in the Sudan they had all been insurgents, apart from Nijam who had been somehow swept along by his brother's fire. During those long nights when they had discussed the injustice, their cause had seemed valid. A new administration for their country, one that would open it up to business opportunities, wealth and progress for all, not just the corrupt few. But here, in Paris, Wiraj's plans seemed almost laughable. Even with the money they would make from doing this job for Joseph Smith, Wiraj's conviction that they could be crusaders against their own broken nation seemed ambitious at best.

NOT FOR THE first time, Tahir wondered whether Wiraj had really thought through the association with Joseph Smith. Tahir remembered Joseph Smith from school. He had been a loner as a child, the kind of boy who liked to pull the wings off birds and torture stray dogs. Tahir felt little empathy for the creatures that were hurt, but he thought that this behaviour showed that Smith did not understand how the world worked. He left the victims of his torture sessions on the road for all to see, and worse, he did what he did in public. Whilst Tahir was no saint—once he had beaten his girlfriend so hard after a disagreement that she was hospitalised for a week—he was at least clever about what he did. He had simply claimed there had been an intruder, a burglar. He filed a police report for lost cash and a stolen watch and ensured no one would ever speak of it by implying his girlfriend had let the man in to sleep with her. No one had ever challenged his version of events and the blame—as well as the shame—had fallen squarely on her. But Joseph Smith seemed to lack both sense and foresight and, as far as Tahir was concerned, that made him a bad associate. He didn't understand what Wiraj thought Smith could offer them in the way of assistance, unless there was something he knew that he hadn't shared with the rest of the group. But now was not the time for doubts. Tahir knew he had to act. He had done this kind of work before and the best time to catch a victim was when they were at their most vulnerable—asleep, having sex or engaged in any activity in the bathroom, where most people tended to feel they were safe. Eva Scott had just turned on the shower, which meant that now was his moment, the best chance he was going to get to do this cleanly.

According to Wiraj, the receptionist had been bribed so there would be no trouble getting in or out of the hotel as long as he made no mess. The hotel security cameras were off, only two other rooms were occupied, and there was no CCTV in the vicinity, so the risks were few.

HE TUCKED THE leather syringe case under his arm and walked towards the end of the alley where he had been hiding, turning in the direction of the entrance to the hotel. But as he went to step onto the pavement, he suddenly found himself being pushed backwards and propelled in reverse into the alleyway. A fist crashed with incredible force into the side of his head, shattering the bone of his left cheek and he dropped the leather case to bring up the flick knife in his pocket. Hearing the sssssh of Tahir's blade, his assailant expertly head-butted him, sending rivers of pain shimmering across the front of his nose and skull. Tahir grunted, stumbled back, one hand still brandishing the knife, the other pressed against his nose. He tried to get a glimpse of whose fists he was on the receiving end of, but the narrow street was dark and the assailant was dressed all in black. Tahir took several steps back, then positioned himself defensively, ready for the mystery attacker's next hit. The man in front of him did not hesitate. He aimed a sharp kick at Tahir's wrist, sending the knife skittering away. As Tahir hit out, making contact with the assailant's chest and left arm, the man delivered a sharp, disabling blow to the side of Tahir's head that made him see stars. With unnatural force, a shaky, disorientated Tahir felt himself being pulled towards the man and locked into a strange embrace. He felt one arm wrap around his torso, the other around his head and he was held for just a second. Then his neck was broken.

TWELVE

AT 4:00 A.M., Eva awoke with a start in the cold dimness of her room. There's someone here. Her heartbeat spiked as she sensed movement in the thick darkness. She had turned out her light an hour before, after finally forcing herself to ignore a barrage of fearful thoughts about everything that had been happening to her. But she knew she wasn't imagining it and there was someone else in the room. She resisted calling out or shouting for help. As long as the intruder thought she was asleep she had a slight advantage. Very slowly, she began pushing herself upright on the bed, her left hand stealthily reaching for the bedside lamp, the only weapon she could think of. Just as she felt her fingers close around the wire at the base of the cheap, pottery lamp, a figure appeared out of the shadows and moved like lightning across the room to the bed. Quickly, Eva yanked at the lamp and heard the loose plug pop out of the socket. She tried to get out of bed, but the oval of a face loomed over her and she was pushed backwards. She brought the lamp heavily into contact with the shadowy figure but it seemed to have no effect and, as a piece of material was shoved into her open mouth, she started to choke. She hit out again with the lamp, this time with more force, and heard a grunt as the pottery base broke against a shoulder. But the pieces of the shattered lamp just fell on the floor and the dark force above her kept on pushing her down, covering more of her face with the strange-smelling piece of material that now filled her mouth. Weaponless and barely able to breathe, Eva beat out with her fists and kicked with her feet but she could feel herself becoming nauseous and dizzy. She tried to scream through the material but the strong arms pinned her to the bed and her strength faded as the room started to spin.

Suddenly there was a light bright in her eyes and she felt whoever was holding her down loosen their grip as they turned towards the overhead light. She fought the nausea and dizziness drowning her and lashed out with one arm, willing her eyes to adjust quickly to the bright overhead light. Her eyes cleared and she could see the dark skin of an enormous hand holding the drugged fabric over her mouth and nose. Weakly she tried to push the arm away and then the man stood up, dropped the piece of fabric and gripped her head instead, pulling her backwards and upright in the bed by her hair. Woozily, Eva saw the bright flash of a knife in his left hand. Then everything seemed to just stand still. The man dropped the knife harmlessly onto her chest and began to fall forward over her; with the last of her energy she scrabbled out of the way and fell over the edge of the bed and onto the floor on the other side, her vision swimming. When she looked up over the side of the bed the man was face down on the bed, breathing heavily, his eyes closed.

'Get up.' Leon's voice. She turned her head and looked up at him as he loomed at her fuzzily in front of the light.

'Turn the light off,' she said breathlessly and leaned back against the bed trying to draw deep, stabilising breaths.

Leon leaned over her and flicked on the switch for

the remaining bedside lamp that was positioned on the table by her head then strode back across the room and turned off the main light.

The two stared at each other from opposite sides of the room. Eva was fighting a heavy combination of adrenaline and dizziness.

'I have no idea what the fuck you are doing, Leon. Or what the hell is going on.' She was still breathing heavily and her mind was unable to focus.

'I understand.'

'This amateur special ops crap is really wearing me out.' Even as she spoke in a voice that sounded nothing like her own, and despite the heaviness in her head, Eva was acutely aware of the unconscious man on the bed and her body was rigid with tension. But her head still felt dizzy and she could feel herself going into shock. None of this felt real. Leon slowly walked towards her and crouched in front of her on the floor.

'Eva.' He handed her a bottle of water from the bedside table.

'Eva, I don't know much of what is going on here either.' She drank the water and tried to focus on his face. She started to feel better.

'I hope you understand that I had to let you experience this. It was the only way to flush these people out.'

She looked at him uncomprehending. Then the penny dropped. 'You've been using me as bait.'

He nodded.

'That's just great.'

'I wouldn't have let anything happen to you.'

'Oh, don't be such a fucking idiot. Do you think this is a film?'

'That's why I tried to warn you before…'

She laughed. 'That was your way of warning me?'

'It is a complex situation.'

'You really need to take some lessons in communication.' A flash of anger rippled across his face.

'What have you done to him?' she said, nodding at the man on the bed. She heard herself speak—matter-of-factly, in a calm, thick voice—and she wondered how on earth she wasn't having some sort of panic attack after what had just happened. But she wasn't, and that was good.

'Tranquiliser.'

'Why not just kill him? Add another to your tally?'

'I had enough trouble disposing of the first body. We have fifteen minutes until he wakes up.'

'We?'

'You have to come with me now. I have a safe house, in the country.'

'You must be joking.'

Leon looked at her. 'I don't understand.'

'I'm not sure I feel any safer with you than on my own. You behave like a psychopath.' A tense silence fell in the room. Eva felt impressed at her own honesty. But she just wanted him to leave. Wherever Leon was there seemed to be chaos.

'If you stay on your own they will kill you today.'

'I've done OK so far.'

'No,' he said firmly. 'No, you haven't.' And then, before she could protest, 'Go and open your bathroom window.'

'It has bars.'

'Open it.'

Eva looked at him for several seconds and then stood up, put the bottle down on the bedside table and walked unsteadily into the bathroom. She pushed open the window and stuck her head out. 'What am I looking for?'

'There.' She jumped as Leon—now right behind her—spoke.

As she looked down, she gradually began to make out the outline of a human being propped up against some bins. She turned and looked at him.

'He would have killed you whilst you showered.' Eva looked back down at the bins. Her heart was beating wildly, her head swimming with questions. She didn't know what to think.

'You don't understand what you're caught up in here, Eva.'

'And you do?'

JUST BEFORE THEY reached the outskirts of Paris, Eva and Leon pulled in at a garage. Eva had agreed to go with him because she simply didn't know what else to do. The body by the bins had scared her enough to make her feel like she didn't want to be on her own and, in the short time she'd had to reason it through, Leon seemed like a better option than facing the increasing numbers of assailants by herself. He'd also had several opportunities to harm her if he'd wanted to and he hadn't. If he was playing a game, it was a much more complex and manipulative one than the other men threatening her and, for now at least, it seemed he wanted her alive.

As they sped through the dark city streets, the tension in the car was almost unbearable. However, once they passed the city limits, Leon seemed to relax.

Eva, on the other hand, was still unsteady after the most recent attack. She didn't know who to trust. As she tried to work through her situation, her normally clear and rational mind had become a confusion of assorted anxieties and arguments, magnified by being stuck in a confined space with Leon. When the lonely petrol station appeared on the horizon, she had insisted they stop. She desperately needed to create the chance to have five minutes alone. As soon as the car had come to a halt Eva stepped out and crunched over the gravel of the deserted forecourt to a sign that indicated a women's toilet. She glanced back warily at Leon before she pushed open the toilet door. She still had no idea whether he was really on her side.

As soon as she had disappeared into the building, Leon pulled out his phone.

'Where are you?'

'I'm still in Paris.'

'I told you to get out.'

'Leon, I have nowhere to go.'

'It's not safe.'

'I don't care. Do you have Eva Scott?'

'Yes.'

'Bring her to me.'

'I don't think that's a good idea.'

'It doesn't matter what you think, just bring her to me. If you don't, I will find a way to get to her myself.' Leon hung up and angrily shoved the phone into his pocket. He locked the car and walked over to the other side of the petrol station building, glancing briefly over towards a solitary row of trees to the right of the forecourt as he did so.

WHEN EVA EMERGED five minutes later, she noticed the empty car immediately. Assuming Leon had gone to use the facilities, Eva walked over to the Citroen and tried to open the passenger door but it was locked. The window was slightly open but not enough to fit her arm through and reach down to unlock the door. She looked around. They were on the outskirts of Paris, so far from the city that they were surrounded on all sides by fields. Other than a small line of trees silhouetted on the far side of the garage car park everything else was open farmland. The petrol station was just one building, economically designed, glass-fronted and eerily empty. Light was just beginning to filter through the clouds behind it as the pre-dawn began and all around her she could hear the first birds finding their voices. Other than that, Eva couldn't hear anything at all. She stood awkwardly by the car.

An owl called out in the darkness and she jumped violently. Quickly, she tried all the doors to the car but despite its decrepit shell the Citroen seemed to have central locking and she couldn't get in. Where the hell was Leon? Eva decided to find the men's toilets and get the keys from him. She crossed the forecourt to a door marked with the outline of a stick man and pushed the door. It opened with a creak.

'Leon?' She waited. Nothing.

Eva's senses roared into action. The hairs on the back of her neck stood up and she felt her face burning as she stood listening for sounds of occupation. Breathe, Eva.

She stepped inside the stinking space and checked both stalls in the small, grubby bathroom but they were empty. Cautiously, she walked back over to the exit, pushed the door open and poked her head out. Leon was right there.

'Be quiet,' he said in a low voice, 'there are people here.'

ROB GORBEN GOT up with the dawn that morning. In the night, news had come through that the first shipment of algae plants was on its way from Africa to populate his newly built ponds. He had received specific instructions, relayed to all the crew of the plane and the handlers, that the plants must not be exposed to oxygen in transit. If a single box didn't survive the journey, the entire contents would have to be burned and there would be heavy discounts in the fees of the handlers, and also in Rob's bonus. Rob was nervous. It was not a condition he had ever agreed to before—whilst he hadn't seen the transport boxes themselves, he knew each of the algae boxes had a filter that ensured the right mix of nutrients was pumped into it to keep the artificial algae alive. Unfortunately, he knew from experience that these boxes often became damaged in transit—even the smallest crack could expose the algae inside to the oxygen in the air. However, the deciding factor had been the fee he had been offered—so big that even when he had factored in a discount for a few dead plants, he was still looking at enough for a down payment on that little town-house in Amsterdam that his wife had always wanted. Gorben rubbed his gloved hands together to ward off the cold and then jammed them into his pockets as he waited outside the tented side of the site for the vans to appear. Professionally, he was interested to see the containers used to transport the plants, as they had been developed specifically for the project and were of a kind never used before.

He was also intrigued as to what would happen if oxygen should reach the algae plants. Normal algae required oxygen to survive but apparently this genetically modified plant did not. How then would it grow in the open raceway ponds he had been ordered to construct?

Why would the plants only be ready to be exposed to oxygen once they were in the UK? But Rob Gorben had learned to keep the questions to a minimum with this particular employer.

JUST AS HE was contemplating going to buy a coffee, several large refrigerated trucks appeared around the corner of the frost-covered street. He directed the lorries to a large parking lot inside the site, secured the gates and then greeted the drivers as they finished what would be their first job of the morning. Once the lorries were stationary, he opened the back doors to take a look inside and saw the special containers he had heard so much about. They were clear and completely sealed, other than having small ducts in the top that let in filtered air but contained the water within the unit. Each box was fitted with a soundless motorised pump, which, by means of an additional filtered duct, was conveying nutrients crucial to the survival of the algae on their gruelling journey from Khartoum.

Once the driver had disconnected the air ducts and stalled the motors, they removed the first of the giant boxes of algae and used a pick-up truck to take it through to the waiting raceway pond, already filled with water and gleaming in the strange light beneath the huge tented ceiling. They unloaded four boxes and stacked them next to the pond, Gorben supervising each one, the bonus always at the front of his mind. When they pulled the fifth container away, revealing the box behind, Gorben drew a sharp breath. Whilst most of the algae boxes contained just three or four plants, in this box there were so many that its sides were convex. He exchanged looks with the handlers and then ordered the box be drained and taken into his office. Once the box had been emptied of water and the trucks had driven off again, he bought himself a coffee and then spent some time examining it. He noticed a small hairline crack that was leaking the tiniest amount of water. From the look of the box it would not hold much longer, even without the pressure of the water. It looked almost as if the algae inside were trying to escape.

Eva STEPPED OUTSIDE the toilet and noiselessly shut the door.

She realised she was shaking. Leon directed her to a mid height stone wall behind which she dropped into a squat and he came and crouched next to her. 'I saw a figure as I was coming into the bathroom,' he whispered.

'Where?' she said incredulously, indicating the vast expanse of empty countryside.

'There,' he replied and pointed to the far side of the car park where the dark brown frozen earth of a field began in the line of trees she had noticed when she came out of the bathroom.

'But I didn't see or hear a car.'

'If someone was tailing us then that's exactly what they would want.' He was right.

'Are they still there?'

'I haven't seen any other movement.'

Eva frowned. 'And you left me out there, standing by the car?' She noticed something flicker in his eyes. 'You were using me as bait again,' she said stonily.

'I could have dealt with them. You were in no danger.' There was no point arguing with him.

'Who are they?' He broke her gaze and glanced over

his shoulder before looking out from behind the wall and scanning the immediate horizon.

'The same people who were at my apartment and in your hotel room.'

'You sound like you know who they are.'

'I don't.' She looked sideways at Leon and instinctively felt like he was lying. Why was he here? Why bother to get himself caught up in this? She didn't understand why he was playing her hero. He didn't seem the altruistic type. Not for the first time she wondered whether this was all simply a complex ruse to get her away from the city and dispose of her. If it was, all she could do now was to wait and see what happened next and then try and react to it. It wasn't a comfortable position to be in.

She shifted so that she was beside him, scanning the forecourt; it was still completely empty and totally still.

'Here.' Leon dug into his jeans and handed her the car keys. 'Go to the car, get inside and lock the doors. I'm going to flush them out of the trees.' He began to stalk towards the edge of the wall.

When Eva didn't reply, he turned, his dark eyes boring into her.

'I'm not completely OK being the helpless bait, Leon.' And I don't trust you.

'Eva, if we don't go now, there will be more of them and we will have no hope of getting away. Just do it.' He stared at her. His eyes were hard, his body was tense and his fists were almost completely clenched.

Suddenly it dawned on Eva why he looked like that— he was working hard to conceal it but Leon was afraid.

She nodded silently at him and he turned away. If he was afraid, she reasoned, then this threat was real. And if this threat was real then maybe he wasn't the enemy after all. For now at least.

Eva looked again around the forecourt for signs of movement. Nothing. The garage building looked empty, the surrounding countryside looked empty and there wasn't even a gust of wind blowing the trees in the ditch where Leon had decided their watchers were positioned. It was eerily quiet. Eva clenched her fists, summoned up every ounce of fight that she had, stood up and began to run.

As Eva NOW DISCOVERED, a natural ability to run, and an athletic physique, do not always guarantee speed. Running on a treadmill was easy, and road-running had become her meditation, but running across a large, empty space in the morning half-light, trees, plants and buildings in her peripheral vision, expecting at any moment to feel the sharp sting of a bullet, she now discovered was very difficult indeed. She could hardly get a breath out, her chest was so tight, and she couldn't run nearly as fast as she wanted to—fast enough to outrun bullets. As soon as she took off, she stumbled slightly on the gravel but righted herself and carried on, arms pumping. As she rounded the side of the garage building her breath was coming in big, noisy bursts and her legs felt like jelly, but she kept going, head down, heart thumping, every nerve ending jangling like a set of keys.

Keys. The car keys.

As she ran, she held them up and readied the one she would need to unlock the door. Aside from a key for a Chubb lock and a thin silver key, there was one battered old key with moulded plastic around the top and Eva reasoned in the short time she had to make the decision that this would be the car key.

Suddenly the car was almost in front of her. She slowed her pace and then put her hands up, bracing herself for the impact of the car and ready to jam the key into the lock and wrench the door open.

The impact came, but not from the front.

AS SOMETHING DARK, hard and heavy came out of nowhere and hit her from the right-hand side, Eva was thrown left along the side of the car and away from the door. She scrabbled at the slippery surface of the bonnet trying to get some kind of grip but her nails scraped across it and suddenly she was on the floor, face down. She shouted out as her knee hit the rocky ground and immediately blood began to flow from the side of her left hand where she had landed on the gravel.

Winded, Eva looked up, dragged a breath through her lungs and started frantically to push herself up on all fours. That force had been a person. Where were they? The answer was instant. Strong hands looped underneath her arms from behind and dragged her upright.

'No! NO!' She struggled and kicked but the hands simply lifted her off the floor. As her pursuer turned towards the car with her in his arms, Eva suddenly had purchase, landed the soles of both feet against the side of the car and pushed off with all her strength. She heard the man holding her swear in a foreign language as they fell backwards, severely unbalanced, and then both of them hit the ground, Eva on her back on top. She lashed out with her elbows and suddenly she was released and on her feet, running back around the other side of the car.

'Eva!' She heard Leon shout somewhere in her vicinity but when she looked up all she saw was a blur that could have been anyone. She reached the driver's side and fumbled with the key in the lock, swearing at herself as her hands shook and shook. Finally, the key drove home and she flicked the lock, wrenched open the door and threw herself inside, slamming it behind her and central-locking it from the inside. She sat looking at her knees and took a single breath before she realised that she was not really any safer in the car than out—these people had guns. She looked up towards the passenger's side to try and locate Leon or her attacker in the half-light of the early dawn. Why couldn't she see them? Why hadn't the man caught her as she was trying to get into the car? Suddenly a face slammed against the partially open window on the passenger side. Eva screamed and with a start realised she was staring at the features of the same man who had been in her hotel room earlier that night. His eyes were bulging horribly, not even looking at her, and squashed against the glass she could see a mouth opening and closing in silent expressions of pain. She sat, frozen to the spot as the eyes bulged further, became bloodshot and began opening and shutting. Suddenly, a great spurt of blood made her gasp out loud and the glass of the window was suddenly covered in red. Eva's hand flew to her mouth and she forced herself not to retch. The person on the other side of the glass slipped slowly down the outside of the car, blood coating and then running down the window in bright red smears.

Eva stared at the blood-covered window. There was a figure still moving outside. She heard a dragging noise and then there was a thud on her window, which almost sent her jumping out of her skin. She turned around and

Leon stood there, breathless and blood-covered, wiping a knife on his thigh.

'Get out of the driver's seat!' She stared at him.

'NOW, Eva! Open the door and move over!' Suddenly Eva's brain reconnected and she hastily shifted herself across the gear stick into the passenger seat, then reached back over and unlocked the door. Leon threw himself into the driver's seat.

'Where are the keys?' She handed them to him and he took them silently before starting the engine and reversing back into the yard.

Eva numbly held on to her bag. As she looked down she noticed that the squashy leather was spotted with droplets of thick, red blood.

THEY DROVE FOR some time before Eva felt able to speak. Her hand was seeping red and her head was throbbing, but for several minutes she just sat in shock. Finally, she began trying to clean the dirt from around the side of the cut on her hand with the edge of her coat. The wound was small, but deep.

'I need to know what's going on, Leon. I don't understand why you're helping me.'

'Why?'

'Yes.' Leon stared at the road ahead and Eva noticed the muscle working in the side of his jaw. She stopped cleaning the cut on her hand. 'This situation is confusing enough without my not being able to trust you.' He turned his face to look at her, then turned back to the road. He looked as if he was clenching his teeth. When he spoke he was much calmer than Eva had ever heard him. 'I should have done more to help Jackson. We went through so much together when he was alive but, when he needed me the most, I wasn't there for him. That's why I feel I must be here for you.'

'Why didn't you help him?' she said bluntly.

'I was scared.' Eva glanced over at him in surprise. Fear didn't seem to be something Leon suffered from.

'Of what?'

'Of going back.'

'Back to what?'

'Addiction is a frightening place, Eva. It completely changes you. I have done things when I was high, or wanting to get high, that I would never have done without that influence in my life.' Eva remembered Leon confessing at his flat that he had met Jackson in rehab.

'I see.'

'You don't. You couldn't, nobody can until they have felt the urgency and shame that comes with that kind of need. The things you do. Sometimes, I…' His voice tailed off.

Eva didn't know what to say. She hardly knew this man and she wasn't even particularly good at dealing with the problems of people she knew really well. Her solution for her own issues had been to never talk about them; then it was easier to believe they didn't exist.

Outside the car the sky had darkened and fat drops of rain started to fall lethargically, landing against the windscreen with heavy thuds.

'I know that you know about Sophie.'

Eva looked over at him in surprise. 'How do you know about that?'

'I have been monitoring your internet usage. I know that you contacted her.'

'How the hell have you been doing that?'

'Several days ago, I broke into your hotel room and

put a device into your laptop. It was important I knew. Now I think you need to meet her.'

'So what, we're going back to Paris now?' Leon nodded.

They sat in silence for several minutes before Leon spoke.

'I am sorry about the laptop—I needed to know whether I could trust you.'

'And you know that now, do you? Because I sure as hell don't feel like I can trust you.' They both sat in silence and stared at the road ahead.

Then Leon spoke quietly. 'I don't think either of us really has a choice.'

As FAR AS Rob Gorben was concerned no-one needed to know about the exploding box of algae. When all the other containers were empty he had simply unloaded the algae himself into a tough industrial sack and taken it to the local dump. After that, he had instructed that the covers be taken off the ponds—a huge job in itself, given the size of the raceways—then, with the tents taken down and the ponds open to the air, his job was complete. Rob was relieved not to be a permanent caretaker to this kind of project. He hadn't been instructed to hand anything over to anyone, so it wasn't clear to him who would be managing it going forward. But at least it wasn't him. As an engineer with a specialism in structures for algae growth and development, he knew unplanned algae spread was an annoyance at the best of times. He had no desire to be the one on the receiving end of all the complaints from the locals who found their fish ponds were clogged with plants spread by the spores carried on the wind. God only knew how the company proposed to deal with that kind of problem.

HE'D CHECKED SEVERAL times that they wanted open ponds when he'd had the initial briefings. Since the site was near the centre of a city, what about the local waterways and supply reservoirs? he'd said. No, he had been told, the raceway ponds were specifically required and without any covering. The company representative, 'Mr Smith', had even refused to divulge the genetically altered code of the algae, despite Rob's insistence that it would assist his designs. When he'd taken a sample of the plant to try and work it out himself, he found that, bizarrely, he couldn't confirm the genetic make-up because it seemed to keep changing. It was as if the plant itself was disguising it. Which was, of course, impossible. But his protests had fallen on deaf ears. All he was told was that the algae were genetically engineered for two purposes: firstly, to produce a massively high yield of algae for a new type of health supplement; and secondly, to be entirely resilient to anything and everything either man or nature could throw at them.

THIRTEEN

It wasn't long before they were nearing the outskirts of Paris again. Eva had been silently watching the sun rise, deep in thought, but suddenly she sensed a tensing across the car. She looked at Leon who was staring into the rearview mirror. He switched his gaze to the wing mirror, took a sudden left turn and looked again. They had turned off the main road now and were driving through a small, picturesque town with an old church and the customary smattering of *boulangerie* and *tabac*. The rain had stopped but the streets were still slick with wetness from the earlier showers.

'We're being followed.' Eva felt the hairs on the back of her neck begin to rise.

'It's a black car. They have been three lengths behind us for around five kilometres but when we left the main road they turned too.' Eva twisted in her seat and looked behind her as the nose of a large black, very conspicuous off-road vehicle appeared around the last bend they had traversed and then came into full view behind them. The windows were ominously blacked out.

'We're going to have to lose them before we meet Sophie.' Despite talks of a safe house, Leon seemed now to be utterly set on getting Eva into a room—or rather a church—with Sophie. They were to meet at the Sacré Coeur in the Montmartre area of Paris, somewhere that Eva had never been.

He glanced over at her body and Eva realised he was looking to see if she was wearing her seatbelt.

'Hold on,' he said and suddenly the car took a turn down a small bumpy track that Eva couldn't even have seen if she'd been looking for it. Eva's hands flailed for something to hold on to as the battered old car flew around the dirt road, the suspension handling the curves remarkably efficiently. With another violent lurch they reached the end of the track and suddenly they were driving over a field of bright yellow rapeseed, the wheels of the car sticking slightly in the damp earth. Eva glanced behind. The black car had turned down the track too and it was gaining on them.

'Leon, they're nearly behind us.' Leon didn't react.

'Do you know where you're going?'

'I think so.'

'Do you think we can lose them in this car?'

'Yes.' Eva wished she had the same faith as Leon, but the Citroen was an old model, not made for off-roading. The car took another swing to the left and they were suddenly careering downhill through some low-lying vegetation towards what looked like a river. A slow-moving but substantial enough river. A river that did not seem to have a bridge… Eva gritted her teeth as the car suddenly reached the end of the foliage. She tightened her fingers around her seatbelt and waited for the splash as they hit the water but, instead, the car flew right over.

Eva opened her eyes as she heard the wheels bumping over the rough surface of a broad plank bridge. She saw Leon glance over at her. All at once her mobile phone began to ring and the first gunshot rang out behind them.

BACK IN HIS bedroom in his three-storey detached house in Surrey, Rob Gorben was struggling to breathe. He gazed around the room, decorated so tastefully by his wife Marnie, and representing the collective fifteen years and three children that made up their life together. Light was streaming in through the open window and a crisp breeze lifted the ends of the gauze curtains Marnie had hung to keep out prying neighbours. Not everyone in this wealthy neighbourhood had been happy to find a Dutch man and a black woman arriving on their exclusive suburban street back then.

Rob had woken that morning and struggled to keep his eyelids open, as if, he told his wife, he had lost control of the muscles. Marnie had laughed at him, kissed him and called him lazy then gone downstairs to wake the kids and make some coffee. Even now he could smell the bitter richness of the Ethiopian blend they both loved so much drifting up the stairs.

'Rob, breakfast is ready!' Her call travelled up the stairs and Rob Gorben's brain sent a message to his mouth to respond. Before the message reached his mouth it faded away—under his skin, antibodies produced by his own immune system were blocking his neuroreceptors and so he remained motionless on the bed. He moved his eyes to the left and, through almost completely lowered lids, he could just about see his BlackBerry lying on the floor where it had fallen after his hands had suddenly become numb and unresponsive. He had been sending an email, his last for the job, instructing that the algae be deposited into the raceway ponds at all of the fifty-six locations around the UK. Oh, how he wished he had not used the last of his energy to press send, but to call for help instead! But the paralysis had been quick and he had not been expecting it. He tried to open his mouth to shout to his wife, tried to move his hands and feet but he lay motionless, helpless as a baby, his throat steadily constricting, crushing his voice box.

Sunlight continued to flow in through the open window and the sounds of the early morning school run went on as usual downstairs. Rob's breathing became laboured, as if his lungs had shrunk to a tenth of their normal size, leaving him no space in which to draw a breath. He tried again and again but his gasps went unsatisfied as his lungs gradually filled up with the fibrotic tissue being produced in response to the foreign bodies in his system. Finally, the muscular walls of his now-useless lungs gave way and slowly, his eyes opening wide for his final breath, staring at the ceiling, he died. Behind his motionless head the curtains continued to flutter in the breeze.

'WE HAVE TO be at the Sacré Cœur in an hour,' said Leon, checking his watch and forcing the car up the bank on the other side of the river as the engine started to scream.

Eva looked at him, eyes wide, then ducked down in her seat as more gunshots pinged off the car's bodywork. She glanced at the incoming call on her own phone, recognised the number as Valerie's and chose to 'ignore' it. She almost dropped the phone as the car's rear windscreen was shattered in a hail of bullets.

'We have to lose them before we get into Paris,' shouted Leon above the noise of the car.

Again Eva didn't respond. She heard words forming in her head but all she could do at that moment was cling to the seatbelt and grit her teeth.

Leon looked at her again, then put his foot to the floor

and took the car up a gear as another bullet hit the top of the wing mirror on Eva's side. He floored the accelerator as the car tore across another field and then through a small gap in a hedgerow as Eva hunched further down in her seat. How many gears did this car have?

As THE LITTLE Citroen bounced onto the solid tarmac of the main road on the other side of the hedge, Eva risked another glance behind her in the wing mirror. The black car had managed to negotiate the exit in the foliage they had come through and was still behind, but seemed to be slowing down. As she watched, the car backed off completely so that it was now following at some distance, apparently not trying to get any closer. The shooter Eva had seen leaning out of the window had pulled himself back inside. She suddenly realised that he had been sitting in what appeared to be the driver's seat. That was weird. A right-hand drive car? She tried to see whether the plates were English but the car was now too far behind.

Eva turned back to the front and exhaled, not knowing how long she had been holding her breath. She looked at Leon but he ignored her. There were so many questions flying around in her head about what had just happened, but she sensed he had no answers. She switched her gaze stared to the road ahead. They were out of the fields now, back onto a main road and Paris was fast approaching. She thought about what she was about to do at the Sacré Coeur. It wasn't exactly a scenario calculated to allay anxiety, but it was necessary. She had come to the conclusion that the only way to survive this situation was to end it. To do that she needed to know what it was that Jackson had known and apparently the only person who could tell her that was Sophie.

'Presumably you are going to come to the Sacré Coeur?'

'Yes,' Leon replied.

'Why don't you meet her, why does it have to be me?'

'She said it had to be you.' Leon looked at her doubt-fully across the car but Eva ignored him. It was a logi-cal question: Leon had already proved he was far better equipped to defend himself than she was.

'Where exactly do I meet her?'

'She has your phone number so she can communicate with you that way.'

'Right. Do you have a gun with you?' she asked Leon casually.

He hesitated. Just for a moment, but it was a definite hesitation. 'No.' Eva looked straight ahead. He's lying.

The old familiar tension descended on the car again. They both sat in silence and stared at the road ahead as suburban Paris began to surround them. Rough blocks of flats ran along both sides of the road with a restau-rant, bar or small shop at irregular distances.

'Are we on time?'

'Yes, no more than half an hour away.' He looked at his watch. 'It's still early. The Sacré Coeur is in Mont-martre, which is at the northern end of Paris. Once we are through the suburbs we will reach the Périphérique. Once we are on that road it is a steady, circular traffic flow around the outside of Paris. We need to get off at Porte de Clignancourt and then we are less than fifteen minutes from our destination.' His voice had taken on an oddly robotic tone. Once again he seemed to have changed, Jekyll-and-Hyde-like, from one personality to another. Any trust Eva had felt in Leon earlier in the night began to evaporate. Why had she allowed their in-terests to become intertwined? He was a manic paranoid and his methods were completely illogical. But then had he ever really given her any choice other than to go along with him... Not for the first time she wondered how much of the situation she was in was of Leon's design.

'What do we do about them?' she said, indicating the huge car behind them, still following at a distance on the public road.

'Leave them to me.' Eva didn't want to think about what he was planning to do and she knew he wouldn't tell her even if she asked. She held on to her seatbelt with both hands and stared out of the window of the stationary car. They were waiting at a level-crossing for a train to pass. The barrier was down, the lights red, the warning sounding and in the distance Eva could hear the rumble of the high-speed train as it came thundering towards the spot where they were waiting. Behind them, the black car was just slowing in order to come to a stop at the crossing. It seemed strange to Eva that the attack had stopped as soon as they were back on the public highway but, at the same time, it made perfect sense if the driver was also the shooter. It was one thing to fire a gun in a field, but quite another to be attempting to handle traffic lights and crossings with one hand and a weapon with the other. Besides, the more attention they attracted, the less likely they would get away with whatever they were trying to do. And so the two cars waited in line. In the queue behind the black car was a family station-wagon full of children, and behind that two small Peugeots.

As Eva was about to reach for her bag, the car suddenly lurched forward. She stared at the situation in front of her. The lights had not changed, they were still red, but

Leon was driving the car around the barrier, right across the tracks at the lowered gate on the other side. Coming the other way, to their right, at speed, was the train.

Before Eva even had time to scream, the train let out a huge blare of its horn, Leon jammed his foot down even harder on the accelerator and the front of their car smashed through the barrier on the other side of the track. As one of the back wheels seemed to hesitate over the metal rail, Eva held her breath, shut her eyes and—for the first time in her life—prayed. She waited for the collision but it never came. Or, at least, not to their car. Opening her eyes she heard an almighty crash and the sound of splintering glass and metal and, turning in her seat, she saw a brief flash of the black car as it was swept along in front of the train, which was still travelling at full speed.

THEY ARRIVED IN Montmartre at 10:05 a.m. and Leon parked the Citroen in a quiet side street. As she got out, Eva took a good look at the car that had just survived the ordeal with them. It was covered in mud, there were pieces of fern hanging from the doors and the back windscreen was gaping where the bullets had shattered the glass. It looked a mess but it wasn't any of these details that caused Eva to hesitate. It was the tyres. As Leon busied himself trying to tape some newspaper over the back window and clean the blood of the man at the petrol station from the passenger door, Eva bent down and took a closer look. The tyres were huge. Although she had limited knowledge of cars and their component parts, she was sure that she had never seen one of these iconic little cars with tyres like this. Not only were they enormous, looking completely out of place on the little roadster, but they were the thick, studded type that Eva had never seen on a normal car before. The tyres looked like they belonged on a seriously heavy duty off-road vehicle.

'What are you doing?' She looked up to see Leon staring down at her, annoyance written all over his face. He was pulling on a new shirt to replace the jumper he had been wearing that was now soaked with blood from the attack at the petrol station.

She stood up. 'I was just wondering how this little car managed all that off-roading.' Leon looked at her then walked around to the driver's side, threw the dirty jumper inside and slammed the door hard.

'We should go.' The sinking feeling she had felt in the car started working its way down Eva's spine. Something wasn't right. There was something about Leon that wasn't right.

She felt the phone in her bag vibrate with the receipt of a text message: 'Meet me at the Altar of The Virgin, third row, fourth seat in. Ten minutes'.

'It's Sophie,' Eva said, reading the location in the text out loud and then replacing the phone in her bag. 'We have ten minutes.'

'This way.' Leon started off away from the car at a swift pace and Eva had to run slightly to catch up with him. They were walking through a residential area that seemed unnaturally quiet to Eva. The sound of their footsteps echoed around the walls of the houses, many of which were built at strange angles as a result of the uphill slant to the road. Each house was of a different design to its neighbour, there was no cohesion or uniformity. The street they were walking up was gradually getting steeper and Eva's lungs were starting to burn. She drew level with Leon.

'How much further is it?'

'Five minutes.' His tone had become clipped and terse and he was walking very quickly, as if intentionally trying to get away from her. If this behaviour was the result of anxiety, he was making no effort to control it.

She looked at him; he glanced over at her. 'We are nearly there.' They reached the top of the hill and Eva was surprised to find herself standing opposite a windmill that was built into one of the houses on an otherwise normal-looking street. As they continued walking, the streets started to fill up. Tourists of every nationality thronged around them, having caricatures painted by street artists, filling up on hot chocolate or coffee and spending all their hard-earned money on pink plastic Eiffel Towers and snow globes containing a miniature model of the Sacré Coeur. Eva glanced up and saw the white domes and curved structures of the cathedral, towering over them. Even on such a dull day it looked bright and beautiful, the intricate carving and smooth workmanship as impressive from ground level.

'This way,' said Leon attracting her attention. He led her around a small side street and they emerged at the front of the cathedral, to their left a large bank of stairs leading up to the entrance and to their right a breathtaking view out over the whole of Paris.

Leon turned, stopped suddenly and Eva came up short, almost colliding with his chest. Their faces were uncomfortably close.

'I will be standing a short distance away in front and to your right,' said Leon not moving. Eva took several paces back from him as he continued. 'If you feel like you are in trouble or you need some help you will start to cough. Make sure you put your hand right over your

mouth so I can see because I won't be able to hear you.'
It didn't sound like the most amazing plan but it was,
at least, a plan.

'OK.'

'You must make sure you get as much from her as you
can and then get out, she may be being followed, which
will compromise us both. If she gives you any information don't lose it, if she tells you anything, you must
focus your mind entirely and not let any other thoughts
enter it, as you must remember everything you are told.'

'Fine,' said Eva, not enjoying being patronised.

They set off up the steps together, with Eva fighting
a strong flight reflex. Inside, the cathedral was dark
and warm and smelled comfortingly of wood polish and
old fabric. It was also packed with people, despite the
early hour. As they walked through the entrance there
were people queuing to light candles on a candle tree
or stopping to pick up paper information leaflets about
the cathedral. To their left was a large tourist party, all
listening intently to a tour guide speaking very quietly
in German. They squeezed in between the tourists and
the candle-lighters and started on the circular, carpeted
walkway that wound around the building.

'It's smaller than I expected inside.'

Leon ignored her. 'That's the Altar,' he said, indicating an alcove housing a statue of the Virgin Mary, eyes
cast upwards, hands clasped in prayer. All around her
were candles, smaller religious icons, human heads bent
in supplication and in front were rows of chairs. Eva
glanced around her and wondered whether Sophie was
already there and watching them. Perhaps she wasn't
the only one.

'I will wait over there.' Again Leon indicated an area to the right of the chairs with another head movement.

'Communicate as we discussed if you feel you are in trouble.'

'OK, fine. Wait…' Eva's voice faded away as she turned to Leon and realised he had already gone.

FOURTEEN

EVA FORCED HERSELF to put one foot in front of the other. A sort of woodenness was threatening to overtake her limbs. She glanced at her surroundings and wondered whether she was under surveillance by parties other than Leon. Briefly, she considered using this as a chance to extricate herself from the situation, but the reality was that the only option was to do what they had agreed. Sophie knew how and why the papers from the sports bag had come into Jackson's possession—and possibly how and why he died—and Sophie was here somewhere. As she approached the row of chairs in front of the altar Eva realised there was already someone sitting in the place she had been told to take. She stood motionless. Was this the person she was meant to meet? It was a blonde woman but her hair wasn't the natural-looking blonde she had seen on Sophie's social networking profile but a white, platinum blonde and much longer. Eva checked the text message again: third row, fourth seat in. This was definitely the right seat. She moved out of the way of a couple walking in the direction of a pyramid of candles in front of the altar and glanced to the right of the rows of seats where she spotted Leon. He looked directly at her for several seconds and then bowed his head as if in prayer. Eva turned back to the row of seats. The fourth seat was now empty.

Starting as if she had been poked in the back, Eva

slipped past the seated worshippers until she was at the end of the third row. She counted the seats as she walked along the row—just to be sure—and carefully sat down in the fourth one. There she remained completely still, waiting. After several minutes the rigid position she was sitting in became incredibly uncomfortable and she forced herself to release some of the tension and relax her shoulders. She looked around the building at all the people milling past.

Leon was now standing next to a huge stone pillar, apparently reading one of the paper information leaflets that hung in wooden boxes all around the cathedral. Occasionally, he would look from the leaflet to the ceiling, across the room or straight at Eva, each time appearing simply to be taking in whatever he was reading about. He looked pretty much like any other tourist.

Suddenly someone sat down in the seat next to her.

'Don't look at me.' Immediately, Eva tensed up.

'You are Eva?' A woman's voice.

'Yes.' They sat in silence for several seconds and it was all Eva could do not to turn around and get a good look at who was sitting next to her. 'And you are Sophie.'

'…Yes.' Eva turned her head very slightly towards where the woman was sitting. Out of the corner of her eye she could see thin legs clad in dark blue denim, a pair of plain, expensive-looking brown brogues and the sleeves of a thick, dark coat. Sophie had her hands in her lap, thin fingers intertwined and squeezed together, alarmingly white where she was gripping herself with tension.

'You are in danger, Eva.'

'I know,' Eva replied. Sophie was almost gouging the flesh from her hands and there was a note of such anxiety in her voice that Eva could feel her own carefully controlled heartbeat begin to rise again.

'I am so sorry that you have ended up in this position, I know that Jackson would never have wanted that.' At the mention of her brother's name, Eva turned to face Sophie. She couldn't help it. She was met by a pair of wide, warm blue eyes, a thin face with highly defined cheekbones, framed by that short, light blond hair. She was wearing a dark fur hat jammed down on her head and small diamond earrings, one in each ear. Unexpectedly, Sophie smiled. 'You look a little like him.' The two women stared at each other for several seconds before a wariness seemed to gradually filter back behind Sophie's eyes.

'Tell me what happened,' said Eva, taking the lead.

'I met your brother in a bar,' Sophie said, cutting straight to the chase. 'Nothing happened but we were both drunk; we talked for several hours. Unfortunately, I became quite attached to him.' Eva nodded and then broke Sophie's gaze, for some reason feeling slightly embarrassed at prying into her brother's life in this way.

'After that night I tried to contact him and get him to meet up with me again. It was more forward than I was used to being but I felt there was such a connection I just couldn't ignore it.'

'Did he respond?'

'Yes. But he was a good man your brother, he was faithful to his girlfriend.' Sophie sighed. 'Unfortunately, I did not let it go and I pursued him. I am 35 years old, Eva, I am unmarried and I have no children. I feel a huge pressure to not be alone any more. At my age, when someone comes along that you feel something like that for, you don't let him go without a fight.'

'Even if he wasn't yours to fight for in the first place?'

Sophie held Eva with a steady gaze. 'I know I did the wrong thing. I was overcome by the fear of being alone. It was stupid. Oh, you have no idea how much I regret pursuing your brother now.' She looked like she might cry. Eva knew that there was no time for that.

'Tell me what happened next.'

'I was trying to find a way to get your brother to see me again and then I came across an email at work. It concerned a project in the Sudan and I knew your brother was passionately committed to his work there. I sent it to him.'

'Where is it you work?' Eva didn't want to give away what she knew. Not yet.

'A company called Bioavancement S.a.r.l. I am—I was—a PA to one of the Directors.' Eva remembered Sophie's name printed across all the documents from Jackson's sports bag—her position explained why she would have had access to all that information. 'What did the email say?'

'It was a confidential email, I should never have sent it.'

'But what did it say?'

'Bioavancement S.a.r.l. had set up a laboratory in the Sudan.'

'That's an odd location for a lab.'

'Not really. Bioavancement S.a.r.l. is an enormously private company—so in a way, the Sudan was perfect— vast, lawless in places, and plenty of scope for bribing the local law enforcers. Most of us who worked at Bioavancement S.a.r.l. had no idea what they really did, other than that it was pharmaceutical research.'

'Did you know?'

'Not initially, no. I was a PA so anything I came into contact with was communication from the man I worked for to others within the business. It all seemed harmless—I later realised much of it was in code.' Eva thought of the batch of emails she had discovered in Jackson's sports bag that had seemed out of place in his stash. The discussion of weekend plans and meeting schedules must have been using the code Sophie was talking about. She wanted to ask what the code was but Sophie was already speaking again.

'I forwarded that initial email to Jackson—about the laboratory. I hardly read it first, I was just so desperate to make contact,' Sophie continued. 'But later, when I had sent it on I realised that it was uncoded. They were discussing this secret laboratory in barely concealed terms and with some considerable urgency.'

'What were they saying?'

'There had been some kind of leak. An outbreak of something in the local area resulting from their tests. It was the second time it had happened—first in 2009/10— and they were really scared about what would happen if it went public. People had died so there was an urgent need to contain reporting of it. I thought that perhaps Jackson could take it to a journalist and gain some leverage. I didn't care about being fired, I hated my job.'

'And you hoped he would want to see you again.'

Sophie nodded. 'Yes. And he did want to see me again. But of course it wasn't actually me he wanted to see, it was because of my connection to his work.' She sighed heavily.

'Unfortunately, it didn't stop there, that first email wasn't enough. After that he wanted more and more information. He started making connections between events in the Sudan and Bioavancement S.a.r.l.—and then in other locations. He wanted me to help him expose them.'

'Did you?'

'Of course. I printed off reams and reams of emails for him and I stole so much information. But when we found out what they were really doing, we got so much more than we bargained for.'

'In what way?' Eva shifted nervously in her seat and glanced over Sophie's shoulder. She was beginning to feel like a sitting duck. She looked over at Leon's position. He wasn't there. 'Is Jackson's death linked to the Sudan issue?'

'No. That email led us to details of a land purchase in Paraguay, then another that concerned a group of people in Paris the company was using for...for something else.' She suddenly turned to Eva, eyes wide. 'It's all about profit, Eva, a lethal profit.'

What? Eva was starting to feel even more confused. 'A lethal profit...' she repeated.

'Yes, I...' Sophie's voice faded away and she looked at the floor. Eva glanced over at her. She must have been pretty once but now her skin was drawn tight across her bones like a thin, sallow mask; her lips were marked with cuts as if she had been constantly biting them and there were dark, sunken hollows underneath her eyes that seemed to be the result of months of lack of sleep. She kept looking around her fearfully and Eva noticed that where she had been pinching one hand with the other she had drawn blood.

'Sophie?' Sophie looked up at Eva, her face calm but her eyes wide and distrustful. Although she was obviously intent on attempting to keep up an outward appearance of stability and control, Eva sensed desperation, as if at any moment the anxiety Sophie had been holding at bay might rise up and completely overwhelm her. Such naked fear sent a tremor down Eva's spine.

Finally, Sophie spoke in a hushed voice, unable to hold Eva's gaze. 'I don't know, Eva, I don't know if this is something real or…or perhaps I am going insane!' She laughed unsteadily.

Eva didn't reply.

'The only thing that makes me know it's all real is that people who possess this information, who try to do something about it, end up dead.'

'Can you give me any more details?' Eva asked gently.

'What we found was just the tip of the iceberg.'

'What do you mean?'

'The repercussions of what they are about to do, it goes so much further. That's why I had to get Leon to bring you to me. I thought Jackson must have told you everything if you had come to Paris. We must stop them, Eva—no one knows who they are, no one can even see them!'

'No, he… Who? Bioavancement S.a.r.l.? I don't understand Sophie.' Eva was beginning to get frustrated. She needed cold hard facts not this emotional outpouring.

Sophie ignored the questions and began to search in the small leather bag she held on her lap. She found what she was looking for and closed her hands around it. 'Don't look at me. I need to give you something. For your own safety no one must see.' Eva turned to face forwards again and stared ahead.

'It's a memory stick. It doesn't contain everything, but once you have read it you will understand and I…' Suddenly, with a slight shudder, Sophie fell quiet and Eva wondered if she was crying. She didn't know whether to turn around and offer help or to continue to face the front as she had been instructed to do.

She sat and waited for several seconds. 'Sophie?' she asked, still facing away from her. There was no response and for a horrible moment Eva thought Sophie had asked her to face forward and had made her escape. But she could still sense Sophie's body next to her and besides that made no sense. Why mention the memory stick and then make a run for it without actually handing it over?

She softly nudged her right leg against Sophie's leg to make sure she was still there. She could see out of the corner of her eye the same pair of trousers. 'Sophie,' she hissed, 'what are you doing?' There was no response. She nudged the leg again, hard this time. It fell back towards her like a dead weight. Eva turned. Sophie was staring straight ahead, unmoving. Her eyes were open but unblinking. Eva looked closer. Suddenly she saw it. In the centre of Sophie's forehead, just below the bottom of her hat was a single bullet hole.

IT TOOK EVERY ounce of composure Eva had not to scream. She glanced around her, looking for a smoking gun but of course there was no-one. Fighting the urge to panic, she sat frozen to her seat. She looked over at the spot where Leon had been reading the information leaflet. In his place was an old woman attempting to light a small candle with shaky hands, a look of rapt concentration on her face. Eva's gaze moved quickly to the right and left of the old woman. Where the hell was Leon? She considered giving the signal Leon had instructed her to use and put her hand right over her mouth, but in the end she made no noise. The last thing she needed was to draw attention to herself. Whoever had fired the fatal shot at Sophie probably had the very same gun trained on her head right now. Realising the danger she was in, Eva quickly ducked down so that her head was below the level of the person in front and sat crouched on the floor trying to regulate her breathing, fiddling with the prayer book slotted into the back of the seat in front.

She looked quickly back at Sophie. The hole in her forehead was starting to ooze the tiniest trickle of blood, which was soaking into the fabric of her hat. At any moment it would start running down her face. Oh God, poor woman, Eva thought. Then she remembered the memory stick. She looked down at Sophie's left hand and saw that it was curled around the stick, the fingers still locked tight to the inside of her palm. She had to get that memory stick. There was no way she could leave without it. Eva began gently pulling at Sophie's clenched fingers. Anger welled up in her throat at the same time as sickness at what she was doing, but she fought it down and carried on tugging and pulling at Sophie's poor, scarred hands. Eva couldn't stop a small gasp escaping as she began to think she could feel the sights of the gun trained on her head right at that moment.

'Oh God,' she muttered quietly, wrenching at Sophie's hands which seemed to have become like stone. A surge of panic gripped Eva and finally, almost ripping Sophie's fingers from their sockets, she managed to open her hands. Inside was a small black memory stick. Eva grabbed it, stuffed it into her pocket, picked up her bag and got ready to move.

'I'm so sorry,' she whispered, as she took a final look at Sophie's sad, shocked face. Then she quickly made her way to the end of the row, keeping as low as she could, thankful that the low light in the cathedral, and Sophie's large hat, meant no one had yet noticed she had been shot. When she reached the end of the row, the desire to be outside had gone beyond urgent. As she pushed through the milling crowds of tourists, attracting angry curses and frowns for her haste, Eva tried to think through the situation.

She looked up at the roof to try and locate where the shot could have come from. There was no mezzanine and apparently no upper floor. Unless the killer had found a hidden upper level then the shot must have come from someone in the church. Given that they had shot Sophie square between the eyes, they must have been standing right in front of them. In exactly the direction she was heading.

But she could see no other way out of the circular building. Eva was near the doors now, the daylight was shining through and she could feel the cold of the air outside. The crush of people around her slowed her pace painfully but she was nearly there.

Suddenly, a shrill scream filled the cathedral and echoed, bouncing off the ancient curved walls. They had found Sophie. She had to get out. Now.

WAITING SEVERAL SECONDS to try to avoid any connection with the scream, Eva began stealthily pushing her way more quickly through the crowd, many of whom had stopped and were looking back in the direction of the scream. A general muttering in the cathedral was turning into something more high-pitched and panicked as word of the grisly discovery spread through the building. Eva was only about ten people away from the door as she ducked and weaved, smiled apologetically and then

forcefully pushed her way through, ignoring the excla-
mations and treading on feet that wouldn't move. Only
six people away. Four people. Two.

Suddenly she was swept through the remaining
crowds and into the watery sunshine outside by someone else. Eva attempted to wrench her arm free from the
person dragging her. She was being propelled down the
steps so fast she could hardly keep up and had to keep
her eyes on her feet for fear of being dragged down the
steps head first. They got to the bottom and Eva finally
managed to look up.

'Come,' said Leon as he turned to her. 'We have to
go. Now.'

WIRAJ COULD HAVE kicked himself. From his position
standing on the seat behind the curtained lattice of an
unused confessional he'd had a clear shot of Eva Scott
when she'd been sitting down. His gun had jammed after
he fired the first shot and, just as he'd pulled the trigger
a second time, she'd ducked down and the bullet had embedded itself harmlessly in the wood of the tall chair behind. She'd remained crouched for several minutes next
to the corpse and then suddenly she had moved down the
line of chairs and, once again, the shot he'd squeezed off
had missed, this time ineffectively grazing one of the religious icons at the back of the section of the church. He
had to eliminate her, he thought grimly, as he dismantled
the assault rifle which Joseph Smith had given him, and
secreted the parts in the inside pocket of his small rucksack. Otherwise he would pay with his life. He pulled out
a hand gun and tucked this into the back of the waistband
of his trousers. Inside the confessional he drew a knife
from the inside of his bag that had once belonged to his

brother Nijam. He had retrieved it from his body at the petrol station where he had been murdered. It would be only fitting that he should use it to silence this woman, once and for all. An eye for an eye. The irony of the intense religious significance of the site was not lost on him, either—this building represented to him the religion Nijam had fallen into before his death, the religion that had weakened him. Wiraj firmly believed that Nijam would still be alive today if he had not allowed himself to be drawn into something so distracting, so directionless, that was not part of his culture. He had lost all his fight. The fact that Wiraj had now committed murder in a building that was iconic of the religion he blamed for his brother's loss was satisfying to him.

Zipping up his rucksack, Wiraj secreted the knife on the opposite side of his body from the gun then pulled on a long coat, grabbed his bag and set out in pursuit of the fleeing girl. It was only once he was out of the confessional he realised he had left it too late. The throng of tourists kept him from getting closer than five people to Eva's dark head, moving as quickly as she was towards the door. He had considered using his knife to hack people out of his way but that, of course, would draw far too much attention to him and the crowd was packed in so tightly that, if he were identified as the perpetrator, he would most certainly not be able to escape. Then he had glanced up at the doorway and seen that strange, intense man appear from nowhere, grab the girl and sweep her off her feet, down the steps and out of Wiraj's range.

FIFTEEN

THE JOURNEY BACK to the car was a haze. Leon kept hold of Eva and continued dragging her forward at a blistering pace so that her arms felt as though they were being wrenched from their sockets. She allowed him to pull her along, not wanting to stop in the middle of the street because of the sniper from the cathedral, but it took all her self-control not to force him to let go of her. Finally, as they reached the car, she pulled her wrist free.

He looked at her. 'Get in.' She did as she was told, slamming the door and sitting rigidly in the passenger seat.

'Put your seat belt on.' Silently, Eva obeyed.

At first, Leon's harsh tone and the violence of his actions had angered and confused her; he seemed constantly to change from friend to foe. But in the ten minutes it had taken for them to rush back to the car, a more sinister thought had occurred to Eva: Leon had disappeared minutes before Sophie had sat down next to her in the Sacré Coeur. He had not been standing where he had said he would be. She had looked for him just before Sophie had arrived and just after she had been shot and he had not been there, either time. Then he had suddenly appeared at the exit to the cathedral in precisely the area where she had worked out that the fatal shot would have come from. He had arrived exactly as Eva had been leaving and he seemed to know what had happened, even though no one else in that area of the cathedral had been aware of the murder. And he had lied to her earlier when she had asked him if he had a gun.

Leon had both means and opportunity to have been Sophie's killer. But what could be his motive? Had he just been using Eva to get to Sophie?

She glanced up as she felt Leon's gaze on her in the rearview mirror. He looked away again as he took the Citroën up another gear and tore through some back streets, scattering pigeons and tourists. Eva felt an urgent need to get away from him. Leon left too much chaos in his wake and she never felt in control when he was around.

'Are you OK?'

'I'm fine.'

'Did you see where the shot came from?'

'No. Did you?'

'No.'

'What did she give you?' If Leon had seen Sophie take the memory stick from her bag then he had been watching them only seconds before the shot was fired. And yet Eva hadn't seen him anywhere.

'She didn't give me anything,' Eva lied.

Once again, she caught him looking at her in the mirror. She met his gaze evenly, and then looked away.

THEY WERE DRIVING back down through the centre of Paris and Eva was beginning to recognise some of the streets and the Métro stops. She sat tensely in the passenger seat, wondering how she could best remove herself from Leon's company, when suddenly a situation presented itself. As they waited at a set of traffic lights, a large fat man with very red cheeks, brandishing a map, began knocking on Leon's window. The street was so narrow that he could reach the car from where he was standing on the pavement. Leon ignored him but the man kept knocking.

Eva saw a muscle in Leon's jaw start to twitch and she knew it was only a matter of time before he would respond. She sat still and waited.

The man knocked again and Leon glanced impatiently at the lights, evidently willing them to change. Eva prayed that they wouldn't.

Once again the tourist, obviously now just persisting for the sheer hell of it, banged on the window, three short sharp raps. All at once, Leon exhaled violently, reached over, wound down the window and began shouting at the tourist in French. In the same instant, Eva threw open the passenger door and launched herself out into the street, running for the corner at the end of the road where she could hopefully lose herself in the connected streets. Turning briefly, she saw Leon's shocked face wearing almost the same expression as the fat tourist, then in an instant it turned to anger as the lights changed and the cars behind began impatiently sounding their horns.

EVA TURNED AGAIN and ran. When she reached the end of the street she took a hard left, hearing the slam of a car door in the distance as she did so. She took the corner tightly and began running along a wide, flat pavement, her legs pumping as fast as they could go, adrenaline surging through her veins. Two blocks ahead she could see the yellow, circled 'M' of a Métro station. She ran faster. She was travelling down a broad road and realised that at any minute Leon, having the advantage of the car, would be able to catch her. She briefly considered turning off and trying to lose him in the side streets but she didn't know her way around them and the Métro would provide a far more efficient escape route.

Alert for the sound of a speeding car behind her, Eva pushed herself through pain barrier after pain barrier until finally she was within spitting distance of the Métro. Breathlessly, she turned her head again and looked behind, expecting to see Leon chasing after her, but there was only one car, a red Peugeot. Odd, she thought, but continued running until she reached the Métro where she extracted a single carnet ticket from her purse, threw herself down the stairs onto the platform and jumped on the waiting train.

The train left the station and Eva tried to catch her breath. As she sat down and fought to take in great gasps of air, she glanced back at the platform, once again expecting to see Leon in pursuit. He was nowhere to be seen.

GIVEN THE EFFICIENCY with which he moved, Leon would have had no problem slamming the passenger door shut and tailing her around the corner to the Métro before she had managed to run down the steps to the safety of the train. With his athlete's physique and agility he probably could have chased her down the road on foot and still caught her. But he had been nowhere in the vicinity when she had turned round and now there was no sign of him at all. His lack of reaction went against everything she had learned about him and that made Eva very uneasy.

She brushed aside the shiver of fear and focused her mind on what had just happened. Sophie had been about to tell her something back at the Sacré Coeur, something that Jackson had died for and that Sophie had now also paid for with her life. Something that was on the memory stick now in Eva's possession. She felt in her pocket for the small stick and was relieved to find its tiny bulk still there. She pulled it out and looked at it and then realised she had no laptop. It was still at the hotel. Damn.

Eva sat and thought as the train pulled into another station, slowly pushing west underneath the city, towards the Champs Elysées and, further on, the business district. She had to get to a computer where she could open this memory stick without the risk of anyone interrupting her. She couldn't return to the hotel and risk Leon catching up with her there but a public internet café would be too risky. There was only one other person she knew in Paris. She checked her watch: 11.35am. The whole drama at the Sacré Coeur had taken less than two hours. Eva pulled out her phone and accessed the phone's memory. She put the slim device to her ear and then waited as it rang three times and was answered.

'Valerie.'

SIXTEEN

VALERIE OPENED THE door to her flat in a pair of black jeans and a tight white T-shirt that clung to every curve. 'Eva, come in,' she said and opened the door wide. Immediately, Eva was struck by the change in her demeanour since the last time they had met; she seemed confident and self-possessed, rather than haunted and uncomfortable. The way she was standing made her appear several inches taller.

Eva smiled warily and stepped into the flat, hearing the door click shut behind her.

The space inside was modest; a tiny hallway leading down to several smaller rooms, a bedroom, bathroom and a second, larger bedroom. At the other end, Eva could see a kitchen with a small dining-table and to the left of that, a huge open living-room with floor-to-ceiling French windows framed on either side by heavy, dark drapes. The flat had beautiful wooden floors, and a pleasant, airy feel, with the sounds from the streets of the expensive and well-to-do 16th arrondissement drifting in through an open window. Eva couldn't help wondering how Valerie could afford a flat like this on a receptionist's salary, now that she didn't have Jackson to support her.

Valerie led her into the light of the living-room, to a huge peach-coloured sofa positioned opposite a wide-screen TV that was attached to the opposite wall.

'Would you like a drink?' Valerie said hospitably.

'No, thanks.' Suspicion began to seep into Eva's bones. This woman was nothing like the Valerie she had met at the café, who had seemed fragile and almost broken. Whilst Eva had never met Valerie before that day, so knew very little about her, she now felt like she was meeting her brother's ex-girlfriend for the first time. Which one was the real woman?

'Can I get you some food? You look very tired.'

'No, thanks, I'm not hungry.' Almost as soon as she said the word 'hungry' her stomach let out an almighty growl that seemed to echo around the room.

'I'll get you a sandwich,' said Valerie, smiling and heading out of the room.

'Valerie,' said Eva at the retreating back, 'where is your computer?'

Without even checking her pace Valerie said, 'In the bedroom.' Eva turned and walked out of the living room, choosing the first of the two bedroom doors, which opened to reveal a small bedroom with a low bed, polished wooden chest of drawers and more dark antique drapes. As she walked in she caught sight of herself in a large oval mirror; her cheeks were flushed but underneath her skin looked pale against the dark leather of her jacket. In the corner of the room sat a brand-new iMac complete with printer, huge speakers and a second monitor to the right of the first. Again, Eva experienced surprise. It was a very professional looking set-up. Why did Valerie need two screens? Eva remembered Leon insisting Valerie was at the heart of everything that had happened to Jackson. It gave her an uneasy feeling in the pit of her stomach. For a second, she stopped and considered what she was doing. Was this a stupid move?

She thought about the risk she might be taking coming here—there was a chance that Valerie wasn't who she seemed, but it was Leon who had obsessed on that and the fact that Eva didn't trust his judgement made her dismiss what he had said. If the worst did happen, Valerie was a woman so at least she and Eva were relatively evenly matched physically. Eva drove the confusion of thoughts from her head and flicked a button on the back of the slim, white machine before it sprang into life. She was minutes away from unlocking the contents of the memory stick. The rest she could figure out afterwards.

FIVE MINUTES LATER, Eva was reading a news website, unwilling to open the memory stick before she could be sure there would be no interruptions. She soon heard footsteps coming down the hall and then Valerie appeared around the door, balancing a tray of food and a can of drink. 'Here, eat.' She set the tray down on the bed and left without another word, closing the door with a click. Her unquestioning response to Eva's phone call asking to use her computer was extremely unnerving and Eva couldn't help feeling that she had just wandered into a lioness's den. Nevertheless, she had to press on. Press on or go back—although where she could safely retreat to now she had no idea.

At first, Eva tried to ignore the sandwich but the howls in her stomach were stopping her from thinking straight so she reached for the baguette and took a huge bite as she pulled the USB stick out of her pocket. The sandwich was delicious—creamy cheese, rich ham and some kind of slightly tart sauce, probably mustard. She took another bite, then a long drink from the open can and waited for the USB stick's folder to open up on the screen. The computer was fast and it took less than a couple of seconds before she was looking at the contents of 'Mfiles', Sophie's name for the stick on which she had loaded all the information.

Eva stared at the folder names and four jumped out at her: 'briefing', 'forecast', 'test results' and 'read me'. She opened 'briefing' first and found it was a folder of collated newspaper articles and web research on a new type of health supplement that it was claimed could regenerate human cells. It was being launched by the company that Sophie had worked for. Eva skimmed through the commentators' conclusions, which seemed first to challenge the idea that this was possible and then—six months later according to the dates on the clippings— to accept it.

Eva was inclined to dismiss the idea as fantasy, a way for big business to make money by milking the human obsession with being young. However, when she came to the paragraphs on the make up of the algae, she was surprised to discover that it had been genetically engineered. That made it a whole different ballgame, as who knew what was possible in a plant that wasn't cultivated from nature? She took a slow drink from the can and then opened an internet window on Valerie's computer and typed the name of the supplement into the search box. Immediately hundreds of hits sprang up on most of the major news networks, indicating that a marketing campaign for the supplement was already under way. It was due to go on sale in the UK in just a week and commentators were predicting the first batches would sell out in hours. As one said, 'in the quest for youth and health that most pharmaceutical companies peddle, Bioavancement S.a.r.l. seems to have found the Holy Grail.'

WAS IT STRANGE that a pharmaceutical company should be manufacturing a health supplement? Eva wasn't sure but she tended to take a cynical approach to those who made money from human insecurity for a living—it wouldn't be the first time she had been surprised to discover insidious corporate links she had not been aware of that connected other businesses. Her favourite 'quality', 'fresh' sandwich company, for example, which had turned out to be owned by one of the biggest fast food giants in the world. Who really knew what kinds of corporate manipulation of the public psyche went on behind the scenes? It seemed more sensible to assume it was happening than not.

Eva opened another document, which seemed to be one that Sophie had stolen from Bioavancement S.a.r.l. itself, setting out the genetic structure of the algae the company had developed, and which they had named 'PX 3.' Unfortunately, the scientific equations meant nothing to Eva so she had no way of deciphering what made the PX 3 so special. She closed the folder.

Next she opened 'test results' and clicked on the first document. As soon as the document was on the screen Eva's heart began to pound. The opened file was a scanned image and, stamped across the top in block printing, were the words 'Highly Confidential'.

The scanned file was actually two documents, both of which were identically laid out and part of a standard form documentation process for Bioavancement S.a.r.l.. The first form contained information on a test of the PX 3 algae on mice, showing that it seemed to have quite a dramatic effect on the liver, although Eva struggled to understand exactly what that was. The second form was identical but related to a different test which concluded that the genetically modified algae was capable of something called 'super speed algal bloom', which would cause it to grow at more than a thousand times the speed of a normal algae plant. In another document in the 'test results' folder, she found a summary of the plant's hardiness, concluding that it was 'utterly resilient to every type of industrial algaecide'.

Eva closed the file and then opened the 'Read Me' folder, which consisted of a single document of the same name that seemed to be a collection of copy and paste reports and paragraphs that Sophie had put together herself. She stared at the screen, realising that the words suddenly looked a little fuzzy, shifting uncomfortably in her chair as she felt a twinge of indigestion in her stomach.

The document was composed of almost incomprehensible scientific jargon. Symbols, numbers and words jumped off the page at her and Eva wished she had paid more attention to science at school. Finally, towards the end of the last page, she noticed a report with a summary written in language she could understand. According to the summary, the algae's reproduction rate meant that it was actually capable of spreading so fast that it could not be controlled. She looked for evidence that Bioavancement S.a.r.l. recommended the use of ways to prevent the spread of the algae, but she found the exact opposite— they had actually insisted the algae must be grown in pools open to the air, despite the fact that this would effectively turn the algae loose. Eva felt a knot of tension forming in her stomach as she read on.

The summary's author returned to the algae's unprecedented growth rate and concluded that, as a result of this uncontrollable population, the sites allocated as the development pools for the algae in the UK would not be able to contain the plants. The spores would be carried—on the wind or by insects or animals—outside the company's official raceway pond sites, where they would settle in any hospitably wet surface or waterway. Suddenly Eva leaned against the hard back of the chair as a wave of pain rippled through her stomach. She rubbed a hand across her belly to try and soothe the aggravation that was most likely being caused by not having eaten all day then consuming an entire sandwich in the space of thirty seconds.

She had to keep reading.

As SHE FOLLOWED the words on the page, it became clear that the breakthrough algae, that had the potential for such positive things, had not been developed as a health supplement at all. Eva found herself struggling to make sense of the scientific language but it seemed that the effect that it actually had on the liver was to increase its resistance to insulin, causing the body to create vast amounts of unnecessary insulin that interfered with the brain's ability to detect fat cells. She stared at the screen and tried to connect what she had read about the algae's ability to spread, and this odd effect that it had on the liver. Both of these issues seemed to present a significant barrier to a supplement like this being produced and sold to the public—didn't this kind of thing have to be approved?—and yet she had seen just moments ago on the net that it was already out there. Was this what Sophie was talking about when she said that the people behind this couldn't even be seen? Eva pushed a strand of hair away from the damp skin of her face and realised she was sweating heavily despite the cold of the room.

As she reached the end of the paragraph it all started to become clear, but Eva suddenly stopped reading, pushed her chair back and staggered sideways, trying to hold on to the desk for support. She was going to be sick. Her vision started to swim and her head was spinning as if she had just got off a fairground ride. She lurched back towards the computer and tried to read the document once more. When she realised she was about to pass out, she made a grab for the USB stick.

FROM HER POSITION leaning against the sink in the kitchen Valerie heard the crash as the rohypnol took effect and Eva fell crashing to the floor. She was pleased that the girl had not just slumped in her chair; it was a far better result if she had fallen and caused herself some damage. Valerie did not like Eva.

She stood up straight and stalked over to a small cupboard on the other side of the kitchen where she extracted a black fabric square, some small lengths of plastic and a small handgun.

She checked and loaded the gun and once she was satisfied it was prepped, she pushed it into the waistband of her jeans, nestling the cold steel in the warm hollow at the base of her back.

In the bedroom, Eva was lying on her side where she had fallen. Valerie glanced at the screen to see what she had been looking at. The white page of a blank document filled it with only an error message about the incorrect removal of a device. She checked the side of the white screen that housed the USB points, as well as the USB extension port, looking for a memory stick, but there was nothing there. She frowned. She bent down, rolled Eva over and began methodically searching her but she found nothing. A car horn sounded outside and she realised it was too late to do anything now. She would first deal with this and then she would track down any missing items.

Valerie flipped Eva over with the ease of someone who had trained long and hard to have a subtle strength that never compromised those winning curves. She pulled Eva's wrists together at the base of her spine and used one of the lengths of plastic to bind her. The custom-made bands locked into place, unbreakable without a knife. As she was finishing, she heard the boy come bounding up the stairs.

'She's ready,' she said as he came in the room.

ONCE HE HAD disabled the driver downstairs, Wiraj had taken his car keys and run up the stairs to the flat where he had observed Eva Scott arrive only half an hour before. As he walked through the door he had heard a woman's voice say 'she's ready' and then he had spotted the dark-haired British woman lying face down on the floor, her arms bound behind her back, apparently unconscious. He had quickly taken his gun to the back of the head of the redhead and she had gone down straight away, her head hitting the corner of the desk before landing face down on the floor. Wiraj noticed the shape of a gun in the waistband of her trousers as she fell forward and wondered who the hell she was.

As he bent down to pick up the unconscious woman, he noticed the black felt hood on the floor, picked it up and shoved it in his pocket before heaving Eva over his

shoulder and setting off out of the flat and down the stairs
to where he had left the car with the engine running.

ON THE BANKS of the Thames, twelve miles west of central London, in the six raceway ponds so carefully con-
structed by Rob Gorben and his team, a savage act of
cannibalism was taking place. As several of the algae
plants began to die, the others started to feed off the nutrients deposited into the gently moving water of those
oval-shaped ponds. The genetically modified algae
worked at an unusually high speed to feed and repro-
duce its own population, which only the day before had
been relatively dormant. The species had been developed
to be aggressive, to ensure its survival by eliminating
any other minor organism that got in its way, efficiently
turning it into food by feeding on the dead cells, even
if the plant was one of its own. In the twenty-four hours
since the dead plants had been introduced to the water,
there had been a feeding frenzy, so much so that by the
next morning, the PX 3 would officially have reached its
first formal milestone—'a rapid increase or accumula-
tion in the population of algae in an aquatic system': an
algal bloom. And with each new organism that came into
being, a new life cycle was begun, a life cycle unnaturally manipulated to move at great speed until the algae
was nothing but decaying matter, floating on the surface
of the water, to be recycled once again into food for the
new plants. But as each algae plant died it had one last
function to perform to ensure the survival of a species
unrecognised and out of place in the natural world—the
release of spores, the lightest in nature, so featherweight
and small that as soon as they were released they were
carried up into the air and out into the world beyond.

SEVENTEEN

'MR PORTER, I think you need to look at this.' At the Thames regional office of the UK Environment and Waterways Agency, Regional Director Don Porter was drawn to the computer screen of one of his newest and keenest assistants.

'What is it, Fred?' The newcomer, Fred Humphries, had started to make a habit of trying to attract Porter's attention on issues that Porter's usual team knew not to trouble him with. He was in the middle of a horrendously busy day, including a battle with a new company that had set up some kind of facility within the boundaries of his geographical remit, with no thought whatsoever for local planning or environmental regulations. The company was not supposed to take over the site for another two months, until all the permits and licences were in place, but it had appeared almost overnight and none of his staff had been able to get into the site or even speak to anyone involved in the company. He was going to be completely hung out to dry on this one if he didn't do something about it and soon. The last thing he needed was these distractions.

Don Porter gazed at Fred's screen. 'What is it?'

'It's a chat room—' Porter wondered if this was a sackable offence. Humphries had obviously been browsing the internet after all and that was misuse of the company's computer. He was in the mood for a sacking, particularly when it came to anyone unnecessarily taking up his precious time.

'Yes, I can see that, Fred. Why are you showing it to me?'

'It's going mad, Mr Porter. Ever since yesterday evening there are all these posts that have started going up about algae appearing in people's ponds. There's even one here about someone noticing the same plants in a local river.' Porter thought he could at least get away with giving the boy a severe and very public dressing down.

'We get this kind of thing all the time, Fred. Honestly, it's really nothing to write home about.'

'But don't you think it's a little odd? All of it suddenly appearing at the same time?'

'Well, is it all over the country?' There was something about Fred's enthusiasm that stopped the Regional Director from giving him a reprimand. Not many of the Environment Agency's employees had much of this kind of enthusiasm any more—working there for more than a year seemed to knock that firmly out of people. But Fred was new and fresh and that, Porter reasoned wearily, should probably be encouraged.

'I don't think so, Mr Porter, it seems to be only happening around London at the moment.'

'Whereabouts exactly?'

'Seems to be mostly concentrated just west of Richmond. There's a lot of open water around there—waterworks, as well as a number of reservoirs and public gardens.'

'Right. So it seems fairly contained?'

Fred frowned. 'I guess.'

'Well, for the moment I suggest we monitor the situation. No point in alarming anyone—all those open waterworks are treated with algaecide so we're not going to be overcome with a "red tide" any time soon.'

'It's not red algae, Mr Porter. As far as I can tell from these posts the algae seem to be black.'

'Black? Black algae normally only grow in fish tanks or swimming pools.'

'I know, Mr Porter, that's why I thought it was strange.'

'They must be mistaken—it could very easily just be dark green.' Fred opened his mouth to protest but Don had a meeting and he'd heard enough.

'Monitor the situation for me, Fred,' he said and smiled encouragingly.

THE FIRST THING Eva was aware of when she opened her eyes was a blinding headache. She was in complete darkness, with some sort of material covering her head, but from the pain behind her eyes she felt as if someone was shining a spotlight right into them. She tried to remove the head covering but her hands were bound and her ankles tied together, tough plastic digging into her skin when she tried to move. Eva's first instinct was one of panic. The claustrophobic feeling of the material over her head and her bound hands and feet triggered a surge of adrenaline that she fought from escalating. I can't afford to lose control, she told herself over and over again. If she panicked she would not be able to think rationally and, right at this moment, that was just about her only defence and her only weapon.

She leaned to one side and felt around with her hands for several seconds and realised she was sitting on a rough, uneven floor covered in small rocks and grains of sand. She was not in Leon's flat once again, or at her

hotel. Was she even still in Paris? The last thing she remembered was sitting in front of a computer screen but
she had no idea where or why. Her mind had gone completely blank.

As another wave of panic threatened, Eva struggled
briefly with her bonds but she was bound tight. Finally,
she let out a short, frustrated cry and slumped against the
wall, her heart beating hard. To try and release the pressure, she let herself cry and the tears spilled down her
cheeks without being wiped away, hot and salty against
her dry, cracked lips, soaking into the black felt of the
hood over her head. The tears had the desired effect. As
the anxiety dispersed enough for her to think clearly,
pieces of information and images began to crystallise
in her head. She remembered being at the Sacré Coeur
with Sophie and her memories before that were all in-
tact. But how had she come here?

SUDDENLY A DOOR slammed in the distance, drilling a shot
of adrenaline through Eva's system. Memories began
flying faster through her brain. She remembered sprint-
ing away from Leon and then arriving at Valerie's flat.
Opening the memory stick that Sophie gave her at the
Sacré Coeur was one of the last situations she could recall, so it must have been Valerie's computer she was
looking at. Eva tried to feel for the shape of the memory
stick in the pocket of her jeans, but she couldn't move
her hands and she knew instinctively that the device
was not there. She realised she no longer had any idea
what was on it.

Again she felt a sense of overwhelming anxiety. She
tried to ignore the chasm of possibilities opening up
below her—where she was, why was she there, what

would happen next? Instead she tried to focus on something inside her body—her breathing, her heartbeat—the only things she had control over.

Suddenly the room was filled with light. Eva sat completely still. Through the thin material of the hood she could make out two figures framed in the doorway, one short and stocky and the other tall and thin.

'Pick her up.' The voice was male and accented, although Eva couldn't place it.

The stocky figure moved across the room towards her and grasped her by the back of her top, pulling her, stumbling, to her feet. Small waves of panic washed over Eva; she was completely at the mercy of these two men, whoever they may be. She tried to keep herself calm and focus on regulating her breathing, keeping all her strength for any opportunities she might get to escape. It wasn't easy—every surge of adrenaline brought a fresh urge to panic.

'Bring her through.' That clipped voice again, accent indecipherable—French? Italian?

Suddenly Eva found herself facing the floor as the stocky man hoisted her over his left shoulder. By moving her head, she managed to loosen and then shake off the black hood as the man carried her, still bound at the hands and feet, out of the dark cell and into the light of a narrow stone corridor. Eva lifted her gaze and glanced back at the room he had taken her from. It looked very much like a prison cell and even had a small wrought-iron door with a tiny window in the centre at the top. As they walked down the corridor, Eva saw other similar doors on either side, all shut. By the time they reached the end of the corridor and turned left, she had counted six.

EVA WAS CARRIED into a room and deposited roughly into a rickety chair. Her carrier then proceeded to fasten a rough rope around her shoulders so that, with her hands and feet bound together and her body fastened to the chair by the rope, she couldn't move at all. Eva looked around. The room was better lit than the corridor and now that she was free of the hood she could clearly see the two men in front of her. She felt the eyes of the taller man boring into her own. His skin was dark; he looked African. Eva remembered the man at her hotel, the same man that Leon had executed at the petrol station. Perhaps this was revenge. Or perhaps it was worse.

The tall man continued to stare at her and then suddenly he spoke, his voice wound tight like a spring. 'Why are you here?' He walked over to her, his dark eyes never once leaving hers. As he grew closer Eva could see a scar running down his left cheek along pockmarked, lumpy skin.

'I said...' He leaned in towards her until she could smell the gum on his breath. She tried not to flinch and stared back at him, waiting for him to finish his sentence.

She blinked and then suddenly a block of hot pain flashed across her right cheek and she was momentarily in the air. She cried out as the chair she was tied to landed roughly on the uneven floor, leaving her stranded on her back. He had hit her so hard that the force of the punch had thrown her into the air. Eva's breathing was coming hard and fast now. The metallic taste of blood filled her mouth and the right side of her face was throbbing painfully. She struggled to try and loosen the ties around her wrists, felt the rope fixing her to the chair loosen, and then suddenly she was upright again. The wiry man had retreated to the other side of the room and it was his stocky second-in-command who now stood behind her, his hands on the back of the chair, having brought her back to an upright position.

Eva was hyperventilating; she couldn't stop herself. The attack had come out of the blue—he hadn't even given her the chance to answer his question.

As the scarred man seemed to take time to compose himself, Eva desperately tried to calm herself down. She tried to think of anyone who might be in a position to help her but the only person who might know what had happened was Valerie and by now it was clear she had some involvement in all this.

SHE LOOKED UP suddenly to see the wiry man coming at her across the room again at an unexpected pace. Eva didn't notice the glass in his right hand until he threw the contents in her face. She screamed; it burned her skin like acid. Overcome by an unexpected burst of rage, Eva kicked out with her feet trying to get to him, uncontrollable anger suddenly coursing through her body. She bucked and kicked until suddenly she felt the rope around her chest give way and she was free from the chair. Standing precariously, ankles and hands still bound, she shook off the chair and launched herself at the man, trying to loop her bound wrists over his head so she could choke him with her bonds. As she hit his shoulder with her head, she could hear him laughing and even as she felt him fall underneath her weight and the force of gravity behind her, Eva knew that this was a small victory. Her arms and legs were still tied and these two men were unbound, stronger than her and probably armed. She had no chance.

'You are angry,' he said as he pushed her aside, dusted

himself off and got back to his feet. 'Good.' His sidekick pulled Eva upright by her hair and the pain made her scream as she struggled to keep her body close enough to her head to stop him pulling her hair out in clumps. He pushed her back into the chair by shoving it violently into the backs of her knees then re-tied the rope, making it so tight this time that it cut into the bare skin over her collarbone. She blinked through still-wet lashes. She was shaking violently. Whatever had been in the glass was not corrosive. He had succeeded in unsettling her and making her lose control, which had no doubt been his intention all along, but she wasn't in pain and, as far as she could tell, he hadn't injured her. The skin on her face had settled to a grim throb as she felt the liquid start to dry. She forced her breathing back to a regular rise and fall, but her nerve endings flared with alertness.

'Why are you here?' The man was opposite her again, closer this time.

'I don't understand what you mean.' Her mouth was thick with blood where he had punched her.

'Don't play games with us, Eva.'

'I'm not.'

'Do you think we are playing games with you, Eva?' He laughed. 'Do you think we are wasting your time? We have planned and executed everything to the letter.' There was something about the way he pronounced 'executed' that made Eva stop breathing for several seconds. She tried to imagine how it would feel to be shot, stabbed or suffocated but she couldn't. Every time she tried to picture it her mind went blank.

'I came to find out what happened to my brother.'

'Ah yes, Jackson.'

Eva inhaled quickly. 'You know him.'

'It was a very short acquaintance.' He laughed.

'You killed him.'

The man smiled. 'Perhaps.' Eva clenched her fists and dug her fingernails into the soft palms of her hands.

'Do you want to know how we may have killed him?' All the breath left Eva's body. She waited in silence. Was he just playing a game with her or was this real information?

'We may have tortured him for a couple of days before he died. Or maybe we killed him straight away. Or maybe he is still alive and looking for you. How will you ever know?' He laughed and began to walk in the other direction. 'If he was anything like you I would say if we killed him then he would have taken a while to die,' he said as he turned back towards Eva. 'Stubborn and resourceful, both of you.' The man went over to the table and picked up something heavy that made a metallic noise as he dragged it towards him.

'But in the end, there are some forces that are unstoppable.' He took several paces towards her. 'No matter how strong you think you might be, how much you have suffered, or how hard you have fought for your life and how much you think you deserve for that effort, none of us gets what we are due in the end.' He stopped in front of her. 'Death is a great leveller, Eva.' A slight incline of the head from the wiry man and suddenly strong hands came from behind and wrapped themselves around Eva's throat. Slowly they began to tighten their grip. The wiry man continued to talk as if nothing was happening. 'You should know that I am merely a conduit.

Under normal circumstances I would wish you no harm.' Eva stared at him incredulously as she was choked on his orders. He stood motionless in front of her, a huge metal crowbar in his hands. Eva was gasping now, vainly sucking in tiny draughts of air through the vice-like grip slowly closing around her windpipe. If he didn't watch his henchman strangle her, he was going to beat her to death with the crowbar, she thought. This is what it feels like.

'Like everyone else, I'm just trying to make my way.' He looked thoughtfully at the crowbar as Eva started to suffocate.

'We all just run parallel to each other, Eva, alongside all these millions of other people and yet completely separate—until our paths cross.' His eyes drifted back to her reddening face. 'Unfortunately, now our paths have crossed. Yours and mine; mine and your brother's; your friend Leon's and my brother's; your brother's and Sophie's.' He seemed almost philosophical.

Eva could hardly breathe and there was an excruciating pressure building up behind her eyes and around her ears.

'Did…' she spluttered.

The man made a sign and suddenly all the pressure was gone as the hands released her and her airways expanded. Eva opened her throat and took in great, hungry gasps of air.

'Did…did…' She struggled to pull enough breath into her lungs to be able to speak but she was determined now. 'D-did you shoot Sophie?'

'Of course!'

Eva shook her head and took some more deep breaths. It hadn't been Leon. She waited for those hands to close back around her throat but nothing happened.

'We have been searching for her since your brother. For three months we had to stay in this godforsaken city looking for her. Then we found her and still we had to stay, watching to see if she had made contact with any-one else. And then there was you.'

'I don't understand,' said Eva coughing as she spoke.

'No. Why would you? As I said, all that has happened is that our paths have crossed. But only one of us gets to walk away.' He looked at her and smiled.

'That is such a load of shit,' she said still gasping for air. Suddenly the philosophical expression on the man's face broke. He leaned in towards her and propped the crowbar under her chin. 'And. What. The. Fuck. Would. You. Know.'

'You're trying to make out like this is a situation over which you don't have any control. You could walk out of that door right now and leave me here unharmed.'

'I couldn't.'

'You could.'

'There is no choice here.'

'Bullshit.' Eva watched his eyes flare at her and she thought he was about to lash out with the crowbar. Then the flame died.

'I come from the Sudan, Eva. You come from En-gland. You could have no idea how different life is out-side of your democracy.'

The reference to the Sudan confused Eva. Did all this have something to do with Jackson's work there? It didn't make sense. 'Jackson was trying to help you. Why did you kill him?'

Unexpectedly, the man hesitated, an expression of confusion spreading across his savaged face. 'How could he have helped us? He didn't even know who we were or what we are trying to do.'

'No, he was trying to help your country.' She studied

the man's obvious incomprehension. Apparently, he had
no idea who Jackson really was or what he did for a living. Perhaps he had just murdered an anonymous man.
Or maybe he had never even met him.

'Jackson worked to raise awareness of the problems
in the Sudan, that was his job. He was trying to raise
money for your people,' she said. 'He had information—
he could have helped you.' The man opposite continued
to glare at her. Eva stared back at him. He was just a paid
thug. He knew even less than her. He wouldn't be able
to tell her anything about what really happened; maybe
he hadn't even been there.

'You're a liar.' As he spoke, Eva noticed the hesitation
on the man's face had gone. Where before she had seen
questions triggered by what she had said, now only seconds later, he seemed to have made up his mind. 'Joseph
Smith said you would tell lies.' So there was someone
next up the chain of command.

'I'm not lying.'

'You are,' he said, hefting the huge crowbar between
his hands, 'and now I don't want to listen to your lies
anymore.' Eva looked around her; the wiry man was
reaching the end of his capacity for talking.

The man opened his mouth to speak again but got no
further. With an enormous crash, the door flew open
and Eva recoiled as a series of high-pitched shots filled
the room. She stared up at the wiry man as his face suddenly slackened and his body briefly danced before he
fell to the floor, blood oozing from the bullet holes in
his back. Several more shots were fired and Eva heard a
small exhalation and a loud thump behind her.

Then she was alone in the room. With Leon.

EIGHTEEN

'DID YOU HAVE to kill him?' Eva realised her teeth were still gritted as she spoke, clamped together to stop her screaming when the shooting began. Her nerve endings were on fire; the gunshots were still echoing around inside her head. She felt Leon's incredulous stare as she remained sitting on the battered wooden chair, in between the bodies of the two men.

'Is that a serious question?' He walked quickly across the room and began shifting the two bodies to one side before methodically searching them. She could hear that he was breathing heavily, through nerves or exertion.

'What are you doing?'

'Searching them.'

'I…'

'Can we talk about this later?' Leon indicated the bodies on the floor. 'We need to get out of here.' Eva looked down at the man with the scar who was now lying mute, eyes wide, fingers gripping the uneven floor in the position he had died.

Leon seemed to have found what he was looking for; he pulled Eva's phone from the man's pocket. Eva looked it at, surprised.

'Come on.' Having cut the rope around her shoulders and the bonds at her hands and ankles, Leon pulled her to her feet, handed her the phone and began propelling her out of the door. Eva resisted slightly, but for the first time she let him lead. She was exhausted.

They half-walked, half-ran back along the corridor lined with cells, passed through a large metal door that looked like it had been kicked off its hinges, then stepped into a more inhabited building that appeared to Eva to be basement office space. It was empty, eerily so. Leon led Eva along through the dank darkness of the basement and then suddenly took a right and burst through a fire door.

'Up there,' he said, indicating a small doorway. She looked up. They were at the bottom of a long metal spiral staircase that covered at least eight flights. Her legs felt weak, she was still shaking and her head was throbbing, but there was no way out other than up. When they finally reached the top, Leon broke through the outer fire escape door and suddenly they were in the street. A Parisian street—alive with cars, barking dogs and the smell of fresh bread. Eva looked around her in surprise.

'I thought I was outside Paris.'

Leon simply shook his head. 'Come.' He led her around the corner to where the Citroen was parked, and opened the door. Eva got in, sinking gratefully into the soft seat. She was surprised to see the rear windscreen, that had been in pieces the last time she had seen the car, had already been replaced.

Leon started up the engine and pulled out into a flow of traffic whilst Eva glanced in the mirrors. Once they were under way, she looked expectantly over at him, assuming that some kind of explanation would be forthcoming.

'Thank you,' she said in what was probably a fairly

underwhelming expression of gratitude for what he had just done.

'I shouldn't have left you alone at the Sacré Coeur.' He nodded in the rearview mirror at her. 'You look terrible.'

'Thanks.'

'Who did they work for?'

'That's what I was about to find out.'

'Did they say anything at all?'

'There was a name—Joseph Smith.' Leon nodded slowly.

'What did they do to you?' he asked, his voice hard.

'Just what you can see,' Eva replied. And then in a low voice, with a lump in her throat, 'I think they killed Jackson.' Leon remained stony-faced. He seemed heavy, depressed.

They sat in silence for several minutes.

'Look, don't ask me how but I know of this man Joseph Smith,' he said finally. 'If they are working for him then we won't have long before they discover you have escaped and come after us.'

'Who is he?' asked Eva, ignoring Leon's instruction.

He gazed at her in the rearview mirror for several seconds.

'It doesn't matter right now.' Eva locked into his gaze and held it. They stared at each other and then, fearing Leon's pig-headedness would see them end up in a traffic accident, Eva looked away.

'We need to find the memory stick Sophie gave me.'

'Yes.'

Eva thought about how convinced she had been that Leon had been Sophie's murderer. 'How do you know she gave me that? Every time I looked for you at the Sacré Coeur you weren't there.'

'There was someone watching you—it was the larger man back there,' he said, indicating the direction of the cellar he had released her from. 'I left my position because I followed him. I lost him and that's when I saw the gun being aimed at you through the curtain of a confessional near the exit. I couldn't get there in time...' He finished, disappointment heavy in his voice. 'I guessed it must be some kind of device.' Eva nodded silently.

'What was on the stick?'

She looked over at him. 'I don't know. I mean, I did know...but...'

'I think you were drugged.'

'I guessed as much.' Eva rubbed her aching head. 'How did you know where I was?' Leon glanced sideways at her and then back at the road. 'I fitted you with a tracking device when you were at my apartment. That's how I knew you had been at Valerie's flat.' That was why he hadn't bothered to follow her when she ran off after the Sacré Coeur, she realised. 'Where is it?'

'It looks just like skin. It's on your lower back.' Eva reached round and felt all across the skin of her back with one hand until, after several minutes, she finally found a tiny patch that was too smooth. She used her fingertips to find the point at which the too smooth area became real skin then gouged with her nails until she made a ridge. With some considerable effort she ripped the feather-light strip off, pulled it out from under her top and held it up.

'It was for safety.'

'Right. You know if you tried communicating with me in a normal way we might not keep ending up in these situations.'

'It worked, didn't it?' he said, ignoring the comment.

She stared at him, annoyed, and then sighed. She was too tired.

'I went to Valerie's yesterday but she wasn't there,' he continued, apparently keen to gloss over the issue. 'I spoke to her neighbour and he saw her leave several hours after you. He said he noticed blood in her hair.'

'Seriously?' That was a surprise. 'Do you think maybe she didn't hand me over to those people?'

'I considered that, but then why drug you?'

'True.'

'I'm still certain she's caught up in this.' Whilst she wouldn't admit it, deep down, Eva couldn't help feeling stupid. She had walked right into Valerie's hands, despite Leon having warned her, and she hadn't been smart enough to avoid getting herself drugged, despite the fact that all her instincts had told her something was wrong from the moment she had arrived at Valerie's. She wasn't about to admit that to anyone though.

'Where does she fit in all of this?'

'I don't know. But we need to find that out.' Eva glanced at the clock on the dashboard: 11.53 am. She had been there all night.

'Look Leon, this might be crazy, but I don't have the memory stick and I know that I had it before I lost consciousness. I think I might have hidden it at Valerie's somewhere.'

'Before you passed out?' He sounded incredulous.

'It's not impossible, is it?'

'No, but it's not going to be easy to get in there.'

'I thought you said she had gone to see a medic.'

'That was yesterday, right after it happened.'

'It's worth a shot, isn't it?' They pulled up at a set of traffic lights next to a news stand. The headlines blared off the stand at them: 'Bioavancement S.a.r.l. sells youth back!' Eva looked away and the lights turned green.

WHEN THEY ARRIVED at the flat, Leon met a man in a suit standing at a bus stop opposite and they had a short conversation.

'She's out,' he said when he returned to Eva.

'Who was that?'

'A friend.'

'Did your friend also have any idea how we can get in?'

'The best way is just to walk through the door.'

'Fantastic, where's the key?' Leon held up a small set of wire-thin tools.

Once they were outside Valerie's door it took Leon less than a minute to shift the internal mechanism of her lock around so that it sprung open.

'I'm guessing you've done this before.' He ignored her.

'We have an hour maximum.'

'I need to clean up. I'll meet you in the room with the computer, down the hall.' He nodded.

Once Eva had located the bathroom, she gratefully shut the door, sat on the edge of the bath and took a minute to try and collect her thoughts. After allowing herself several deep breaths she quickly used the products she found in the bathroom to wash off the liquid that had been thrown at her and remove the blood from her face, neck and hair. She took one of Valerie's hair-bands and pulled her long dark hair back into a ponytail. Her face was scratched and she was developing another huge royal purple bruise across her right cheek where she had been hit, but nothing felt broken and at least now she was clean and less bloody. She cleaned and dressed the wound on her hand from her fall at the petrol station and wiped antiseptic lotion over the smaller grazes on her face, hands and arms and the cuts on her collarbone. Finally, she borrowed mouthwash and deodorant to try and make herself feel slightly more human and took a couple of painkillers with water from the bathroom tap. Her head was still pounding.

She found Leon sitting at the computer, his broad frame blocking most of the screen. When he heard her come in, unexpectedly he stood up and Eva took up a position in front of the computer. She looked back at him over her shoulder, surprised at the relinquishing of control. Then he handed her the USB stick.

'You found it!'

'Under the table leg. I noticed as soon as I walked in that it wasn't level. I always notice lines that aren't straight—OCD.' Eva took the stick and glanced at him sideways. She'd never met anyone with the same issue she had. She watched him line up an iPad that was sitting on the desk so that it was exactly parallel to the edges of the table. It was satisfying.

As the contents of the USB stick opened up in the window and the folder names came into view, memories suddenly began to filter through Eva's mind.

'I opened "briefing" last time,' she said, hovering the mouse over the file as she remembered.

'What's in it?' asked Leon, his voice tinged with impatience.

Eva thought for a second. 'It's a collection of research sources—articles about a youth supplement. I don't think it's very important.'

'What about "test results"?'

'I don't know. Perhaps that's what I was reading when

I passed out.' She clicked on the folder, selected the first file and the 'Highly Confidential' document appeared on the screen. She felt Leon reading over her shoulder, his eyes like laser beams boring into the page. 'But this...' He began and then stopped and carried on reading. Apparently the scientific jargon was no barrier for Leon. When he didn't say anything else, Eva opened the summary document she had read the day before and Leon made fast work of that too. Then he folded his arms, gave a short whistle and leaned back against a cupboard.

Eva closed the file 'test results' and looked at the remaining folders. There was one labelled 'Read Me', a document rather than a folder of documents. As she looked at it, she knew she had read it before.

'I think this might have some answers.' She moved the mouse over the icon and opened the document. As she began to read, it all came flooding back.

Eva looked away from the screen and up at Leon who seemed to have turned very pale.

'Does it seem serious to you?'

'It could be.'

'But it's just algae.'

'I expect that's the assumption they are relying on everyone making.' Leon scrolled further down the page and whistled.

'Jesus. This stuff is virtually unstoppable.' She looked at him incredulously. 'I know what the document says, Leon, but seriously it's just a plant,' she repeated.

'Have you ever heard of a "red tide"?'

'No.'

'It's a "population explosion" of toxic, naturally occurring microscopic algae. It can kill everything it comes into contact with—fish and plants—it contaminates water and is even harmful to humans. Here.' He reached over Eva and opened up an internet search engine on the computer, typed in 'red tide' and pulled up the results.

All at once Eva was looking at blue-green seas covered in vast swathes of red algae—a 'red tide'. She quickly read the accompanying FAQs.

'But it says here the particles are only harmful if you eat infected fish or shellfish and normally they are filtered out of water by our filtration processes.' Leon frowned and stared ahead. 'This information, Eva, I find it very confusing.' She nodded. 'It doesn't make sense.'

'I don't understand why this company is importing algae plants into the UK, when these plants are clearly going to become a threat to its water system. How can this have been allowed to happen?'

'What I don't understand is why they have done it. I mean, surely this Bioavancement S.a.r.l. company is going to end up getting sued for the damage it causes. No commercial contract would leave a loophole like that.'

'And what about this?' said Leon bringing up the 'Highly Confidential' document once again.

Eva looked blankly at the screen. 'I don't understand the language in that one.'

'It's describing the effects of this strain of algae on the human body if you consume it as a supplement. It doesn't seem to have anything to do with cell regeneration—in fact, quite the opposite. It actually shuts some of the body's functions down.'

'Fatally?'

'Not really. Look,' he pointed to the screen. 'This is the effect that the algae have on the liver. They increase its resistance to insulin, which in turn means the pancreas has to make more.'

'I'm not sure I understand the significance.'

'It's basically blocking the message the liver would normally send to the brain to tell it to stop eating.'

'Eating?' Eva was taken aback. 'The way Sophie described this information made it sound like a life-threatening situation. I don't understand. What use is a supplement that makes you eat a lot?' Leon looked at her. Once again he reached past her to the computer and searched the words 'obesity epidemic'. He pulled up a page from a National Health Service website.

'The UK diet industry is currently worth more than £2 billion. Obesity is predicted to rise by 70% over the next fifteen years,' Eva read quickly.

'An enormous rise in the number of obese people creates a brand-new market,' said Leon still leaning over her shoulder, 'all with one life-threatening problem in common.'

'Of course. Obesity drugs.' Suddenly something dawned on Eva. She began searching through the other documents on the file and sure enough there was a file labelled 'forecast'.

She opened one and they read in silence.

'Look,' said Leon, 'with this supplement they're going to speed up the "natural" advance of obesity. Look at that profit forecast. It's made on the basis of a 200% increase in the level of obesity over just the next two years.'

'Create a market by making us sick and make money by selling us the cure. A classic business strategy,' Eva said.

They sat in silence for several seconds before Eva spoke.

'But what would happen to Bioavancement S.a.r.l. if

someone found out this was what they were doing? Is this really worth killing people like Sophie and Jackson for?'

'It would be the end of their business and I imagine they would be heavily sanctioned, probably imprisoned.'

'There must be a lot of money at stake.'

'People have killed for less.'

'It seems so reckless though. Is it really something that could go unnoticed?'

'They wouldn't be the first company to make money by manipulating the public into harming themselves. But I see what you mean.'

'I don't know, I'm not sure I buy it. How can someone have looked at this and thought they would get away with it. And why use algae that you know will spread uncontrollably. Surely the whole point of this would be that after the initial launch they try to stay below the radar. It specifically says in that report that they intend to withdraw the supplement from the market after two years to stop any association with it.'

'When the damage has been done.'

'But this document says the algae is being shipped to Bioavancement S.a.r.l. sites. When it starts to spread that will draw an intense spotlight on Bioavancement S.a.r.l. and then presumably an investigation into its business.'

Suddenly, a floorboard creaked in the hall. Eva looked at Leon, heart pounding.

'Wait here,' he whispered. 'Take the memory stick.'

'OK.' Eva disconnected the stick as Leon disappeared from the room. The flat was not large so there was little time. She wiped all the recently viewed document records and stored the memory stick in her pocket where she could feel it pressed against her hip. Then she waited, listening for any sounds coming from beyond the door.

After several seconds, Eva realised she could hear scuffling along the corridor and the grunts of some kind of muted fight. There was a crash and the sound of glass smashing and Eva's skin began to burn with adrenaline. Then she heard Valerie's voice, speaking low almost in a whisper. She moved closer to the edge of the door. The voices were coming from further inside the flat.

'I said I'd kill you if I ever saw you again. I should have killed you then.'

'Do you know what fucking chaos you left behind?' Eva's skin began to tingle as she listened to the conversation. They know each other.

'I was never part of a team.'

'That was how it worked!'

'I don't work with anyone.'

'You signed up to work with a team.'

'Honour amongst thieves? You know it doesn't work like that, don't be so fucking naive.'

'You just don't do that, Valerie.'

'I don't have time for this, Leon. I have to be at the airport in an hour. Let me go.'

'Fuck you.' Eva heard a grunt and then the sound of bone crunching on bone. She heard something heavy drop to the floor and then there was silence.

Eva stood beside the door, her entire body rigid. She strained to hear the sound of movement or voices; and then suddenly there were soft steps coming in the direction of the bedroom.

She looked around the room for a potential weapon and settled for a stone Buddha head, the size of a small football. She hefted it with both hands and crept towards the door.

NINETEEN

SUDDENLY EVA FOUND herself face to face with Valerie. The Frenchwoman's eyes were aflame and she was breathing heavily. She had a gun in one hand pointed straight at Eva's chest but her face wore an expression of shock. Eva realised Valerie had not expected to encounter her until she was inside the bedroom and took advantage of the slight delay in the other woman's reactions, swinging the Buddha head like a shot put at the gun in Valerie's hand, before dropping it in the general direction of her feet.

The heavy stone, empowered by gravity, immediately hit Valerie's hands and the gun went skittering across the floor. Valerie let out a scream as the stone landed on the edge of her left foot before she could move it out of the way, crushing the bones beneath it.

EVA LEAPT PAST HER, out of the bedroom door and veered to her left, making a dive for the gun, which had landed underneath a small side-table in the hall that held an ornate antique lamp and a small potted plant. As she fell, she hit the table, which began to pitch over. On all fours, she managed to touch the gun with her fingertips but suddenly she was being dragged away from the tipping table, by hands pulling her ankles.

She twisted onto her back and made a grab for one of the table legs behind her with her hands as she was pulled in the other direction. She missed but managed to get hold of the light cord and pull it, bringing the antique lamp smashing down onto the floor above her head, where the thick glass shade shattered into five pieces, leaving jagged edges reaching upwards from the bulb.

Then Valerie was above her with the Buddha head in her hands, apparently not slowed at all by the broken bones in her foot. Eva rolled away just as Valerie smashed the heavy stone to the floor where Eva's head had been. As soon as she had released the stone head Valerie threw herself at Eva, pinned her to the floor and began trying to strangle her. Eva, flat on her back now, gasped and struggled as her eyes met Valerie's, a frightening shade of green only a few inches from Eva's own.

'Stop!'

'Shut up,' Valerie hissed, spitting at Eva as she continued trying to strangle her.

'Why…?' gasped Eva.

'You would not understand.'

'But Jackson…'

'Unfortunate,' said Valerie and then began to tighten her grip so that Eva could no longer speak.

From the other room there was suddenly the sound of glass smashing and Valerie looked up briefly. Eva wondered what she had done to Leon; he was obviously still alive. Then the pressure of Valerie's stranglehold began to make her see stars. She knew that soon she would lose consciousness. She had to do something. Bringing her hands up in a move she had seen in a film, Eva slammed the flats of both her palms against both of Valerie's ears as hard as she could. Valerie screamed as her eardrums burst, released Eva's throat, pushed herself into a crouch and stumbled back, disorientated and unbalanced.

Eva quickly shunted herself upright and then sideways in the other direction, kicking out at Valerie who dropped to a sitting position on the floor as she rocked away in pain. Eva began struggling to her feet, gasping loudly as she recovered from having her throat crushed, but Valerie, recovering inhumanly quickly, snarled and made a grab for Eva's left leg, locking her hands around her shin and trying to twist it at the knee to break it. My God, thought Eva, breathlessly, this woman is unstoppable.

EVA STUMBLED TO the floor, landing on her left side, instinctively reaching for the shattered light that had fallen from the table with her left hand, the only weapon she could see. She yanked the stem of the light, trying to pull the plug out of its socket but it held fast. Eva cried out as she felt the pressure Valerie was putting on her leg almost reaching breaking point and then with an almighty tug, the lamp was free from its plug.

Eva used all her strength to try to kick Valerie wildly in the head with her free leg and one blow landed square on her temple. As soon as Valerie reacted, releasing the pressure on her leg enough for Eva to move, she leaned forward and sliced the shattered glass lamp into one of Valerie's arms as it held tight to her leg. Blood spurted from a deep cut she had made in the forearm and Valerie howled and jumped backwards. In that split second, Eva was on her feet and running towards the living room, still holding the shattered lamp.

Behind her, Valerie was no slower and she made a grab for Eva's ponytail, yanking it backwards so that she could get an arm around the crook of her neck. Her arms were strong, much stronger than Eva would have anticipated for someone who looked so very feminine, and try as she might, she couldn't break Valerie's stranglehold.

Now with a clear view of the living room, Eva could see Leon lying on his back on the floor; hundreds of glass shards from a smashed coffee table he seem to have collapsed on were all around him. He wasn't moving.

Suddenly Eva felt Valerie start trying to force her down to floor level from behind, whilst still keeping her choking hold around Eva's neck. She resisted the downward pressure but Valerie was stronger. Eva realised Valerie was going to try and get them both onto the floor so she could reach the gun that had fallen under the tipped side-table. She gasped, straining for breath, taking in as much air as she could through the tiny space left as Valerie's arm crushed her windpipe. Then, as Valerie reached for the gun, rocking them both in the direction of the fallen table, the grip loosened, just enough to allow Eva to breathe. She gasped in two large breaths, waited until they were almost on the ground and then jabbed an elbow back as hard as she could into Valerie's torso. She heard Valerie grunt but her arm remained locked around Eva's neck as if it was made from steel. She tried another jab but this time Valerie was prepared and moved her torso slightly away so that the force of the blow was wasted.

CRYING OUT WITH FRUSTRATION, Eva looked around for anything she could use as a weapon. Valerie still had her in a headlock and when they reached the ground she would be within the reach of the gun.

Eva was still clutching the base of the shattered lamp in one hand and was about to throw it to the floor when she realised she could use it. As Valerie lowered them both right to the ground and reached out for the gun under the wreckage of the table, Eva reversed her hold on the lamp so the base of it was now facing forwards and the points of the jagged glass shards backwards towards Valerie behind her. At the same time as Valerie jerked forward, Eva shoved the lamp backwards where she could feel Valerie's body against her. She heard a gasp as the sharp ends of the lamp stuck in flesh and then she shut her eyes, gritted her teeth and shoved the dagger sharp shards further back. Immediately, Eva felt the hold around her neck loosen. She bit down hard on Valerie's forearm and, as the other woman let out a shuddering shout, Eva was released completely.

She pulled away and threw herself forwards, making a grab for the gun and clasping her hands around it at the same time as did Valerie, who had thrown herself in the same direction, reaching for the weapon even with the lamp stuck fast in her side. Eva felt Valerie try and pull the gun towards her from behind, lifting both their arms up over Eva's head as both held on to the gun.

Valerie succeeded in destabilising them so that they fell backwards, each refusing to release the gun and submit to the certain death that would follow. Then the Frenchwoman cried out; Eva's weight was pressing down on the flat base at the end of the glass shards embedded in Valerie's chest, pushing them even deeper into her body to pierce her organs. Positioned uncomfortably close to Valerie, their hands locked together around the gun, Eva suddenly felt Valerie's fingers release as the other woman screamed in pain and her body went limp. Tearing the gun from Valerie's fingers, Eva scrabbled forward into a sitting position and then up onto her feet, turning immediately to face her opponent. As she spun around she shakily raised the gun and pointed it at the spot on the floor where Valerie lay.

The glass shards of the lamp were buried in Valerie up to the bulb and by the looks of it had emerged on the other side of her torso as she was holding herself slightly off the floor behind, trying to wrench the light fixture from her chest.

'Help me…' She looked appealingly at Eva, large green eyes widening, shining with tears. 'Please, I don't want to die.' Eva's heart suddenly went out to her. She kept the gun trained on Valerie but hesitated for just a second. In that tiny moment, sensing Eva's hesitation and with a show of inhuman strength, Valerie wrenched the lamp out of her chest and propelled herself at Eva, blood spraying from her open mouth and the wound in her chest. Terrified and taken by surprise, Eva pulled the trigger.

DON PORTER'S MEETING at the Environment Agency was dragging on and on. He glanced at his watch once again and realised that the meeting would soon have to break for lunch, which would give him an hour's respite at least and time for a cigarette and some more strong coffee. Once again his wife had insisted on making him sandwiches to bring for lunch—limp, white-breaded affairs spread with paste out of a jar. He shuddered. Frankly he would rather put himself through the ordeal of the leaden jacket potatoes in the canteen than risk one of those. But this lunchtime he would just have to eat what he had in his office because there would be no time for anything else. During his meeting he had received details on his BlackBerry about the company that had taken over the Sunbury site in west London, without any heed at all to local environmental and planning regulations. His officers had once again been down to the site and taken photos showing large oval ponds filled with a dark liquid. Without any official sanction, they couldn't break in or take samples and there appeared to be no one there for the whole five hours they had watched the place. They already knew the company was called Bioavancement S.a.r.l. from the official documentation that had been submitted when the company first applied to use the site, but that was all they had to go on. Despite the fact that the company was all over the papers, all the contacts Bioavancement S.a.r.l. had provided connected to dead phone lines and no one could explain why the company had suddenly decided to use the site before permission had been given. It was such reckless behaviour. Don's lunchtime would be spent trying to get hold of someone with some authority at the company that he could give an earful to. He glanced again at his watch before his attention was drawn away from the table of suits to the door, which suddenly burst open to reveal Fred Humphries. What the… 'Mr Porter I must speak with you straight away.'

Don stood, half-tempted to take the opportunity to get out of the meeting early. 'Fred, I really don't think this is the time…'

'Mr Porter, I can assure you that it is. Please, I have to speak to you right away.' Something about Humphries' manner set Porter on edge. He stood and apologised to the four other men in the room, each of whom looked on jealously as he escaped the rest of the agenda. As soon as they were outside he turned to Humphries.

'Fred, this is really not the way to do things, that was a very important meeting.' Fred was flushed and feverish, his straw blond hair pushed over to one side of his head in an unruly mess. Don began to wonder whether there was something rather unstable about him. Perhaps he should have given the job to someone more experienced after all.

'Mr Porter this is urgent. It's that algae, the black algae.'

'Oh Fred, really…'

'I'm serious, we've been inundated with calls, it's not just the chat rooms.' Don stared at him doubtfully, running the various disciplinary options available to him through his head.

Fred exhaled with exasperation. 'Come with me.' He led the way back into the main open plan room where normally Don would occupy the corner office, looking out over the twenty-four desks that housed his team. Don stared. The place was in uproar. Every single person was on the phone making notes, each one of them red-faced and looking as if they had consumed far too much of the cheap vending machine coffee. As he walked in, his second-in-command, a plump, normally jovial, man named Geoff signalled him over to his station. He asked the caller he had been talking with to hold and pushed the pad he was writing on over to Don so he could see. 'Look at this.' The pad was covered with scrawls, each one a concern or complaint about black algae.

He put his hand over the receiver and spoke to Don. 'I've had twenty-seven calls in the past forty minutes concerning black algae that seems to have appeared in every stretch of open water within our jurisdiction. Our phone lines are backed up. This stuff has just appeared overnight. It's *everywhere*.'

'Is it dangerous?'

'As far as we can tell it has killed or contaminated everything it has come into contact with—fish, other fresh water plants, the lot.' Don felt a jolt of energy surge through him. 'It's a red tide.' He glanced an apology at Fred.

'What's the geographical spread of the algae?'

'It seems to be worse around Hampton and Sunbury, just west of London.'

TWENTY

AN HOUR LATER, Eva and Leon were sitting in a small corner café close to the Gare du Nord. They had concealed Leon's Citroen behind the considerable bulk of a 4 x 4 and sought refuge in the tiny establishment. Both were exhausted, hunched over a tiny metal table, unspeaking. Eva had found Leon in Valerie's living room, dazed and cut but not seriously hurt. She had helped him dress his wounds and then they had tried to remove as much trace as possible of their presence from Valerie's flat before climbing out onto the fire escape. After the exertion of the fight with Valerie, Eva had descended into a trance-like state. She could still see the expression on Valerie's face when she had instinctively fired the gun and the bullet had torn straight through the other woman's heart. The guilt burned through her insides like acid. She had taken a life—did that ever go unpunished? Eva was not religious but in her shocked state she felt an impending sense of retribution. She was sitting, staring morosely at the small TV in the corner of the bar, her expression unreadable. She saw Leon look nervously at his watch. She knew they couldn't stay here long. They couldn't stay anywhere very long.

'My God.' Leon felt for the gun in his waistband as Eva spoke.

'Look.' She pointed up at the TV and Leon turned. The news item playing out in French was backed by pictures of a red tide, similar to the one he had shown her on Valerie's computer.

'What is it saying?' she asked him, suddenly alert. Leon called over to the barman and asked him to turn up the volume.

'It concerns the UK,' he said, translating out loud as the reporter spoke in French, 'overnight a spread of algae, not unlike the red tide shown in this picture, has appeared around an area just west of London and in fifty-six other locations around the country. The algae in this case is black and appears highly toxic to plants and fish.' The screen was suddenly filled with pictures of fish floating belly up on water that was so full of algae it had turned an inky, shiny black.

The news anchor crossed over to an on-the-ground reporter interviewing someone called Don Porter, director of the Environment Agency for the affected area.

'We have never seen anything like this,' he was saying, 'it seems to have appeared overnight. We are distributing algaecides to all local residents and farmers. Water companies have been put on alert and asked to instigate their own algal defence systems.'

'Is the algae dangerous to humans?' asked the reporter, shoving a microphone into Mr Porter's face.

'We don't think so but we have never come across this strain before. From the analysis we have done so far—which has been very basic as we have not yet had time to react properly—it is like nothing we have seen before, so we can't predict how it will behave.'

'There are rumours that it is a genetically modified strain.'

'It could be.'

'Who genetically modified it?'

'At the moment we're not sure.'

'But is it dangerous?'

'I think not. It's certainly the fastest growing algae we've ever seen but at the moment I don't think there's any need to panic.'

'But if you don't know its genetic properties how do you know whether an algaecide will work? What happens if it doesn't? Is there a serious threat to the UK's water resources?'

'We're working on that. Thank you for your questions.' Don Porter ended the interview.

Eva locked eyes with Leon.

'We have to warn them. We have the genetic information in here,' she said, indicating the memory stick in her pocket.

'Keep your voice down,' Leon growled. 'We must not draw attention to ourselves.'

But Eva was burning for action. 'We need to *do* something Leon. We have to stop this.' It was the only way. Otherwise she would see the look in Valerie's eyes every time she closed her own for the rest of her life. Suddenly she understood why all his life Jackson had tried to be a hero; that's what this kind of guilt could do.

'I know. But it's not that simple.'

'But…'

'Eva, calm down.'

Eva's fire began to wane and her composure returned. He was right. She took a large gulp of coffee. What was done was done. There was just no time for lengthy sessions of self-hatred.

'How do we do this?'

'I don't know.' A taut silence stretched between them. The familiar feeling of distrust returned to Eva as she looked at Leon, remembering the conversation she had overheard in Valerie's flat. Leon and Valerie clearly knew each other, had existed as part of some kind of team. And yet it appeared to be the case that today she had tried to kill him. Eva decided not to ask him about that—yet. She took a different tack.

'Who is Joseph Smith, Leon?' Surprise showed on Leon's face as if he couldn't keep up with her cantering train of thought.

'He's someone I have heard of, read about in the news.' Instinctively she knew he was lying.

'I don't believe you. You know more than that.'

'That's all I know.'

'Why is it you seem to have such a problem telling me the truth?'

'I am trying to protect you.' His response was trigger-fast.

'Don't be such a fool.'

'You don't understand.'

'Try me.' Leon paused. 'Jackson told me about him.' The calls and texts Eva had been receiving from Jackson's phone flew into her mind. He was dead. Wasn't he? She looked at Leon and despite everything she felt a flicker of something like hope.

He gave a small shake of his head.

'Not recently—it was before he died, there were things that he said to me…although at the time I had no idea that he was telling the truth.'

'Like what?'

'He spoke about someone called Joseph Smith.'

'What did he say?' Leon didn't answer her but leaned forward enthusiastically.

'He must be the link, Eva.'

'But who is he linked to? He was obviously working with the other Sudanese men but they were not working with Valerie. What's the connection—is there more than one?' They looked at each other. That gap in their knowledge was dangerous. It opened up variables and there were too many of those already.

'The connection to the Sudan is just coincidence, that much is clear,' said Eva. 'The men who kidnapped me had no idea who Jackson actually was, or that his work was focused on the Sudan—that at least we do know.' Leon nodded.

Eva downed her brandy. She was beginning to feel very tired. 'I wasn't even sure that they had met Jackson.'

'So do you think they killed him or not?'

'I just don't know.'

'Did you learn anything from their conversation? Why did they take your phone?'

'No, it seemed calculated to confuse. I know that they were under orders from Joseph Smith and I know that they were not personally involved. But as to why they were doing what they were doing—or why they wanted my phone—I have no clue.' He nodded silently.

'I have no idea what to do, Leon. Do we try to find these people?'

Leon sighed heavily. 'I have a feeling they will find us.' He was right; they were being hunted.

They both sat in silence in the cold, damp bar and Eva finished her coffee. 'We have to go to England,' she said suddenly.

Don Porter didn't know whether to be excited by the amount of sudden interest in his regional branch of the Environment Agency, or absolutely terrified. In the space of four hours a giant spotlight had suddenly been turned on their offices, which were now crawling with people he didn't recognise, some drafted in as temps to help deal with the deluge of panicked phone calls, some who were people in suits he had only ever seen named on briefing sheets or being interviewed on the TV news. Don had the distinct impression that despite being Director of the regional office, he was no longer in control. He had been summoned to another meeting in one of his board-rooms, but this time there would be no opportunity for clockwatching and thinking about lunch.

'Please provide us with a briefing on the situation, Mr Porter,' one of the suits said as soon as he had shut the door. From the authoritative tone in his voice and a picture Don had seen in the newspapers on the man's appointment, he deduced that this was the minister in charge of the government-funded Environment Agency.

Don nodded and took up a position at the table, ar-ranged his papers, removed his jacket and then leaned in and began to talk.

'Minister, the algae has spread at a faster rate than we have ever seen before. We currently have at least fifty-six very large and rapidly expanding affected areas threat-ening to join together and cover the whole country. It's spreading like wildfire.'

'Can we stop it?'

'No.'

The minister looked up, shocked. 'What do you mean, no?'

'We can't stop it. It's not an existing species of algae. We don't have information on its genetic profile and it seems to be resistant to every algaecide we have, even the strongest.'

'Surely you can just take a sample of it to determine its genetic make-up?'

'For some reason that isn't possible. Each time we get a different result.'

'Can't we just throw some kind of chemical at it?'

'The problem with that, minister, is that it has taken root in waterworks, streams, rivers, reservoirs around London—and the entire country—in any area of open water. The only chemicals we haven't tried on it are the kinds of chemicals that might kill the algae but would also poison or contaminate everything around it.'

'Hasn't the algae already done that?'

'As yet not to humans, no. These industrial chemicals come under the remit of severe water pollution, the kind we would normally reward with a hefty fine or prosecution if they appeared in any water we tested. We can't dump them in the river ourselves.' The minister frowned and glanced at his two advisers who looked away and quickly began to scribble on their notepads. He turned back to Porter.

'Could we set fire to it?'

'If we do that over such a wide area it would be difficult to control, which could be a disaster, even in this cold weather, particularly as we don't know how—or even if—it would burn. Plus there are issues with the pollution from the smoke.'

'Well what can we do then?'

'At the moment, nothing. We need to be able to identify this species of algae before we attempt to destroy it.'

'How long will it take to identify it?'

'It normally takes around a week. But as I said, at the moment it is proving difficult to even start this process.'

'Oh, for heaven's sake.' The minister brought his fist

slamming down onto the table in front of him. 'Well, if it takes a week, where will we be then?'

'At the rate it's going, the algae will have a critical hold over all the major waterworks and reservoirs within forty-eight hours and every single open waterway in the entire country within four days.'

'Bloody hell.'

'At that point the country's infrastructure will likely start to struggle with the lack of clean water for drinking. This will also affect hospitals and industry such as agriculture. We have stores of bottled water enough for drinking for five days but importing these from non-affected countries would be prohibitively expensive in the long term—even over a period of several weeks—and there just won't be enough to go around to cover everything else we use water for in this country.'

'Where the hell has it come from?'

'We have no idea.'

AFTER WALKING TO the Gare du Nord and buying tickets for a Eurostar leaving at 6:00 p.m., Eva and Leon drove around the city, reluctant to stay still until the moment the train pulled out of the station. They were driving through Montmartre, up and down the winding streets lined with boutiques and cafés that spilled tables out onto the pavement, streets so narrow that a tail would be impossible not to spot.

'Do you know anyone in London who can help?' asked Leon as they drove past an enormous wall of flowers outside one of the shops on the way down to Pigalle.

Eva thought for a second. 'Not really.'

'I thought you were a journalist?'

'Editor. Of a magazine. Not much use in this kind of situation.'

'Is there no one you know who might have some kind of influence?' Leon had allowed himself to be carried away by Eva's conviction that travelling to London was the right course of action but was obviously now having second thoughts. Although even he could see there was clearly more need for the information they had on the memory stick in London than in Paris at that moment.

'N...' Eva stopped herself. She was silent for several seconds and when she spoke there was a hard tone in her voice. 'Only one.'

'Who?'

'Irene Hunt.'

'Who is she?'

'She's the woman who broke up our family.' Leon was silent, apparently taken by surprise.

'She had an affair with my father,' continued Eva. 'They met whilst he was reporting in the Lebanon. At the time she was secret service—MI6 I think. He almost left my mother for her but in the end she refused to leave her husband.' With surprise, Eva heard the bitterness in her voice—even after all these years.

'Do you think she could help us?' Leon said cautiously.

'I don't know anyone else with any connections to that kind of sphere.'

'Can you trust her?'

Eva stopped and thought about that. Irene Hunt and her father had seemed unstoppably drawn into each other's orbit when they had returned from the Lebanon, so much so that he had been willing to forsake decades of marriage for her. After the affair was discovered and the confrontation had ended, Eva's mother had become seri-ously ill. Even though in the end her father didn't leave, knowing that he would have if Irene had been willing to give up her own marriage had left Eva's mother utterly bereft. The life just seemed to seep out of her. Once the fighting had stopped and there was nothing left to say she had simply taken to her bed. When she died, doctors had named her cause of death as *Takotsubo cardiomyopathy*, also known as 'broken heart syndrome'. That affair had also been the reason that Jackson had felt compelled to leave, so in a way Irene Hunt had ruined all their lives. Could Eva really trust her?

'I don't know,' she said honestly.

'What about the man we saw on the TV—Don Por-ter?' said Leon clearly unsure about contacting someone like Irene Hunt who had apparently had such a negative impact on Eva's life.

'How would we even find him, Leon? You said your-self that the algae spreads like wildfire so we can't leave it that long. Even if we find Porter, we'd never get close enough to explain what's on the stick and how we got it in time. We would sound like crazy conspiracy theorists if we tried to tell people what we know. If we try and email this information to someone there's little hope of it falling into the right hands in time and I don't know who else we could contact who wouldn't dismiss us straight away as insane. I can at least get close enough to Irene Hunt to force her to read this information.'

'Can you?'

'Yes,' said Eva a little too forcefully. Leon looked at her.

She looked away.

TWENTY-ONE

INSPECTOR LEGRAND FROM the Préfecture de Police gazed steadily at his sergeant who was busily scribbling notes as he finished a phone call with the pathologist who had carried out the post mortems on the three bodies they had discovered in Seine Saint Denis Département 93. Of the two teenagers found in the playground, the first cause of death had been easy to pinpoint—a slashing of the stomach with some kind of curved blade and nothing more complex—but the other two deaths—the second boy from the playground and the red-haired Englishman from the nearby apartment block—had sent the pathologists into a frenzy and Sergeant Gagnere was currently on the phone trying to find out why.

'Well?' Legrand asked bad-temperedly as soon as Gagnere had replaced the handset.

'We're going to have to go down to the morgue.' Legrand groaned. There was a reason he did the job he did and that was so he could deal with live criminals and victims. He would much rather leave the corpses to that morbid branch of scientists who seemed to relish poking around in the deceased. He reached for his heavy woollen coat. 'Let's get this over with then.' The pathologist on duty was an old colleague of Legrand's—Dr Shume—and the policeman's frosty demeanour melted slightly when he saw who was in charge of the autopsies. At least they wouldn't receive some long, drawn-out lecture on

the biological history of the patients or the rate of oc-
currence of these kinds of deaths since 1975. Legrand
did not have time for that.

'Shume, my friend,' he said, shaking the doctor's
hand, 'how are you?' Dr Shume, a small, wiry man with
a silver halo of remaining hair and the handshake of an
ox, grinned steadily at Legrand.

'I'm puzzled to be frank,' he said, cutting straight to
the chase.

'Why's that?'

'Well, initially I just couldn't figure out how these
men had met such a grisly end. The boy has injuries con-
sistent with being beaten, but not enough to have killed
him; and the Englishman...well, he was a real puzzle.'

'Obviously you opened them up.'

'Yes, that's when it became really confusing—they
seem to have symptoms of several fatal conditions all
rolled into one.'

'That's not so uncommon is it?'

'No, but in this case they are illnesses that would
have taken years to develop. They are normally present in much older people than these two who are virtually children.'

Legrand said nothing.

'Look,' said the doctor, 'I will show you the Englishman.' The doctor whisked a sheet from a metal gurney
to reveal the corpse they had found in the apartment.

'Can't you shut his eyes?' the inspector complained.
The look on the man's face as he had died was quite
frankly rather disturbing.

'Well, I left them open for a reason. You see they
show externally the kind of trauma he was experienc-
ing inside.'

'Right,' said Legrand uneasily. He was eager to get out of the morgue.

'As I said, there's evidence of several diseases here, none of which you would expect to see in someone of this man's age, particularly at such an advanced stage that they would be fatal.'

'What are they?'

'Myasthenia gravis, a chronic autoimmune neuro-muscular disease characterised by varying degrees of weakness of the skeletal muscles. The body is dependent on muscles to function—the diaphragm, heart etc—so if these muscles become so weakened that they no longer work, essential functions like breathing will begin to slow down and then they will stop altogether as the organs collapse. Highly distressing if it occurs because the sufferer can feel it happening.'

'And the other condition?'

'Pulmonary fibrosis—replacement of normal lung tissue with thickened scar tissue that causes irreversible decrease in oxygen diffusion—it's the body's own immune system that triggers this, normally in response to inhaling something like asbestos. It's a really horrible type of death because the patient is acutely aware of not being able to get a breath as the lung capacity is gradually restricted.'

'No wonder he looked so alarmed.'

'It's certainly one of the least pleasant ways to go. Pulmonary fibrosis can be a secondary effect of an autoimmune disease like Myasthenia gravis but it would be rare.'

'So then we're not dealing with a murder?'

For the first time in the conversation, Dr Shume paused. He frowned and then continued, 'Well initially, that's exactly what I thought but the speed at which these two conditions appear to have advanced is medically impossible.'

Legrand looked blankly at Dr Shume. 'I don't understand.'

'It's like I said, these conditions take years— *decades*—to develop. These bodies, in the condition that they are in, should not exist.'

'How do you know that they were not already harbouring this?'

'We have access to this man's medical records,' Dr Shume said, pointing at the corpse. 'He worked at the British Embassy and every one of their employees is required to undergo both a full medical before starting work, as well as an annual check-up. The medical would have picked these up because for these diseases to have killed him now, they would have had to have been at quite an advanced stage in the past twelve months.'

'When was the medical?'

'He's had several. The most recent was a month ago and there was no sign of even the beginnings of either condition.'

'Is it possible for either one to become fatal within a month?'

'Absolutely not.'

'And the boy?'

'He is just fourteen—this could be the first time someone this young has ever died in this way anywhere in the world.' Both men fell silent. Legrand felt out of his depth.

'OK, so it is not possible for this to have happened and yet…'

'It is not possible in nature,' said Shume, interrupting. Legrand frowned. He did not like being interrupted.

'What does that mean?' Shume looked him straight in the eye.

'Although it would require considerable resources, it would—theoretically—be possible for a genetic simulation of these diseases to be manufactured in a lab and then planted into the body.'

'You're not serious...'

'Look at this.' He pushed the corpse onto its side and directed the Inspector's attention to the back of the victim's right thigh.

'A puncture mark,' said the inspector, gazing at the small red welt.

'Indeed. The other victim has one too.'

'So what are you saying?' The inspector was becoming frustrated. The smell of death made him nervous.

'I could be wrong, Inspector, but I think these two were injected with something that artificially implanted the Myasthenia gravis, the Pulmonary fibrosis into their bodies and that subsequently led to their deaths.'

'Artificially implanted?'

'Yes.'

'Forgive me if I say that sounds a little fantastical.'

'Forgiven.' Dr Shume fixed Legrand with a beady eye.

'However, I do think you need to consider the possibility that what you're dealing with here, Inspector, is a very sinister, very clever serial killer.'

AFTER THEY HAD finally been forced to stop driving, Eva and Leon had parked Leon's car and taken shelter in a secluded park five minutes' walk from the station. It was rush hour in Paris, traffic was gridlocked; they couldn't risk getting blocked in and missing the train. The park was really nothing more than a large, hedged garden circled in the centre by a gravel path but it felt far enough from the rush of people to give them space to think. However, it was not a comfortable environment. A group of men crowded around one of the park benches had watched them arrive, staring unashamedly at every inch of Eva's slim frame. It was clearly an action calculated to intimidate but Eva had refused to increase her pace or show any sign of fear, despite her pounding heart. As she and Leon had walked over to a bench on the opposite side from the entrance and sat down, the men continued talking, occasionally glancing over at them, but did nothing.

As THEY WAITED for the minutes to pass, Eva found herself struggling to control her emotions in a way she was not used to. Not once in the past 12 years had she felt this vulnerable and raw. The waiting was excruciating, both because of the pressure of what they needed to do and the feeling of being hunted. There was also an almost overwhelming urge to throw up her hands, push this whole thing on to someone else and run away. Eva had considered heading for the nearest police station— not the most illogical move—but she knew that was an idea that Leon would instantly shoot down and instinctively she felt maybe he would be right. Their story was too strange for it not to be met with suspicion. It would probably stand or fall on their characters and appearance and Leon with his split personality and Eva with her black eye did not meet the superficial requirements for solid and upstanding citizens. Besides, Eva's experience with the fat policeman who had refused to give her any information about Jackson's death had made her less than sure that the police would help them with any degree of speed or efficiency. That had also fed her natural distrust of authority—there was something so strange about Jackson's files having just 'disappeared' that she felt speaking to the police might even be a dangerous move.

Eva tried to silence her racing mind and looked up at the sky. She was exhausted; every fibre of every muscle felt strained. She closed her eyes, leaned back against the seat and took several quiet, deep breaths.

When she opened her eyes, Leon was pacing up and down on the gravel in front of the bench.

'Sit down.' He looked at her and then carried on pacing.

'Seriously, do you want to draw any more attention to us?' She nodded over at one of the nearest huddles of smoking men, a mass of hooded heads, bright white eyes and bent shoulders, who appeared to be becoming increasingly uncomfortable with the pair's presence in the park. They could have chosen somewhere they stood out less, but there was only one entrance to this park and from where they were they could keep a close eye on it.

It was in that direction that Eva was staring when she noticed a shadowy figure enter the park and start to move at speed in their direction.

'Leon.' She stood; instinctively, she grabbed her bag. She took one look at Leon reaching for his gun and then she turned and started to run. Before she had taken two steps she felt as if she was falling. All the breath was knocked from her body as someone caught her from behind. She felt her neck and throat being crushed as she was slammed backwards against the bench she had been sitting on. Another arm came over her head, across her chest and grabbed the belt loop of her jeans as she was lifted bodily from behind over the back of the bench and dragged backwards across the gravel. Panic reflexes seared through her brain and she fought and kicked and tried to scream but remained caught in the iron grip as another hand clasped her throat and fingers tightened around her vocal chords, choking her. The park pathway quickly disappeared from view and suddenly she was behind one of the high privet hedges that surrounded it.

She was dumped on the floor and masking tape was quickly and brutally wrapped around her mouth and head, catching and tearing at her hair. She shouted out in anger but the noise was muted and useless. Eva was flipped over face down onto the ground, which was covered in the brown, wet leaves of autumn. She tried to raise her head to see where she was. Surely someone could see this, they were outside the park now. When she managed to get a glimpse of her surroundings, she realised she was completely hidden in the back of the park where all the hedges converged to create a natural hiding place. She felt her hands being bound once again behind her, this time with some kind of tape, and then a boot obscured her vision before she was flipped over onto her back and roughly propped up against one of the hedges.

Once she was upright Eva tried to calm her breathing, which was coming in raw, ragged gasps through the black tape. Where was Leon?

In the small space with her were two people, both men, both dressed in black and wearing woollen masks over their heads.

ONE OF THE men began trying to fasten the tape around her ankles. She kicked out at him and he delivered a sharp blow just below the knee of her left leg that sent scorching lines of pain travelling up to her hip and down to her ankle before her muscles started to go numb. She tried to struggle but her leg was lifeless and it weighted her in one place. Another of the masked figures produced a small black leather medical case which when opened fully revealed syringes, two of them.

Just behind her on the other side of the hedge Eva could hear street noise. The man with the medical bag pulled out the first syringe and began to hold it up and tap the side. Neither of them spoke. A pre-arranged plan was being executed. Eva listened to the sound of her heartbeat singing in her ears.

She bent her knees up and shunted herself backwards using her one good leg and this time sensed give in the hedge behind her. The men glanced at her but made no move to stop her and carried on with what they were doing. She pushed gently against the foliage with her back once again and realised that the hedge was made up of not one tree but several. There was space between each one, just a tiny amount but if she pushed hard enough she might be able to slide through. Eva began backing herself up more and more against the hedge by pushing with her one good leg and sliding the rest of her body against the floor, whilst the masked man prepared the syringe and his colleague left the sheltered space, presumably to collect Leon. Behind her back she rubbed her wrists together and realised the tape was a poor substitute for plastic cuffs and she could pull her wrists free. For several seconds she worked her wrists until she was able to pull one out of the loop of tape.

She kept her hands behind her back as if they were still bound. She had to avoid anyone holding on to her arms, she couldn't let them hold her down.

Inside her head, calm logic fought with emotional panic. How the hell had this happened? Suddenly, panic won. The surge of adrenaline the anxiety sent through her body seemed to give Eva the energy she needed and, as the masked man turned towards her, she suddenly pushed against the floor with all her might, used her hands to make a grab for the trees on the inside of the hedge and then shunted herself backwards into the foliage. On the first push she was inside the trees and then, with a second, suddenly the top half of her torso was through and she hit the pavement on her back the other side. As she tried frantically to pull the rest of her body through, she heard a shout and she could feel hands trying to catch at her shifting limbs inside the hedge.

FOR SEVERAL SECONDS Eva fought the man on the other side of the hedge but he was stronger and she couldn't free her numb leg from his grip. Gradually, inevitably, she was hauled back into the space behind the hedge. Eva stopped fighting and closed her eyes as she was dragged along the rough ground, until she felt a presence over her. When she opened them she was face to face with a pair of piercing black eyes looking directly into hers. The man above her had pulled her through and was crouching over her, positioning her arms so each of his knees was painfully trapping her hands. For several seconds there was stillness as the man continued to stare. Eva felt the blood begin to drain from her body. What was he going to do?

Slowly he positioned one hand with the thumb and

fingers either side of her throat and began to tighten his grip. Eva felt herself choking and opened her eyes wide with fear. The man stopped instantly; Eva was sure that she saw him smile. She started to struggle and the man hit her hard around the face. Eva felt dizzy; she smelled menthol. The man leaned back and then removed one of his legs from her right hand and crouched at her left side, securing her left hand. Immediately, she raised her fist but his colleague who had returned grabbed both her wrists and fastened them with more tape in front of her, before pushing her back to the floor and holding her there. As the black-eyed man began to walk out of the clearing, out of the corner of her eye Eva saw the other man reach for the syringe.

Again, Eva tried to move, but she was pinned down by just one of his huge hands. The man holding her pushed her further against the cold ground as he positioned him-self above her and began to aim the needle. She realised that the target was not an arm or leg but the left side of her chest, right above her heart.

TWENTY-TWO

INSPECTOR LEGRAND SAT at his desk behind a pile of old notebooks that he had found himself unable to throw away. There was no telling when the notes from old cases would come in useful. He was staring down at the autopsy report from Dr Shume, which was side by side with a report he had arranged to have faxed over from St Thomas's Hospital in London. Inspector Legrand had a photographic memory, the kind that remembered words—headlines—and once he had written down the conditions Dr Shume had identified down in the morgue he realised he had seen them before, and fairly recently. The inspector had Googled the two words together and a whole page of results had appeared concerning the death of a British journalist on the Eurostar only days before. From there it had been a fairly easy step to obtaining the autopsy report.

According to the report, the man had presented with exactly the same causes of death, right down to the shocked expression on his jowled face. The hospital had had access to his medical records and had been able to confirm that a recent medical only two months before he died showed he had none of the symptoms of either disease. Insane as it was, there did seem to be some basis for Dr Shume's suggestion that someone had manufactured the diseases in all three victims. But why? Legrand had called the hospital to ask for confirmation of a red welt anywhere on the journalist's body and an hour later the call had come back with an apology for missing it from the report: his right thigh.

Legrand had spent the rest of the day searching but he could not find anything to connect the three men, one a British journalist in Paris only for the day, one an estate kid and the third a worker in the post room at the British Embassy, also British. Then there was the girl seen running from the scene of the Englishman's Paris flat—another Brit according to a neighbour, dark-haired, average height. They had found a set of fingerprints in the flat but been unable to identify them as the girl obviously had no previous form. If indeed they were hers.

Legrand was now at something of a dead end. Which was a very bad place to be when there was a serial killer on the loose in Paris. Although something told him the killer would not be in Paris that much longer. The only connection he had between everyone involved in this case was that all but one were British. He considered calling his ex-wife Irene—he had helped her out with a young British man she wanted followed in Paris not that long ago so she owed him a favour. However, after some thought he realised this was not something he could do remotely and not something he wanted to involve MI6 in. He would have to go himself to London—and below the radar.

EVA OPENED HER EYES. Everything around her seemed to be moving in slow motion. Above her the man with the syringe seemed paused. Her eyes slipped up towards the blue sky. Such a bright, azure colour it made her heart sing. She found such peace in nature—if there was a god she had always felt the natural world was where she would find evidence of him or her. She took one last look at the strip of blue above her, closed her eyes once again and inhaled the rich scent of the wet leaves and the woody surroundings of the little clearing in the park. As she began to exhale, time sped up once again.

She opened her eyes. The syringe was jammed.

She saw the flicker of panic in the eyes of the man above her. She looked past him to the medical box just out of reach where the second syringe lay. He couldn't reach it without releasing her.

He threw the first useless syringe to one side, stood up and grabbed the front of Eva's jacket, dragging her towards where the medical box lay. As she stumbled after him, one of her ankles came loose from the masking tape.

She pushed herself to her feet and then she tripped him with her numb leg, swinging it into his path. The man fell face down onto the floor next to the medical box. Eva threw herself across his back, reached across him with her bound hands and pulled the second syringe free from the felt fabric lining. She stabbed it into the back of his neck and drove the plunger home.

For several seconds neither moved. Then, as she felt the man below her try to turn over, Eva pushed herself to her feet and limped away, backing up against the hedge behind her.

Slowly, the man on the floor pushed himself to his knees. He looked at her and then back at the empty syringe and then he felt the point on the back of his neck where she had injected him. He seemed as if he might make a grab for her and then suddenly his eyes widened and his body jerked forward. He took a large gulp of air but struggled to do so; then he tried to take another.

Eva took two paces backwards, watching in horrified fascination.

The man was still trying to suck air into his chest but he couldn't. Eva could hear a soft rattling coming from him each time he tried.

Suddenly, he began choking. He pulled off the balaclava to reveal a painfully young face. His hands were at his chest above his heart; he stared at her, eyes wide, his mouth working as he tried desperately to breathe. Then he collapsed to the floor, first to his hands and knees and then onto his back.

Eva felt as if she should help this man, but she couldn't move. She was acutely aware that had the first syringe not jammed that would have been her.

The man on the floor began groaning. He was twisting his body unnaturally, flailing on the floor, his hands clutching and clawing at his chest and throat, a look of sheer terror on his face. Then suddenly he stopped moving. His body remained rigid, arms clasped at his throat. Eva watched the gradual rise and fall of his chest as the movement became less until it stopped completely. He lay there, eyes wide, utterly still.

EVA BLINKED AND looked around her.

She stood for several seconds and then her brain roared into action. *Move.*

With adrenaline still surging in her veins, and aware that at any minute the other men could return, Eva pulled her wrists apart and tore the tape binding them. She ripped the masking tape from her face as she stumbled slightly. She felt like a newborn deer, her balance was shot and the adrenaline in her system made her head spin.

She forced her breathing to slow and tried to empty her mind of all the panicky thoughts so she could think straight and then began working some feeling back into her numb leg.

When she could walk properly again, Eva took a few steps across the small space, back to the opening into the park itself. Her heart was beating like a drum in her ears. Slowly, she looked around the side of the hedge.

Leon seemed to be out cold, lying only a few feet away on his back, hands and feet unbound. Kneeling beside him was a man who looked just like the others she had seen earlier in the park. Eva's eyes widened in surprise. An unlikely knight in shining armour. Next to him lay one of the men in balaclavas, a bright red gash across his neck where his head covering had been lifted and his throat cut. There was no sign of the third masked man.

LOOKING AT THE scene Eva couldn't work out what was going on. Was the hooded man helping Leon? She glanced around the rest of the park but it was completely empty. Not a witness in sight. Her attention was drawn back to Leon as he apparently began to come around. He did not look surprised to see the man leaning over him. They exchanged a few words and then the man stood up. He walked over to the dead body, removed the balaclava, checked the pockets and then rolled the corpse at speed into a huge pile of raked leaves, covering it completely. Then he quickly walked off in the other direction as Leon sat on the ground, rubbing his head.

Eva pulled herself back behind the hedge and shut her eyes. She took a deep breath and when her eyes opened again her gaze fell on the still-full jammed syringe. She picked it up, broke the needle off, tore the felt from the inside of the medical case and wrapped it around the vial before shoving it into her bag as she retrieved it from the floor. Then she ran around the side of the hedge towards Leon. He looked up immediately.

'What happened?' she asked, coming to kneel as she reached his side.

'I don't know. I was out cold.' They stared at each other for several seconds and Eva debated whether or not to ask him about the 'good Samaritan', seeing as he apparently wasn't going to mention it. She looked up at the sky; the sun was setting. There was no time.

'Can you walk?'

'I don't know.' He struggled to stand up but his legs gave way. He tried again and this time managed to pull himself upright. Eva half-dragged him over to the bench and forced him to sit whilst she sat next to him with her ear to his chest, listening for the sound of the death rattle.

'What the hell are you doing?' exclaimed Leon and she heard his heartbeat start to rise, but he didn't push her head away.

His chest sounded clear.

'Back there,' she said sitting up and indicating the hedge behind which the dead man lay. 'They tried to inject me with something but the needle jammed. There was a second syringe and I stabbed a man with it. He died…' She hesitated.

'He died in such an awful way…' The man's face flashed into her mind. All of a sudden it was Jackson's face. She shook her head and banished the image.

'How did he die?' There was an urgency to Leon's tone. Eva ignored him and pulled her phone out of her bag, feeling the felt wrapped around the syringe brush her hand as she did so. 'We have an hour and forty minutes to make the train.'

'We're still going?'

'Of course. We don't have any other option now, not after…that.'

He nodded slowly. 'You never give up, do you?'

'No.'

THE STATION WAS a five-minute walk away so they left the car and set out on foot. Eva checked constantly for the USB stick in the pocket on the front of the right thigh of her jeans. Throughout all the drama that had unfolded since she had first put the stick in there, it had remained wedged tightly against her leg.

Once at the Gare du Nord train station, Eva left Leon sitting at a café under some escalators and went to pick up their tickets, grateful that she'd chosen not to leave her passport at the hotel. Leon kept his in the glove box of his car, which struck her as odd. But there was so much she and Leon needed to straighten out at that moment that it was just another thing to add to a list they didn't have time to go through. She bought them both strong coffees and picked up medical supplies, cleaning wipes and a hairbrush from a pharmacy inside the station. They found the public toilets on the lower ground floor and spent another five minutes making themselves look presentable before climbing the escalators up to the Eurostar departure lounge.

Their train was leaving in twenty minutes and after being rushed through the ticket barriers and English and French customs, they were funnelled straight onto the waiting train, which left the station no more than five minutes after they had boarded it.

At 5:00 A.M., two buses arrived at an area twelve miles west of London and began to spew out people. The figures were clad in waterproof galoshes and raincoats, layered underneath with thick jumpers to keep out the cold of the dark November morning. The sun was not yet up and the figures huddled around the buses, smoking cigarettes and drinking coffee being handed out to them from Thermos flasks. There was an air of grim determination as they stamped their feet on the frozen ground and wrapped gloved fingers around the steaming coffee to keep them warm. Five minutes after they had arrived they began distributing backpacks amongst themselves. The backpacks were the shape of a large cylinder with a hose hanging from the bottom. Each contained a barrel full of algaecide.

Silence was called and instructions were given by the group's leaders—don't touch the algae and try to keep your mouth and nose covered just in case. Several members of the group—a small Asian woman with long dark hair and a tall lanky teen among them—said they had not thought to bring face coverings. For a second the group leader hesitated and then he said, 'Not to worry, I'm sure this stuff isn't harmful to humans.' Then the teams set off to their allocated areas.

Within an hour they had made good progress and several Environment Agency tankers had arrived to pump algaecide into the reservoirs in the area. Everything seemed to be under control. The team leader noticed with satisfaction that much of the algae was already dead.

TWENTY-THREE

As Legrand stepped through the Eurostar exit at St Pancras International, he was happy to see his old friend Tom Chard waiting for him, leaning up against the glass wall of an expensive-looking supermarket.

'Tom,' he smiled.

'Legrand. Your message sounded urgent. Someone stolen your bicycle and onions?' Legrand laughed at the obligatory xenophobic joke.

'The bicycle and onions are safe. Along with the beret.' The two men started walking towards the station exit.

'It's good to see you. How many years has it been?'

'I'd say five at least.'

'Long time.'

'Indeed, my friend. Now what is it you're here for? I take it it has nothing to do with these algae.'

'I'm here mostly on a hunch, Tom. We had this odd case in Paris this week, a man found dead in his flat, and a kid on an estate, both apparently died of natural causes, but the pathologist has this mad theory that it's murder.'

'How so?'

'There are needle marks that could indicate they were injected with something he thinks may have triggered the onset of the conditions that killed them.'

'What were the conditions?' Legrand hesitated. 'Well, I'm not so good with these medical terms but basically I think it's where the muscles give way and the lungs become filled with scar tissue.'

'That sounds pretty nasty.' Chard led Legrand out through the station exit and indicated his unmarked police car sitting in one of the taxi bays. He opened the automatic locking system and the two men climbed inside. As Chard pulled out of the station towards a flow of traffic Legrand continued.

'I didn't believe the doctor at first of course—it all sounds a bit fantastic—but then there was another man who turned up dead with the same symptoms. On the Eurostar.'

'Terry Dowler—that's my case.'

'The journalist, yes. It turns out that he had a strange puncture mark too.' Chard was silent.

'So I'm over here to take a closer look at Dowler's body, try and trace the family of one of the victims to speak to them on an unofficial basis and see if I can't find a common link.' Chard nodded, reached over to the glove-box and pulled out a box of cigarettes and a lighter. He rolled down his window, lit a cigarette, threw the box back in the glove compartment and slammed it shut.

'Unfortunately, I think I may have to throw a spanner in that works,' he said, exhaling out of the window.

Legrand was surprised. And alert. 'Oh? Why's that?'

'Well, we've had another case; another man apparently victim of exactly the same conditions Dowler died of. Timeframe is the same, end result the same, even the look on their faces when they died is exactly the same.'

'So what's the problem?'

'No needle marks.' Legrand frowned. 'Are you sure the conditions weren't naturally occurring?'

'One hundred per cent. The man had a horrendously

expensive medical not more than six months ago and there was no sign of either disease. Apparently it would be impossible for the conditions to advance as far as death in that time.'

'Well, are you sure there's no needle mark?' Chard looked over at Legrand.

'Trust me, mate, we've made sure.'

Legrand felt chastised. 'What was the man's name?'

'Rob Gorben.'

THE ONLY FARES left on the Eurostar had been first-class so Leon and Eva had found themselves cocooned in the enormous seats of the luxurious carriage, being served food and drink as the train flew across the darkening French countryside. As night fell, Eva was becoming more anxious. She had spent the first half of the journey thinking about the episode at the park. It was pretty obvious that whoever had been behind it was keeping tight tabs on them and was not afraid to attack them in public. As she and Leon really had no idea as to why whoever was chasing them was trying to kill them—or what was the significance of the syringes—they were forced into drawing conclusions, a dangerously vague way to proceed. Presumably, they had become targets because of the information they held—because that would influence the outcome of something, somehow, for someone very powerful—which meant that they had no option but to race these people to the point at which they handed the information over to someone else. Although somehow she doubted that would be the end of it. They seemed to have made some very unpleasant enemies.

As they had no real idea who those enemies might

be, that meant that there really wasn't anywhere that they were safe.

Eva glanced at the aisle.

Whilst standard class had been full, their part of the train was almost empty and there were at least three vacant seats behind them; still every time she heard footsteps Eva tensed and prepared to have to defend herself in some way. She took a long drink of a brandy she had ordered after they had eaten, to calm her nerves.

THE MORE SHE thought about the attack at the park, the more puzzled she was about Leon's 'good Samaritan'. He had vanished by the time she had emerged back into the park—not even walking in the other direction but completely vanished—and she still didn't understand what had happened on the other side of that hedge. One masked man had died, the other—the black-eyed man who had seemed to be in charge—had escaped. Leon had apparently not been involved in any of it.

She looked over at Leon who, unexpectedly, was fast asleep. He had gone from being alert and full of adrenaline in Paris to out cold as soon as he had eaten, which surprised Eva given the intense energy of paranoia and suspicion that seemed to drive him. His sleeping face gave nothing away.

Eva shifted in her seat. Her body ached. She felt like she needed a good long soak in a hot bath. But to be honest she was just happy to be alive. After witnessing the shocking death in the park, she knew that were it not for blind luck it could have been her lifeless on that wet ground thanks to whatever was in those syringes. Why were they being used as a weapon rather than a gun or a knife? They seemed an awkward choice for a moving victim and far less efficient than a bullet or a blade. Although whatever was in them was certainly as effective as any other murder weapon, she thought, remembering the dead man's tortured face.

Eva turned away from Leon and rested her temple against the soft, comfortable headrest of the first-class seat as a wave of tiredness swept over her.

WHEN SHE AWOKE an hour later it was to the muted tinkling of the hostesses' trolley distributing coffee and papers. She took a deep, relieved breath and then exhaled slowly; apparently on this train at least, they could sleep safe. When the trolley arrived at her seat she asked for a black coffee and picked up a broadsheet from the pile. They were on the other side of the Channel now and couldn't be far from London. Eva checked the clock on her phone: nearly 9pm UK time, less than an hour until they arrived, and the only plan they had been able to come up with so far was contacting the woman who had broken her family apart and asking her for help. It wasn't ideal. Eva leaned back and rested her head against the soft seat and wondered how much of her suggestion to make contact with Irene Hunt was about resolving this current situation and how much was about the chance finally to confront a woman she had hated in absentia for more than a decade.

Across the table, Leon stretched in his seat and kicked out with one heavy boot, banging it against the table leg. She gazed again at his sleeping features. Dark hair, two-day stubble swathed around his chin and throat, a large bruise forming over his left eye and a deep graze on his right cheek. He had grey hollows under his eyes and his long, black eyelashes flickered against them as

he dreamed. She looked at his muscled arms, tight stomach and thick legs; he exuded some kind of raw strength
even in his sleep. It wasn't something Eva found attractive. He was an unknown quantity: a dangerous, violent unknown quantity who had already killed at least
three people.

And saved her life.

The state of confusion that left her in was not one she
was used to. Eva made immediate judgement calls about
people and they were usually right. After that, she rarely
gave anyone a second chance.

She cut short the thought and turned her attention to
the papers. The algae was quickly spreading through
the UK waterways. However, the front page article that
covered the story seemed to conclude that, although the
plants were a nuisance, they posed no real threat to the
public. Was that panic control or a cover-up? Halfway
through the paper she came across an article, apparently considered non-headline news, positioned between
the sports section and the classifieds, linking the algae
explosion with Bioavancement S.a.r.l.. Why was this
not on the front page? Eva read the article and realised
that it had been 'buried'. It was a trick she recognised
from her editor days. Where there was a piece that could
not be removed completely from a publication but that
wasn't considered newsworthy enough—or was news
that someone wanted to hide—it was kept off the pages
of the paper that drew the most attention. Burying the
article on those dead pages meant that subconsciously
the readers would give its contents short shrift. It was a
clever way of making a molehill out of a mountain. Eva
continued to stare at the page in front of her. Someone
was controlling this situation; the power of the press was

being used to great effect to ensure that the public knew nothing about who was really behind this, what was actually happening and what the consequences might be.

She took her phone and went out into the corridor of the carriage.

'Hello?'

'Dad, it's Eva.'

'Eva. Where are you?'

'I've been away on holiday. Dad, I was wondering if I could ask you a favour.'

'No problem.' Eva heard the sound of liquid being poured from bottle to glass.

'Are you still in contact with Irene Hunt?' There was silence on the other end of the phone and the liquid-pouring stopped.

'Dad, are you still there?'

'Is this a trick question, Eva?'

'No, I need to speak to her.'

'I won't have all this resurrected again.'

'It's got nothing to do with you anymore.'

'Eva, I made a mistake. One mistake. Why must you bring all this up yet again?' For a moment Eva hesitated and the confusion she had felt for years reared up once again. She loved her father, he was a good man. But he had betrayed them and no matter how much she tried to convince herself that she had forgiven him, she wasn't sure that some small piece of resentment didn't still lie buried.

However, she didn't want to behave like a child, raking up the past because she wasn't mature enough to move on. Was she doing this for the right reasons? Was there a better alternative?

No, Eva reasoned, there was no alternative.

'Doesn't she work in intelligence?'

'You know she does.'

'Dad, it's important. Please, I can't explain, I just need to make contact with her, I need her address.' Eva could almost hear her father's mind working on the other end of the phone. Since her mother died, they rarely probed into each other's lives in too much detail, but still it must have sounded like a bizarre and slightly ludicrous request out of the blue.

'I haven't seen or spoken to her since…since I promised you that it was over. I don't break my word, Eva. Especially not after what it did to your mother.' He sounded so sad.

Eva felt the gentle poke of guilt. She spoke more softly this time. 'Dad, this is not about you. I promise I'm not about to do anything stupid. What is there left to say anyway?' After some hesitation her father left the phone and returned with Irene Hunt's address. 'I don't even know if she still lives there. Eva, can't you tell me what this is about?'

'No Dad, I can't.'

'Eva…'

'Look Dad, I'm an adult now and I know that there isn't an age where you just wake up and start getting everything right, even when you're a parent. You did your best with what you had at the time. We're all just human.' She had thrown several self-help slogans at him and she knew it sounded slightly forced.

'Eva, I never wanted to let you down…'

'I know.'

'If I could go back…'

'I know,' she said again. And then it dawned on Eva

that perhaps she really did know what that kind of guilt felt like and just maybe she really could forgive him.

Irene Hunt however was another matter.

Leon was awake when she returned to her seat, looking refreshed and alert, drinking a large black coffee and reading the paper she had left behind.

'Where did you go?'

'I went to phone my dad.'

'Why?' As always, he sounded very suspicious.

'I got an address for Irene Hunt.'

As JOHN MANSFIELD MP put down the phone, his heart began to hammer; an emergency briefing for all members of the cabinet about the algae situation. The country had been put on high alert and the armed forces mobilised to deal with any civil unrest that could ensue if the public somehow discovered just how dire the situation was. Everything was beginning to fall apart, he thought to himself. There was no question in his mind that the algae epidemic must be connected to the Bioavancement S.a.r.l. algae plants that he had personally shepherded into the country. Before long the link to him would no doubt be discovered and he would be made the scapegoat for the entire crisis, as was the way with contemporary politics.

He forced himself to remain controlled. Now was the time to be calm and manufacture himself an escape route. As far as he knew, no one had yet made a solid connection between Bioavancement S.a.r.l., him personally and the algae emergency but he was sure that by the end of the day they would have. He glanced at his watch and then slowly began to pack his briefcase. Soon he could be called to the PM to justify the decision to

associate with Bioavancement S.a.r.l.. He had prepared
and rehearsed his speech for weeks. Given the situation
with the algae and the fact that he had known that the
algae arrived in the UK before the proper licences and
approvals had been granted, he would, of course, be in
for quite a grilling. But he had severed any possible ties
that could connect him to the company as an insider so
he would claim innocent incompetence rather than in-
tentional deception and then offer himself up as a sacrifice. The PM could bundle this whole disaster up and
hang it around Mansfield's neck—the ease of that solution would appeal to him. When it came to preserving his
identity, only the other stakeholders in the project knew
in what way he was tied in and they would no sooner
want to identify themselves with this crisis than he did.
He would no doubt be sacked from his cabinet post but
he didn't expect there to be any further consequences.
If there was no proof of anything other than stupidity
how could they do anything more to him? After that he
would quietly slip away, the apparent victim of a freak
boating accident, his body lost at sea. The Bioavancement S.a.r.l. payment was large enough to last him for
the rest of his life in a country that did not have an ex-
tradition treaty with the UK.

WHEN THEY ARRIVED at St Pancras International, any
sense of safety they had felt during the journey on the
isolated train quickly vanished. In the crowds at the station they were pushed, shoved and poked by evening
commuters and their luggage. Every hand felt like a
sharp knife and every elbow was a blow of some kind.
It didn't help that Eva's body was now a mass of bruises

from where she had been physically pushed around at various times during the last week.

They decided to take the underground to the address Eva's father had given them. Eva could really have done without the commuter crush, which did nothing for her nerves, but in a way the normality of the lives continuing all around them was comforting.

Eva noticed Leon suddenly becoming quite protective of her, shielding her with his body when too many people tried to board the train at one station and pushing his way through to a seat so that she could sit down. She didn't want his help and she tried to make it clear that she didn't need it, but he seemed to be motivated to do it regardless.

As they came out of the station at Warwick Avenue the near-deserted area set them both on edge. They had five broad Maida Vale roads to walk across before they would reach Irene Hunt's house and no idea whether she would even be there when they arrived—or if she even lived there anymore.

LEON—WHO HAD memorised the route they had to take from the map on his phone—guided them across the road and they started walking uphill, taking a right at the next corner and then crossing again onto the road that would lead them to their destination. The pavements were wide and the houses huge with grand interiors. The darkness around them was misty and cold and the orange light of the street lamps provided the perfect setting for an anonymous drive by.

Eva focused on keeping pace with Leon's wide strides. When they were just two streets from the road where Irene Hunt lived, Eva heard a car start to slow behind them. She forced herself to keep walking but glanced briefly over at Leon.

'Keep walking,' he said in a low voice and took a quick glance over his left shoulder towards the road. Apparently not feeling the need to share whatever he saw, he picked up his pace ever so slightly and continued to power forward. Suddenly, without warning, he pulled Eva inside an open front gate of one of the Maida Vale mansions and flipped her around so that he was standing with his back to the approaching car as if he had just taken the opportunity to kiss his girlfriend. Eva stood rigid in his arms, hardly breathing. Their faces were touching, noses, lips and one cheekbone skin on skin. She looked over his shoulder at the car behind his back. She felt his hand move at his side and saw the metallic glint of a gun as he took it from the waistband of his trousers. God only knew how he had got that through customs.

Eva's heart was pounding.

'Leon...' She started to speak. Suddenly he kissed her, apparently to stop her saying anything more. Her eyes opened with surprise. Unexpectedly she didn't feel the urge to pepper spray him. The car passed and he pulled back and released her. They stood still for several seconds as they heard the car driving away and then turned and resumed their original path. Further up the street, the car stopped and appeared to ask another young couple for directions.

TWENTY-FOUR

JOHN MANSFIELD ALLOWED himself an unprecedented afternoon snifter of the vintage cognac the CEO had so kindly dispatched to him that was worth more than most people's cars. He tried to relax back into the plump cushioning of his antique armchair at home and took a deep draught of the amber liquid in his glass. The rich smell filled his nose as the warmth spread from his throat to his chest and the golden drops made their way down to his stomach. Even in the midst of a crisis there were some things that one had to stop and savour. He glanced at the carriage clock on the mantelpiece: 4pm. The CEO had asked him to call exactly on the hour. He had not been expecting more contact—there was supposed to be no more communication between them for fear of risking Mansfield's escape route. He suspected it might be an apology for the situation with the algae—which had not been part of the deal—but he was not entirely sure what was about to happen. This made him rather anxious; he was nervous enough as it was after the earlier phone briefing about the algae, even though he had managed to put off seeing the PM until the morning.

Mansfield delicately deposited the brandy glass back down on the largest of the nest of walnut wood coffee tables his mother had insisted he buy for the house when he'd made the mistake of inviting her over for tea one weekend. He stood and walked over to the desk. From his briefcase, positioned just underneath the enormous leather-topped desk, he extracted a phone that contained just one number.

'You're prompt.'

'I try to be.'

'I appreciate you calling me, I know the risks.' The CEO's voice was utterly expressionless; Mansfield could glean nothing from his tone.

'It's not a problem.' Mansfield waited. The CEO would never be rushed and Mansfield was too in awe of the man to push him.

'We are cutting you loose, John.' Mansfield felt his throat begin to close up. 'I…I'm sorry?'

'Cutting you loose. We can't honour the contract.'

'I don't understand.'

'We no longer have need of you.'

'But everything is done. All that is left is for you to make the payment. I have done everything you asked of me.' The words were tumbling out now; millions of pounds were slipping from his fingertips.

'John, please be calm. We wouldn't be cutting you loose if you couldn't handle it. You will be fine.'

'But I will lose my job, Daniel. I've already offered myself up as a scapegoat as we planned; the axe is about to fall.'

'I'm sorry, John, but we won't be honouring the payment because we don't have it. The project has been compromised.'

'How?'

'An information leak. A girl called Eva Scott.'

'Who?'

'It doesn't matter. We must focus all our resources

on locating her and trying to salvage something from this situation.'

'I don't understand why this is being laid at my door. I didn't even know that the algae would spread like this—you have left me in an impossible position!'

'The decision has been made.' The line went dead.

Mansfield stopped and looked at the phone. It made absolutely no sense. Either they had never intended to pay him the vast amount of money he had staked his entire life on or something had genuinely happened with this girl that had ruined the project. Either way what could he do? Yes, they had a agreement but he could hardly enforce it in a court of law. Mansfield leaned forward on his desk, his head in his hands.

WHEN THEY FINALLY arrived at Irene Hunt's house, jogging most of the rest of the way, Eva was relieved to see lights in all the windows. They let themselves in via a large wooden gate at the front, walked through a small garden surrounded by a high wall and then climbed four steps before ringing the front doorbell. The door was opened by a tall, angular man with thinning hair and a rangy, athletic figure.

'Yes?'

'I'm looking for Irene Hunt.'

He frowned. 'May I ask who you are?' Eva hesitated. Should she reveal her identity? The man seemed to pick up on her hesitation and moved to try and close the door. Immediately, Leon jammed his foot in it and then pushed it open, knocking the man backwards.

Eva stepped forward. 'Look, I'm sorry,' she said smiling and hoping that Leon would just stay behind her. 'My name is Eva Scott.' Immediately, the man's face hardened in recognition as he picked himself up from the spot on which he had fallen.

'What do you want?'

'I want to see Irene Hunt.'

'I very much doubt she will want to see you.'

'It's not what you think. Really. I just want to talk to her about something—something completely unconnected to…what happened.' The man took a step back towards the open door and glanced nervously at Leon.

'Please,' said Eva.

He looked at her. 'OK. But he stays outside.' Leon nodded grimly and turned and sat on the steps, looking the other way. Eva stepped inside the house towards the man who opened the door wide enough to let her in, before shutting it with a bang. He led her through the enormous house, past a large, elegant living room, warmly packed with thick carpets, pictures, art, a television and several small children and ushered them into what appeared to be a study.

Eva was pleased to see a computer.

'I will find Irene. Can I get you anything?'

British hospitality was an amazing thing, even in a situation such as this.

'No, thank you, I'm fine,' said Eva before the man left the room.

When he had gone, Eva looked around her. Right behind the desk was a huge window, black and gaping out onto a moonlit garden. It was making Eva incredibly nervous so she walked over and drew the thick ruby velvet curtains across the empty space and then positioned herself in the chair nearest to the desk. The room was large, with a grand oak-wood writing desk topped with green leather positioned in the centre and bookshelves lining the walls. Photos, certificates, awards and pictures covered one wall and on the other two hung what Eva assumed must be art originals or very good copies.

The certificates and awards on the walls did not belong to Irene though—it would seem that Mr. Hunt was something of a world-renowned journalist, a strange partner for an intelligence officer, and the same profession as her father's, she noted.

After several minutes Eva heard footsteps padding across the carpeted floors she had just walked along, coming in the direction of the study. They stopped outside the room for several seconds and then Eva felt a presence behind her.

WHEN SHE TURNED, Irene Hunt was standing there brandishing a tumbler of amber liquid, ice cubes clinking against the glass. She looked as if she was about to down the lot.

'Eva Scott,' she said expressionlessly. She was petite but held herself with significant presence, almost filling the room without even moving. She had shoulder-length, dark brown hair cut in a no-nonsense style but the ends curled rebelliously. Even though she had apparently finished work for the day she still wore an expensive-looking, teal-coloured suit. No jewellery, no shoes. She fixed Eva with a pair of dark grey eyes, her lips drawn into a thin line.

'Hello.' Eva stood up and the two women stiffly shook hands before Irene moved around her and sat down in the large leather swivel chair behind the desk; she took a long drink from the glass, almost draining it. Then she sat back and looked closely at Eva, who realised she must be noticing the cuts and bruises all over her face.

'You've been in the wars,' she said almost sympatheti-
cally, 'why are you here?'

'I'm not here about the past,' Eva replied quickly.

A brief flicker of almost imperceptible relief crossed
Irene Hunt's face but was quickly replaced by the severe look.

'Then why have you turned up at my house so late
at night?' Eva didn't know what she had expected from
Hunt, but it wasn't this unforgiving, unrepentant hard-
ness.

'I need your help.' It was Irene Hunt's turn to be surprised.

'I don't know how much you know of our family
since…well, since then,' said Eva quickly, taking advantage of the delay in the other woman's reactions, 'but
my brother Jackson has been murdered in Paris.' Irene
Hunt's face wore no expression at all.

'The police say he committed suicide, but I'm now
99.9 per cent certain he was killed because of something he knew. And I believe that I have the evidence
here to prove it.' She slid the memory stick out from the
pocket of her jeans and pushed it across the table. Then
she remembered the vaccine she had taken following
the attack in the park—she had emptied it into a small
perfume diffuser to prevent it being taken by customs.
She pushed that towards Irene Hunt too.

'What's this?'

'The memory stick contains information on the algae
epidemic that the UK is currently in the grip of and also
demonstrates how to stop it. This,' she said, tapping the
small silver diffuser, 'is what someone who knows the
information we have is genuine has been using to try and
attack us. It's some kind of poison—if you test it you will

see how real the threat is to our safety.' Eva was trying very hard to make a convincing argument. She had to at least get Hunt to read what was on the stick.

'Read it,' she said, a little too forcefully.

Hunt looked at the stick and then back at Eva. She didn't move.

'I don't understand why you have come to me.'

'You're intelligence.' No response.

'I know you are. This needs to get into the hands of someone who can do something with it—fast. You are the only person I could think of with that kind of connection.'

'And how do I know this isn't some pathetic little revenge play.'

Eva was taken aback. 'I guess you don't.'

'I know how much your family hates me, Eva. Don't you think that I have known that all this time?' The intensity with which Hunt spoke took Eva by surprise. She found herself reacting, hair-trigger.

'Well, what else did you expect after what you did?' The two women stared at each other. Irene was rigid, sitting slightly forwards in her chair. She held Eva's gaze like a stern headmistress.

'What kind of woman does that to another family?' Eva fought to stop her floodgates from bursting open but failed. But Irene was not cowed.

'And what about your mother, Eva? She and your father got together when he and his ex-wife were only separated.'

'There was no betrayal of trust,' Eva hissed back, 'they had been separated for over a year—that's completely normal, there's nothing wrong with that. How dare you bring my mother into this? She was not the same as you.' Irene put her glass down with a bang and broke Eva's gaze.

'I don't know why you came here,' she said, turning her chair slightly to the right.

'I told you why,' said Eva forcefully.

'I won't help you.'

'You won't even look at this?'

'No.'

'So you expect me and my family to move on, to forgive and forget, but you won't.'

'I tried once to help your brother and look where he ended up. I won't take on any more guilt related to your family.' Eva stopped. 'My brother?'

'The car crash.'

'What?' Eva was out of her chair, her face rapidly turning pink.

'He came to us; we helped him fake the crash.' Eva was breathing hard now.

'I thought you knew,' said Irene Hunt, although she did not look surprised at Eva's reaction.

'No, I did not know. I don't understand. Why would he come to you? How did he come to you?'

'I think it's time you left.'

'No. Tell me what happened, I have a right to know!' Irene Hunt stood up and leaned across the desk. Her eyes had turned almost liquid. 'You have no right to anything.' Eva stood still, shock penetrating every pore. This was not the way she had thought this would go. Shouldn't this woman be showing some contrition? And what did she mean about Jackson?

'I'm not going anywhere until you tell me what I want to know.'

'You will leave.' The quiet voice came from behind

her and Eva turned to see an unobtrusive man in a dark suit.

'And who is this, your fucking minder?' She realised she was out of control now. The swearing, the shouting, the red face. This was not how she wanted to be. She reached across the desk and snatched the memory stick, knocking the diffuser off the table, and then pushed past the man at the door.

AS SOON AS they were outside Irene Hunt's gate, Eva felt the familiar sense of unease return. She was fuming about what had just happened but they needed to be inside, away from all these dark roads.

'We need to find a hotel.'

'Ten minutes away. I've booked a room.'

'Fine.'

'One room is safer than separate,' Leon said as if it needed an explanation.

They walked in silence, at speed, all the way to the hotel.

Eva said nothing about her encounter with Irene Hunt and Leon didn't ask. Once they were in the room, Leon locked the door.

Eva paced the floor; her body was alive with adrenaline. Memories, emotions, thoughts and fears flew uncontrolled around her brain as if Irene had unlocked some kind of Pandora's Box. She had to calm down or she would never be able to think clearly. She needed a release.

As Leon returned from the bathroom and went to take off his boots, she grasped the front of his shirt and pulled him to her. Ignoring the shocked look on his face she kissed him hard and pushed him back underneath her onto the bed.

TWENTY-FIVE

WHEN EVA OPENED her eyes the next morning Leon was lying across the other side of the bed facing her. He was staring at her, unblinking. Eva stared back for several seconds and waited for him to look away. He didn't. His look was cold, appraising and unemotional. It was not the starry-eyed look of love.

Eva pushed herself up in the bed, thankful that she had remembered to put some clothes on before she slept the night before. She felt uneasy and uncomfortable now that a line had been crossed but there was also a kind of acceptance that it had been inevitable. She had instigated what had happened and for once, Leon had been completely in her control.

Eventually, Leon too sat up and reached for his T-shirt.

'What now,' he asked as if trying to gauge her feelings. His tone was flat.

Eva climbed out of bed, plucked a towel from the back of the chair in the soulless modern hotel room and headed for the shower in her underwear.

'We carry on.'

WHEN SHE EMERGED from the bathroom half an hour later the room was empty. For a split second Eva thought Leon had disappeared but then she saw a note on the bed telling her he had gone to hire a car. There was no explanation as to why he felt that they needed to hire a car, just that he would be back in an hour.

Uneasily, Eva locked the hotel room door from the inside.

She debated ordering some room service and then decided against it. When she had combed out her hair and pulled on her clothes, she made the bed and then lay down on it. She flicked on the TV. The early morning news was reporting on the algae crisis, trying to make the most out of the same information that had been in circulation for several days. However, it was clear that the story was considered to be on the wane. She could almost sense the disappointment in the news anchors, who would now be reduced to covering the number of shopping days until Christmas once again.

JUST BEFORE THE programme ended at 9:00 a.m. there was a final interview with the environment agency head Don Porter. It was live from the road in front of his office. Whether it was the early start or the reporter's attempts at harassing him into saying something news-worthy, Porter did not look comfortable. Eva sat up and moved closer to the large flat-screen TV attached to the wall opposite. Don Porter did not look like he had slept. Tell-tale bags hovered under his eyes and uneasy glances to his left spoke of the presence of someone else carefully controlling his responses. What he was say-ing sounded rehearsed, without a doubt. And when the reporter tried to engage him in unplanned speculation he simply ended the interview. Eva flicked off the TV and sat back against the soft pillows, her hands behind her head. Was he really displaying the signs of some-one operating under great stress on little sleep or was she imagining it because she thought she knew what was really happening? If Don Porter was in the middle of crisis management then someone else other than her and Leon understood that the algae was much more of a threat than was being publicly reported. Again, Eva wondered to herself—cover-up or crisis management?

Her thoughts were interrupted by the door being unlocked and Leon stalking through. He threw several packages on the bed and handed her a black coffee without speaking.

Eva began to unwrap the haul. A new pair of jeans—surprisingly the right size and the same style as she had on—a new T-shirt—slightly too large—a black hooded top and even new underwear (white cotton, nothing too provocative). Quickly and unselfconsciously Eva changed into the new clothes, thankful that she could leave her much-worn outfit behind. She reached for her old pair of jeans and pulled out the memory stick as Leon produced a small, brand-new notebook computer.

'We need to make copies of that stick,' he said and shoved it across the bed at her along with a pack of two new memory sticks. Eva nodded, unwrapped the computer and began the business of copying all the information on the stick she held onto the duplicates. As she worked, Leon produced the last of his purchases, tightly-wrapped bacon sandwiches, steaming hot and juicy with ketchup.

Whilst it was never mentioned, Eva had a sense that what had happened last night had been put into a box and shelved in Leon's mind. He may have been vulnerable enough to show how uncomfortable he felt first thing that morning but the shutters had firmly come back down now. Frankly, Eva was relieved; the last thing she wanted was to have a conversation about what it meant or how it made her feel.

WHILST LEON SHOWERED, Eva finished her coffee and began looking once again through the memory stick to see if they had missed anything. She searched the same documents and folders that she had perused before but there was nothing there that was new. She read again the obesity predictions and the projected profits Bioavancement S.a.r.l. assumed would be achieved by setting a light under such an epidemic with their algae 'health supplement'. She found that she felt little shock that a company would sacrifice all those lives to such a horrible end for the sake of profit. Perhaps she had become entirely cynical; but then it wasn't as if it hadn't happened before.

She was about to remove the memory stick from the computer when she noticed that it had a 'trash' folder. She clicked on the file; inside was a single document. She opened it and began to read—it appeared to be a record of attempts that Sophie had made at passing on the information she had and the people she had tried to make contact with. Eva's own name was on the top of the list as the most recent entry, along with the address of the hotel where she had been staying in Paris. The next name down was 'Terry Dowler' and a date next to it. The name rang a bell so Eva accessed the hotel's wireless internet and searched his name. He had been a tabloid journalist who had died suddenly on a Eurostar from Paris to London on the date that Sophie had entered into the document. The article written about him attributed his death to a heart attack. Eva looked at where

Sophie had noted 'EXECUTED' in stark capital letters. She began to get a sick feeling in the pit of her stomach.

She started to read the rest of the names and then suddenly she froze. There, towards the end of the short list was the name 'Irene Hunt'.

AN HOUR LATER and they were on the road. With no real option other than to try and contact the only person who looked as if he had any knowledge of the real extent of the crisis unfolding around them, Eva and Leon had decided to try their luck and schedule a meeting with Don Porter. It was nonsensical to Eva that she should be 'scheduling meetings' when the information that she held was of such critical importance but there was a need to preserve some kind of sanity and not to behave in a way that would make their information less credible. That meant carrying on as normal; but it didn't make it any less surreal.

They had posed as journalists to try and schedule the meeting—borrowing the name of one of the biggest environmental commentators in the field to secure an hour with Porter that morning at midday. A harassed secretary had said that she was sure Porter had fifteen minutes he could spare them as long as they were there on time. Neither had any idea how they would explain that they were not the famous journalist—or convince Porter that they weren't certifiable—but without any other options they were just pressing ahead with what they had.

Eva had shown Leon Irene Hunt's name at the bottom of the contact list on Sophie's memory stick. Sophie had contacted her the week after Jackson had disappeared, which made Eva think that maybe the contact had been left by Jackson for Sophie; or that Irene Hunt had tracked Sophie down—but why? The connection between the secret servicewoman and her brother was baffling and, once her anger had died down, Eva was not yet sure whether it was as sinister as it seemed. She had told Leon about Hunt's bizarre non sequitur confession about being involved in Jackson's disappearance—staging the car crash. Leon had barely reacted to any of the information other than an imperceptible cooling of the air around him. As she sat in silence staring out of the window at the rain falling over the suburbs, Eva knew that Hunt was much more wrapped up in any of this than they had first realised.

WHEN DON PORTER was told that the PA of a rather famous journalist had set up a meeting with him for midday he almost bit his secretary's head off. Apart from the fact that he simply didn't have the time to deal with anything other than what was unfolding in front of him— if he wanted to keep his job—he queried what she had been thinking, inviting a journalist out here when there was so much information that they were trying to stop leaking out. The last thing he needed right now was an investigative journalist sniffing around. If he thought he was going to get the inside scoop on this algae mess he had another thing coming—Don could legitimately tell him to get lost and would do so without hesitation.

A complete media shut-down had been put in place to avoid any further scaremongering and all that was being fed to the waiting hacks was the news that the clean-up teams had been sent out to some of the affected areas that morning and had so far made good progress. They had been sent images of the dead algae which had been broadcast across the country and people had begun to go

back to their lives after the panic of the day before. The
phone calls the Agency had been receiving had dwin-
dled in the morning, as everyone was given collection
points for the algaecide and reassured that the situation
was under control.

The reality, of course, was very different. Don knew
from the research of Fred Humphries that the dead algae
was in fact much more dangerous than the live plants.
Due to the cannibalistic nature of the algae, it would
simply grow stronger and more bountiful by feeding on
the corpses of the dead plants. Plus, as each plant died
it released its spores into the air which were carried on
the wind, by animals, even on people's shoes to new watery homes. The more the algae died, the more it would
spread. The algaecide had so far done absolutely nothing to slow the sinister progress, in fact in some areas it
seemed to have speeded it up, and several of the clean-
up team members had reported feeling unwell and had
to leave the site which was a worrying development. Not
only that but they had not been able to get hold of a single
responsible person at the company occupying the premises in Sunbury, which still appeared to be at the centre of the geographical area of the algae explosion near
London. If nothing else they had to get the company to
take algaecide for any open water areas it had within its
grounds. Discussions of their lack of licences and breaking of regulations could wait until this crisis was over.
Don sighed and scratched his head as his phone began
to ring once again. He thought of Fred's over-excitement
when he had reported back to Don on what he had found
inside the company premises they thought was at the
centre of it all: Large pools. Filled with algae.

Eva was thrown violently against her seatbelt as the force of the car hit them on a quiet country road they had taken to avoid heavy traffic. Throughout the two minutes it took to unfold, the only thing she saw as the car flew forwards, spinning out of control, was Leon's hand suddenly appear on the handbrake to her right and yank the stick back. The car immediately pulled up and turned into a violent skid as the brakes slammed down, screeching and screaming and flinging Eva backwards against the leather headrest of her seat. The car eventually came to a halt facing the way it had come.

An eerie silence fell, broken only by the smell of burned rubber.

Eva looked up, her breath coming in raw, rasping bursts. She expected Leon to spring into action but he seemed dazed and didn't move.

Suddenly there was another impact and they were moving sideways, being shunted off the empty public road and in through the open entrance of what looked like a scrap yard. Within seconds the huge powerful vehicle that had hit them had used its bull bars to push their car into the yard. A large metal gate swung closed behind them.

Eva and Leon stayed in the car as the other vehicle reversed and then came to a halt around a hundred metres away from them, between their own car and the metal gate. Nothing happened. The vehicle had blacked-out windows but inside nothing appeared to be moving.

Eva looked at Leon, who nodded over to her left, towards a small Portakabin where the door was opening.

The petite figure of Irene Hunt emerged clad in a long, dark trench coat and a large dark purple scarf. Eva inhaled sharply when she saw her.

Apparently in no hurry, Hunt slowly made her way over to the Land Rover. She tapped on the window and Eva wound it down.

'Get out.' Eva knew Leon had a gun, but he hadn't produced it. Perhaps he didn't feel threatened enough yet. She stepped down onto the rough earth; as her foot made contact with the floor she realised her legs were shaking.

'What are you doing, Irene?' The other woman looked at her.

'I think the more pertinent question is what are you doing?'

'I'm going to assume that you already know.'

'You're taking part in a game that you cannot win, Eva.'

'How are you involved in this?' Irene looked at Leon and then took Eva by the arm and led her towards the Portakabin. Her grip was steely and utterly unbreakable. Eva glanced back to see Leon sitting in the car, his exit being impeded by two armed men who had emerged from the vehicle with blacked-out windows and were positioned on either side of him.

Once inside the Portakabin, Irene Hunt let go of her arm. It was cold and smelled damp inside the metal shell. There was a rough dark blue carpet on the floor, several desks and filing cabinets. Eva noticed a steaming cup of coffee and some kind of wrapped sandwich on one of the desks that she assumed couldn't be Irene's. She wondered how they had managed to take possession of this quiet spot and who had been removed so that they could.

'Sit down.' She glanced at Irene, a hard look. Eva didn't like being told what to do, particularly by this woman.

As Irene Hunt opened her mouth to begin speaking,

Eva jumped straight in. 'I don't understand how or why you were involved in Jackson's disappearance as a teenager but I know that you must have been in contact with him since.' Irene Hunt shut her mouth as Eva carried on. 'I don't like you, Irene. You broke my family apart with what you did with my father, you virtually killed my mother.' Irene stared at Eva with her hard, grey eyes.

'This isn't about you, Eva,' she said eventually. 'It's never been about you.'

'No, it seems as if it has always just been about you.' Unexpectedly, Irene smiled. She let out a small, bitter laugh and then sat down at the chair behind the desk.

'It's not even about me, Eva.' Eva said nothing.

'Sit down,' Irene repeated. Again Eva ignored her.

Irene sighed and took a seat herself. She folded her hands in front of her. 'Your brother had been working for me—since the car accident after which he disappeared.' Eva sat down in the chair opposite. She felt as if her legs might go from under her. 'I...'

'You know I work for the government. So did he. I helped him arrange that accident because he needed to disappear and start afresh. He was supposed to sever all contact with your family and he was supposed to change his name. Things didn't quite go to plan.' Eva was utterly speechless. Apparently Irene didn't believe in breaking news gently.

'When he found out about the affair I was having with your father, Jackson tracked me down and he confronted me. He was dangerously out of control; he had been snooping about in my life—private and professional— and he had too much information so I had him followed. When your father confessed the affair to your mother, Jackson was unable to handle the fall-out. We could see he wanted to escape. So I contacted him and I offered him a way out—maybe to make up for what I had done.'

'So he really did just run away.'

'Yes.' Somehow Eva had been hoping for a more honourable motivation.

'If it's any consolation, I think the guilt pretty much ate him up.'

'It's not.' Irene Hunt didn't respond.

'What happened after that?'

'The effect on him of leaving your family with the extra burden of his mother's death at such a difficult time, the guilt, was immediate. He clearly had not thought it through. Jackson went completely off the rails—drugs, drink, self-harm—you name it, he went there. For a year he kept trying to re-establish contact with you but each time we prevented him. It would have been too confusing for all of you.'

'And you had other plans for Jackson.' Irene stopped and Eva realised she had hit the nail right on the head. 'What was it that you planned to get him to do in return for helping him "escape"?' Irene seemed to realise there was no point in hiding the truth. She pushed her dark, glossy hair behind her ears.

'We offered him an opportunity, that was all. Once we thought he had the emotion out of his system we sent him to one of our drying-out facilities and after several tries he got clean. He then took a year in France on his own to get strong, fit and back together. And then we placed him.'

'You placed him?'

'At the aid agency.'

'What for?'

'There's a huge op we've been working on for a decade.'

'The algae.'

'No. This algae business is low-level. My ex-husband is a policeman in Paris and I had him follow Jackson for several weeks and it became clear that he had become obsessed, that he had entirely lost his focus. We don't want to know whatever you know about it—we didn't want to know what Jackson or his friend Sophie knew. We didn't kill him, Eva. He got distracted by the algae. In this business you have to be able to focus only on your specific task, without taking responsibility for the rest of the world. That's what got him into trouble, he tried to be a hero—the algae story wasn't what we had trained him for, or what he was meant to be in the agency for.'

'What was he there for?'

'Not what, who—Joseph Smith.'

Eva sat up. 'I've heard of him. He was mentioned in a conversation—I was held hostage briefly by a group of Sudanese men, they mentioned his name.' Irene didn't seem in the least bit surprised that Eva had been a hostage.

'It's likely that they would have noticed you because of your connection to Jackson.'

'Did they kill him?'

'We still don't know.'

'But I think they're connected to the algae problem and this information.' Eva went to reach for the stick in her pocket.

Irene Hunt held up one hand. 'They're not—he's not. It's something entirely different. They have only found you because of the connection with Jackson—because he never kept his identity anonymous as we assumed he had done—and you must stop pursuing them.'

'Irene, I think you're wrong.' The older woman's eyes flashed. 'I'm not.'

'So you want me to what…go home?' Irene Hunt nodded.

'I don't think you realise the position I'm in, Irene. I'm being pursued. I've never been attacked so many times in my life.'

'I can't help you with that.' Eva was taken aback. She had assumed this confession meant some kind of assistance might be offered.

'My life is in danger.'

'I'm not a policewoman, Eva. I'm a specialist intelligence officer. I don't have responsibility for individual citizens.'

'And I'm not one of your employees. I don't have to do what you tell me to.' There was silence in the Portakabin. Outside Eva could hear the mechanical drone of a large piece of heavy equipment.

'What do you want then, Eva,' said Irene finally, 'what will make you go away?'

'I want a contact, someone inside government who I can give this information to.'

'And then you'll stop.'

'Yes.'

'Who?'

Eva thought quickly. 'The Secretary of State for Health,' she said. That was presumably the person within the government who might have the most in-depth understanding of the severity of an obesity epidemic.

Irene Hunt didn't reply. She walked outside the Portakabin, leaving Eva to her own thoughts. The conversation had moved so fast that she hadn't really had time to process the information. Jackson, a spy. It was fairly

fantastical but she was kidding herself if she thought
she had ever really known Jackson and instinctively she
felt that there was something to it. When he had reappeared in their lives Jackson had seemed haunted and
none of what he told them ever really made sense. He
was always eaten up with guilt for having disappeared
when he did—although the first time she had seen him
again he had claimed amnesia after the accident, rather
than embarking on a career as an intelligence officer.
Why do we never tell each other the truth? she thought.

The door opened and Irene Hunt walked back in.

'You have a meeting at two this afternoon with the
Health Minister, John Mansfield.'

TWENTY-SIX

For almost an hour their car ploughed through the lunchtime traffic before they finally reached the central London destination. It took them several minutes of circling before they eventually found a space but Leon proved himself to be as aggressive behind the wheel as he was out of it and other cars soon backed away when they saw the enormous dents in the side of vehicle that Irene's 'friends' had made. As they climbed out of the car, Eva stopped and checked her pocket for her copy of the memory stick and once she was satisfied it was there she set off alongside Leon up the busy West End shopping street and away from the throngs, towards the quieter end of Mayfair. Traffic flew past them on the road and all around well-dressed pedestrians were pushing and shoving their way to lunch breaks, shopping sprees and appointments. Eva realised she had not missed the overcrowded streets of London.

Checking the address Irene Hunt had given them as they rounded the corner, Eva led them on to a quieter street, populated by designer shops and expensive coffee houses which opened onto a pretty square lined with gleaming cars. The square had a small park in the middle surrounded by sleek black railings and was edged by red brick houses with Victorian façades and bay windows. They came to a halt in front of one of the most impressive buildings on the square that, if the windows were anything to go by, gave John Mansfield MP access to no fewer than seven floors, including a huge basement kitchen they could see through the lower ground floor window. Eva was surprised that they appeared to be at a private residence, rather than the MP's public office. Was this how a meeting such as this was normally done?

At the entrance they were searched by a single security guard. Once the search was over, a smart assistant in a tightly conservative suit appeared from a door to the right and they were ushered up to the third floor via some plushly carpeted stairs.

She led them to a comfortable dining room, complete with a huge, highly polished mahogany table and giant silver candelabras. On the table were a silver coffee service and a plate of thickly sliced English shortbread covered with a dusting of white sugar.

'Help yourself,' she said, before shutting the door behind her.

As THE DOOR closed Leon moved silently across the room and filled a china cup with coffee. Eva was preoccupied. The conversation with Irene Hunt had left her feeling incredibly uneasy; she felt like she was walking on very thin ice, totally unaware of the cracks that would drop her through to the deathly cold water below. Not for the first time in all of this, she wished that she could speak to Jackson, ask him what he knew, even just to get his opinion on everything that was happening. Knowing that he was simply no longer there still triggered an almost physical pain. That had to be the worst thing about death—there was no way through it to the person on the other side. She had felt exactly the same when her mother had died. You couldn't argue your way out of it, or bully someone out of being dead, once they were gone there wasn't even anything to rail against.

Suddenly the door was opened and in walked a short, smartly dressed man in a well-cut grey wool suit with dark grey hair and narrow, dark eyes.

'Hello,' he said as he reached out a hand to shake Eva's, a smile creasing his well-polished features. He looked very well preserved, thought Eva as she shook the outstretched hand.

'I'm Eva Scott and this is Leon...' She waited for Leon to fill in the blank where his surname should be but he didn't.

Mansfield nodded. 'Please take a seat,' he said, indicating a number of high-backed chairs that matched the dark wood of the enormous dining table.

They all sat, Leon helping himself to the plate of biscuits from the coffee tray which he positioned on the table in front of him, three seats away from where Eva and Mansfield sat opposite each other. He obviously planned to take no part at all in the discussions.

'I'm afraid I didn't get much information from the message I received, but I think the urgency with which this meeting was set up means it must be important?' He sounded slightly tense and Eva was struck by the fact that he apparently had no idea what kind of information she had, but had somehow been convinced to see them—at home—anyway. Was that odd? Irene obviously held considerable influence.

When Eva started speaking, it was with an uncharacteristic lack of confidence. 'My brother works...well, he worked...only that is to say he's...well he's dead. But...' To her horror, Eva heard herself stumbling over her words. This did not happen to her.

She immediately shut her mouth to stop the flow of confusion. Mansfield was looking at her expectantly; she gazed back at him and suddenly realised that she didn't want to tell him anything. She sat there mute, as the atmosphere in the room started to get strained.

Finally, she forced herself to speak. But she chose her words carefully.

'This situation—with the algae—it wasn't an accident.' She looked for a reaction; Mansfield's face registered nothing.

'Although the algae was genetically engineered to be the main ingredient in a health supplement, from the information we have here…' she produced the memory stick '…there seems to be another, rather more sinister motive for the distribution of the algae—a profit motive.' Eva looked over at Mansfield. She was surprised to see that he didn't look at all shocked. Perhaps as a politician he was used to this kind of thing, perhaps he didn't believe her, or perhaps he already knew all about this. Eva had no doubt that governments often had big business's interests at their heart, maybe even to the detriment of the public at large. The question was whether that was happening here or not.

Suddenly he spoke.

'Well, I wasn't expecting that!' Eva smiled tensely and Mansfield shifted in his seat, crossing one leg over the other and studying Eva and Leon's faces in great detail. Eva felt like she was sitting on a knife edge. Had this been a mistake?

'I have to say that if you had walked in off the street and given me this spiel I would have had you committed. We have had quite a few nutters claiming this algae business is a government conspiracy, the first step on the road to Armageddon, that kind of thing.' He smiled as he spoke jovially. 'But as you seem to have the backing of someone rather powerful, I feel like I should at least read these documents.' Mansfield leaned across the table and picked up the stick, examining it as if he expected to see some revelation inscribed across the outside. 'Is this the only one?'

'No,' Eva replied, failing to notice Leon's slight shake of the head. 'Leon has a copy and there is one other copied stick.' Her voice trailed away.

'Of course,' said Mansfield. 'Well, we won't need them all if they're identical.' Mansfield stood up. 'I think I should go and see what this contains and then perhaps we can reconvene to further these discussions?' Eva stood up and smiled as Mansfield pushed his chair back under the table.

'Feel free to use the facilities on this floor or request any refreshments you might need. My assistant will be pleased to help,' he said, indicating the smart-suited woman who once again appeared at the door.

Leon pulled himself to his feet and the two men nodded at each other before Mansfield delivered a corporate smile to Eva and walked out of the room with the memory stick in his hand.

Turning to Leon, she opened her mouth to speak but he got in there first.

'I have to go.'

'What?'

'I have to go.'

'WHAT? Where?'

'There is something I must do.'

'What do you have to do right now that is more important than this?'

'I'm sorry.' He stood up. 'I will be back soon.'

'Leon…' Eva kept her voice low, not wanting Mansfield to hear them.

'Leon.' He didn't respond, but turned away from her. Eva made a grab for his arm. She had to talk to him about Mansfield. During their short time with him, all her bullshit censors had gone off. She started walking after him towards the door, but when she realised he wasn't going to stop, she stopped herself, watching his broad back disappear through the mahogany door frame as he marched away along the carpeted corridor.

Eva's mind began to whir. There had to be a reasonable explanation. She didn't have the energy to stop trusting him again, she needed a fucking ally in this situation. She looked around at the cosy office, reminiscent of a gentleman's club complete with stuffed stags and priceless crystal and tried to calm herself down. The room was panelled on all sides with a dark wood and smelled deliciously of pine furniture polish. It was furnished opulently with plenty of red velvet, gold brocade and extravagant displays of enormous lilies. Rather outlandish tastes for an MP.

Eva gazed at the open door and waited several minutes to see if Leon would reappear. Then she walked over to it and stepped outside. Someone was standing with his back to her at the far end of the corridor, gesticulating frantically, one hand pinning a phone to the side of his head. It was Leon.

TWENTY-SEVEN

'I HAVE THEM, right here.'

'John, I must ask you to destroy the phone I gave you. Or, at the very least, to refrain from calling this number any more. I have already explained our position and now you must take whatever action you need to in order to survive this. But don't call me anymore.' Mansfield was irritated by the CEO's logical, calm tone; as if he were a wise parent giving advice to a panicking child, not a corrupt businessman who had just reneged on a deal that would effectively cost Mansfield his life.

'Wait, you don't understand.'

'I don't wish to have to end your involvement in this with any kind of finality, John.' Mansfield hesitated for a second whilst the implication behind the CEO's words sunk in. For the first time in this whole episode he could suddenly see how much danger he might be in. He was entirely disposable; once he had fulfilled his side of the deal he had very little leverage. Until the appearance of Eva Scott. Thanks to her, perhaps he could save his own skin and get the money that was rightly his. Mansfield took a deep breath and then he started his attack.

'Eva Scott, she's here, in my house.' There was silence on the other end of the line and Mansfield heard the phone click onto hold.

Several seconds later the CEO returned. 'How has this happened?'

'She has a memory stick with documents on—I've looked through it and it's enormously incriminating, it contains a lot of information on the real purpose of the supplements.'

'Have you read it all?'

'Yes. And I can see now that making money from… from fat people wasn't your only motivation.' Silence.

'The algae spreads uncontrollably,' Mansfield continued, purposefully trying to increase the level of aggression in his tone. 'That was never part of the original plan. I'm assuming if investors have asked any questions up to now you have been claiming this was all a mistake, that you never knew the algae would spread like it does.' The CEO said nothing.

'Well, this memory stick proves that's not the case; that you have been using those companies the entire time and you are basically going to make them the scapegoats for whatever it is you are about to do. They won't be happy. We both know what these people would do to you if I passed this information on to the investors.' Mansfield sat back in his chair; he was breathless and his chest was tight. He had never threatened anyone before.

After several minutes had elapsed the CEO spoke. Gone were the polite tones of his cut-glass accent. All pretence at manners had vanished.

'I should have you killed.'

'I wouldn't do that if I were you. You're not in a position to survive if I send this information out. I could do that right now before you have time to action anything.'

'What do you want?'

'I just want what I have always wanted, that is all. I want my money and I want to disappear.'

By the time Leon returned to the room they were to

wait in, Eva was once again composed. She was angry and uneasy but she couldn't bring herself to confront Leon. If she lost him as a collaborator at this critical moment then she would be carrying the considerable burden of everything that was going on alone. He was the closest thing she had to an ally and, even though he behaved erratically, so far he hadn't actually done anything against her interests. As far as she knew. Even so, when he walked back into the room, she couldn't stop herself from looking for some kind of indication that he wasn't who he appeared to be.

'Mansfield isn't back yet.'

'No.' Eva waited to see if Leon would provide an explanation for his quick exit but he took a seat back at the table by the biscuits.

'Why did you tell him there was more than one copy of the stick?' Not only was there going to be no explanation for the disappearing act but there was also criticism for Eva's handling of the situation. She was about to spit out a sharp reply and then she stopped.

'You don't trust him, do you?'

'No.'

'Why not?'

'Habit.'

'Would you like to follow me please?' Before Eva could ask any more questions they were interrupted by Mansfield's assistant. Leon was clearly unnerved at her almost silent arrival.

'We were asked to wait here,' he said, remaining at the table and meeting her glacial smile with a little Arctic charm of his own.

'Mr Mansfield has asked me to take you downstairs

whilst he finishes some business. He won't be long.' Eva looked from Leon to the woman and then back again.

Leon inclined his head slightly, sighed and then pushed himself up from his chair and began walking towards the door.

'Are we going back down to the ground floor?' asked Eva.

'No,' was the reply, 'I'm to take you to the first floor. Mr Mansfield will meet you there. Shall we go?' Eva nodded and the suited woman turned quickly out of the room with Leon behind her.

She was leading them back towards the stairs, her light, trotting footfalls in direct contrast to Leon's heavy, powerful tread. All around them the house was completely silent and still, almost as if waiting to see what would happen next.

'I will leave you here,' she said as they reached the first floor, an altogether less comfortable environment than the plush surroundings of the third. 'If you could just wait in that room over there, third on the left.'

'Sure.' Eva nodded and glanced at Leon who now seemed a lot more tense than he had been up on the third floor. His violent mood swings were unnerving.

Leon stopped halfway down the hall, halting them both just outside the door they had been instructed to go through. Blinding afternoon sun was streaming through the doorway, making it impossible to see what lay on the other side.

He stood motionless, staring at the light as if waiting for something or someone to appear. When no-one did, he took a few paces in front of Eva and stepped through the gap into the light-filled door space. And then disappeared.

By the time Eva had realised the trick the brightness of the light had played on her eyes another figure was already filling the doorway. A slighter figure with quick movements who immediately reached out towards her and took a painful grip of her right arm.

Instinctively, Eva tried to wrench herself away and run in the other direction but the fingers around her arm were like a vice and she felt herself being propelled through into the larger room as if she weighed no more than a feather.

A sick feeling overwhelmed her. This had been a big mistake.

'Miss Scott.'

BLINKING AT THE white spots swimming in front of her eyes, Eva recognised John Mansfield's voice coming from somewhere directly in front of her. As her vision cleared she saw him sitting behind an enormous desk, a huge piece of modern art behind him and indecipherable sculptures framing the desk to the left and the right. He was smiling but the smile made Eva's skin crawl.

She found herself propelled forwards towards an uncomfortable-looking, high-backed chair where she was unceremoniously pushed down onto the cushioned seat and then lashed tight with tape to the arms. As her wrists were tied down, the smell of menthol drifted up into her nostrils. She remembered it from the park in Paris and looked up at the man fastening her to the chair. Black eyes smiled back at her. Hello again, Eva.

A shiver travelled down her spine.

Leon was seated in a similar chair to her right where he was staring at John Mansfield. To Leon's right was a man holding a gun trained on Leon's head.

'Administer it, Joseph,' said Mansfield, his voice shaking slightly. Eva got the impression that no matter how much he might be enjoying his powerful position, Mansfield hadn't done this before.

Her mind began to rush. 'Administer it…' The black-eyed man moved over to a small wooden flip-top desk in the corner of the room. The design reminded Eva of her desk at school but this one was polished and varnished until it shone in the early afternoon sun streaming in through the open windows. He opened the top of the desk and removed a small leather case of the type Eva had seen before in the park in Paris.

She started to struggle in her chair. One of the guards forced her to sit still by punching her in the side of the head and Eva groggily aimed a savage kick at any part of him near enough to reach. She heard him grunt as her heel made contact with his calf and was rewarded with another blow to the side of the skull, this one so hard that it made her head start to spin. She heard Leon protesting and then vaguely registered the sounds of a fight on the other side of the room. Then she felt a sharp pain in her right arm before the dizziness gave way to black.

Tom Chard took Legrand straight to the morgue to look at the bodies of Rob Gorben and Terry Dowler. Legrand spotted and made a note of the red mark on Dowler's right thigh, the result of a needle being inserted under the skin and a substance injected into his body. On Gorben, Legrand could find nothing. He and Chard had turned and turned the body, to the great chagrin of the pathologist who insisted that he had already done this himself and could they please not disturb the corpse, but still they had found nothing. There wasn't even anywhere the injection could have been administered without leaving an obvious mark—the man didn't have pierced ears or tattoos, the skin over his skull was smooth and they had checked every other orifice but there was no sign of anything unusual.

'So, they both died in exactly the same way,' said Legrand as the pair sat down in a local pub with a pint as they waited for their late lunch order of ham and mustard sandwiches on white bread. Legrand looked at his watch. 3pm in London, 4pm in Paris, no wonder he was so hungry.

'Yep,' said Chard. 'Both had the same odd combination of diseases and that same implausible advancement of the conditions.'

'And yet they both seem to have managed to contract whatever it was from different sources.'

'It can't be a coincidence, there must be a link.'

'Agreed,' said Legrand as the waitress delivered two enormous plates of triangle-cut sandwiches lined on the outside with crisps.

'Do you think the second man ingested something?' said Chard, nodding his thanks at the waitress.

'You saw the autopsy report, nothing in his stomach at all. He died in the morning. His wife said he skipped dinner the night before.'

'The only other way it could have got into his system is if he absorbed it.'

'Nothing on the skin.'

'What about his lungs?'

'Youngish man, non-smoker, should have been in peak condition but, according to the report, the lungs were full of scar tissue because of the fibrosis.'

'Bad.'

'Yes. That would have made it difficult to see if there was anything else in his lungs right?'

'I guess so. But they must have taken a sample of the lung tissue.'

'What if he inhaled something?' said Legrand suddenly as the thought struck him. The other man hesitated for a second and then the idea seemed to fall into place.

'We need to speak to the pathologist again. I'll call him now, ask him to go back and check the lungs,' said Chard, retrieving his phone from his pocket and punching in a number.

Legrand took a bite of the thick sandwich and recoiled slightly at the overly soft, unfamiliar bread. He washed the mouthful down with a large gulp of the strange, bitter ale his friend liked to drink and wished he had a baguette and a cold pression in front of him instead.

Everything had taken a rather strange turn and he had an uneasy feeling about the way this case was going. He glanced up at the TV in the pub which was reporting the same disaster he had read about on the train on the way over—the UK being overcome by some strange algae. Given the reported scale of the problem he had been surprised to find such vague coverage in all the papers he had been able to get hold of. Legrand's mother had been a keen environmentalist and after a lifetime of lectures he knew the dangers of water pollution to countries so dependent on fresh water. Surely this strain of algae was a really big deal? But since he had arrived the situation seemed to have calmed. He had received a call confirming his return Eurostar tomorrow and there seemed to be no hint of a water shortage in this London pub.

Chard put down the phone, looking slightly aggrieved, and took a long draught of his drink.

'What is it?'

'I spoke to the pathologist again and he was pretty annoyed with me.' Legrand laughed at the offended expression on Chard's face.

'Why?'

'He accused me of all sorts—telling him how to do his job, accusing him of not doing it properly. He is a very angry man.' Legrand risked another bite of the sandwich, quickly followed by more beer.

'So what did he say?'

'He says he's already carried out a thorough inspection of the skin and there's nothing to suggest any suspicious contact with anything that could have caused the death.'

'And the lungs?'

'Despite the fibrosis he said he got a completely clear picture of what was in them and there was only one thing that would not normally be there.'

'What was that?'

'Algae spores.'

TWENTY-EIGHT

MANSFIELD WAS SURPRISED, and slightly annoyed, when Joseph Smith re-entered his study. The man had no manners and simply opened the door, rather than knocking first. He shut the door carefully behind him and locked it so quietly that Mansfield didn't hear the bolt slide home.

'Are they dispatched?'

'I've sent them with some of my best men. We had a girl to deliver, along with a small consignment and so they have gone on one of our private scheduled flights.'

'Girl?' Mansfield was confused.

'Yes. She will work there for the CEO—if you know what I mean.' Joseph Smith's eyes flashed, challenging Mansfield to be outraged.

Suddenly Mansfield felt nervous. There was no reason for Smith to be telling him this. In fact, passing over such incriminating information about the CEO's business affairs would give Mansfield even more of a hold over him. Mansfield had always suspected that the CEO's organisation sat more on the dirty side of business but he had chosen to ignore it to pursue his own goal of a well-lined purse. But now Smith seemed to be feeding him a story of a 'consignment'—drugs?—and a 'girl'—trafficking? Was he trying to undermine the CEO, looking for another paymaster like a rat off a sinking ship?

'Has the CEO made the payment?' Mansfield just wanted to extricate himself from this mess.

'He said to call him.' Irritated, Mansfield reached for the phone. He had done his part now—twice—and he expected to be paid. He was a government minister and he still held considerable power—no matter what the CEO thought, there was action he could take if the payment wasn't forthcoming this time.

He entered the pass code into the slim metal device and watched the screen light up. Out of the corner of his eye he noticed Smith moving around the room, handling Mansfield's precious objets d'art. The other man stopped at the small wooden flip-top desk that had been Mansfield's school desk at Eton, which still had his initials carved into the side above the leg. On a sentimental whim Mansfield had offered the school an obscene amount of money for the desk and then later regretted it, but looking at it now he realised having it in his office was a constant reminder of what had been the happiest days of his life.

He was about to tell Smith to stop playing with it when the CEO answered the phone and all Mansfield's attention was focused on the sound of his voice.

'Well done, John. We are most grateful.'

'It was a pleasure.' Mansfield said, his voice hard and flat to disguise the nerves that were flaring at every ending.

'And they are on the plane.'

'Yes, they left with your…consignment.' After momentary consideration, Mansfield had concluded that he had been taken somewhat into the CEO's confidence when Smith had imparted that information. He wanted somehow to convey to the CEO that, as long as he upheld his end of the bargain, knowledge he held about the CEO's business dealings would remain confidential.

The CEO ignored him.

'Where are the memory sticks?'

'Joseph Smith has them all.'

'Very good work.'

'And the girl's phone?'

'That too.'

'What about my payment?'

'It is being arranged.'

'I don't have long before I need to be on a plane out of here.'

'Don't worry, Mansfield, you won't be around to take the flak.' Mansfield smiled. Finally, he thought. 'I'm glad we could bring this to a satisfactory conclusion.'

'So am I.' At that moment Mansfield realised Joseph Smith was standing right behind him, but it was too late to move before Smith plunged the needle into the back of his shoulder. The shock of the impact forced Mansfield to drop the phone and his arm was completely immobilised as Smith drove the plunger home.

Stunned, he tried to stagger to his feet, but Smith— the stronger man by far—pushed him back down into the chair.

He silently pulled the syringe from Mansfield's shoulder and began methodically putting it back in the medical case he had left on top of the flip-top desk.

Mansfield leant forward on the desk. He realised he was struggling for breath.

'You can't do this to me. I am a member of Her Majesty's Government. I know things!'

Smith turned and smiled. 'Do you know what was in this?' he said, holding up the case.

Mansfield shook his head. 'Whatever it is, they will trace it. They will know this is murder.'

'Trust me, they won't,' smiled Smith. 'You will be just one of many.'

GROGGILY, EVA OPENED her eyes. Pain immediately seared through her frontal lobe so she shut her eyes again to stop the strip-lighting burning into her retinas. The air around her was cool, air conditioned and odourless and she could hear a low hum like the noise of a loud refrigerator. She struggled to place where she was or how she had got there but she couldn't. She remained for several minutes with her eyes shut, taking deep breaths and keeping herself calm so that her brain could attempt to form pictures of the journey that had led here. As she started to feel her body come to life again, she instinctively went to move her hands up to her face to rub the points on her head that hurt so much; her hands wouldn't reach. She tried to move her legs but they too seemed stuck fast. She opened her eyes and looked down at her body. She was tied fast to the arms and legs of an aeroplane seat.

EVA TRIED NOT to panic. She pulled at the tape fixing her hands to the armrests of the chair but she was bound tightly. Looking around, she appeared to be on a small plane with wide padded leather seats in rows of two on either side of a narrow aisle, stretching ten or twelve rows forward. She could see that the front four rows were occupied, four dark heads resting against the soft leather headrests of the plush seating. This had to be a private plane, she realised, it was too small to be a commercial flight and there was no way they'd have been able to tie her up like this if it was. She looked for Leon and spotted another dark head, this one tilted to one side as if asleep, two rows in front of her on the left-hand side. Then she remembered the needles at Mansfield's house and her heartbeat began to soar again. Had she been injected with the same thing that had killed the man in the park? Or had it just been the sedative they must have used to knock her out? She took a quick inventory of her limbs and tried to work out whether she felt any different to normal. There was no way of telling at this point.

Suddenly out of the corner of her eye she saw Leon's head move; he was awake. Eva watched carefully as Leon's head movements showed signs of him beginning to come round, taking in his surroundings and then registering the ties at his hands and feet. He struggled briefly and then stopped. How short-sighted to try and secure him with this flimsy tape, she thought, remembering Leon's powerful arms. She glanced at the heads of the men at the front but they didn't seem to have noticed the stirring eight rows back and were busy drinking a round of whatever a girl with a bright platinum dye job had just deposited in front of them. The woman turned away from Eva back towards the hospitality area of the plane. She was wearing a tiny, tight shiny dress and her hair looked messy; Eva saw a flash of bright red lipstick, as the woman struggled back into the cockpit on a pair of ludicrously high, spiked heels.

Eva turned her attention back to Leon who was now perfectly still. She noticed he was staring intently at a huge widescreen TV positioned slightly above the seat in front of him. The screen was some distance away from him because of the extensive leg room of his seat and he was leaning forward and peering into its darkness. Eva realised that because he couldn't turn in his seat and risk attracting attention, he was using the screen to try and see who or what was behind him. Smart.

Now, she had to get his attention.

As Leon continued to stare at the screen, Eva slowly shook her head from side to side. As she did so the hair that had hung down either side of her face fell back revealing the flat gold studs she wore in her ears. She moved her head again and noticed a tiny pinprick of light on Leon's screen as it reflected off the flat surface of her earring. Leon tensed. She moved again. Leon continued to stare intently at the screen. Once more Eva moved, turning her head one way and then the other. This time Leon was completely still. He had seen her.

But what now?, she thought. Where were they even going? She glanced at the men at the front of the plane, wondering if they would be able to give her any indication, but she could only see the sides of two of their faces and the others were just heads on headrests. She looked down at her bonds and once again tried to pull her hands free but to no avail. Then she glanced back in Leon's direction; he wasn't there. Quickly, she scanned the cabin, wondering where he could have disappeared to in such a tiny space and hoping that he was not going to leave her fastened to the chair whilst he took on four armed men. Her eyes roamed the area where he had been sitting. The only place she didn't have a clear view of was the floor.

FRUSTRATED AT NOT being able to communicate with Leon, Eva began to focus on getting herself free. She watched as the blonde woman reappeared in the cabin at the other end of the plane, glancing in Eva's direction as she did so. Eva quickly shut her eyes. She waited for the woman to report that one of the prisoners was awake; nothing happened. The men at the front of the plane continued to talk and the volume of their voices rose as suddenly Eva heard the slap of a hand against skin. She puzzled over the sound but remained still with her eyes shut as the men's voices rose further, this time in jeering tones. From the reckless noises they were making, the men were clearly drunk. Eva listened carefully but they weren't speaking English and she had no idea what they were saying. Suddenly she heard a thud and then a female gasp. Gradually, cold fingers of awareness plucked at her consciousness.

Eva opened her eyes, stared down at the tape around her wrists and realised that if she could bend herself down as far as the armrests she might be able to rip the tape with her teeth. These men had obviously been told their two prisoners would remain sedated until their destination or why else would they have been so poorly secured?

She started to bend forward slowly, not wanting to make any sudden movements lest she draw attention to herself. Because she had been positioned in the last row of seats, there was a wall behind her which meant her seat had less give and less room for her body to move backwards as she bent her head forward. She shifted her body slightly to the left and then continued inching her face down towards her right wrist until her lips made contact with the tape. She bared her teeth and then felt around with her tongue for a rough surface she could grab hold of with her teeth to pull the tape apart. Then all she would need to do would be to quietly rip the tape and she could use her free hand to unbind her other wrist and feet. There was now much more noise from the front of the cabin. Eva glanced up through her hair but all she could see was that three of the men were all looking in one direction, whilst the other seemed to have disappeared. Suddenly Eva heard the tearing of material and the woman cried out. She felt her stomach flip with unease.

THEN SUDDENLY LEON was crouched in the aisle opposite looking over at her. He put one finger to his lips, signalling she was to remain quiet, and then glanced briefly down the aisle. The men were busy and presumably, from what they were doing, it had clearly not even crossed their minds that their prisoners might be awake. Staying low, Leon crawled quickly across the aisle and then he was beside her. She sat up and he squeezed past her so that he was inside the row of seats and then slowly and excruciatingly painfully, peeled the tape from her wrists, taking the hairs around the top of her hands with it. Then he did the same with the tape around her ankles, which was an easier job as it was wrapped around the fabric of her jeans.

When Eva was free, she spread her hands in an open gesture and in response Leon produced a gun.

Eva drew back in surprise. How on earth had he managed to get that? But he shook his head denying her any explanation. Eva frowned at him. He mouthed the words 'trust me'. Her heart began to hammer in her chest. What was he going to do? She nodded in the direction of the woman and the men at the front of the plane. Help her.

Leon rose up on his haunches and leaned in so close to her ear that his lips brushed the soft skin of one of her lobes.

'Stay here,' Leon whispered, 'and stay down.' Eva stared at him. Was he really going to take on four no doubt armed men on his own? On a plane?

He stared back at her, dark eyes boring into her face.

'STAY. HERE,' he repeated, mouthing it this time. Before she had any time to respond he was crossing the aisle to the seats on the left hand side, fast and agile. Eva ducked down from the seat and positioned herself up against the wall in the cavity created by the seat to her right and the seat in front of that. Then, realising she couldn't see what was going on, she shuffled forwards on her hands and knees almost to the end of the row and laid her head on the floor. She now had a view of the aisle and the seats on the left-hand side all the way to the front but she couldn't see the seats on the right. At the front of the cabin there were noises of a scuffle and Eva could hear small gasps escaping from the woman. The male laughter continued. As she was forced to listen, Eva felt a stab of anger inside her rising to the surface. It wasn't difficult to work out what was happening.

LEON WAS NOW crossing the aisle once again so that he was in the seats behind the two occupied rows. In front of him were the four men he would have to dispose of, three still seated and one on the floor with the woman. The wisdom of firing bullets in a pressurised cabin fleetingly crossed Eva's mind but she had no time to vocalise her concerns because Leon had sprung into action.

From her position on the floor, Eva watched as Leon quietly drew his weapon then quickly stood and fired into the top of the head of the man two seats to the right in the row in front of him, and then shot a second man sitting further away through the ear. A splattering of blood and bone flew into the air from the two dead men and the other seated man who was directly in front of him leapt to his feet. Eva briefly wondered why Leon hadn't chosen to shoot that man first, and then as that man felt for his gun, she realised it was in Leon's hand. Leon shot the weapon-less man in the chest as the other on the floor, who had quickly buckled his trousers, suddenly sprang forward and chopped his hand down viciously on Leon's wrist sending the gun flying to the floor. Leon launched himself at the man, making contact with his shoulder and sending both of them flying to the floor. Eva's heart was in her throat as she saw Leon land a bone-shattering punch on his opponent who was now underneath him but by no means beaten——with the strength of an ox he flicked his pelvis up and launched Leon over his head. The half-clothed woman ran for the cabin and disappeared through the curtain and, as she did so, suddenly Eva realised that there could be other people on the other side of that divide. She assumed Leon had considered that and concluded there was no way he could know how many, so he would have had to take the chance that there was no-one else who could come to the other man's aid. If he was wrong, they were in imminent danger of being overwhelmed.

Then Eva spotted the gun that Leon had dropped only four rows in front of her.

She remembered his instructions to stay where she was… Glancing quickly up at Leon who was now facing the cockpit, held from behind in a headlock by the man he was fighting, Eva pushed through a paralysing moment of panic and then began to crawl out from behind the shelter of the seats and along the aisle floor towards the gun. She was now completely exposed. If anyone armed came out from behind the curtain they would simply shoot her. She crawled faster towards the gun and then looked up as another crash sounded from a metre in front of her, where Leon had thrown his attacker against the curved wall of the aircraft and was pulling him up to head height, preparing to head-butt him. She heard the blow delivered and then her hand was around the handle of the gun. Stand up! Suddenly she was on her feet. At exactly the same moment another man in a white shirt emerged from inside the cockpit and threw himself on Leon's back, trying to pull him away. Eva ducked down behind the nearest row of seats with the gun, watching as the newcomer locked his elbow around Leon's neck and then Eva heard a gurgling sound as Leon started to choke. Leon clawed his hands around the first man's neck and suddenly Eva saw a flash of steel. Leon's original opponent had a fruit knife that must have fallen from the drinks table the two had felled when they started fighting and was turning it in his hand preparing to use it on Leon. Eva had only a split second to decide what to do. She didn't have a clear shot at the man with the knife and risked hitting Leon instead, but if she aimed at the man on his back, she realised she might distract Leon, giving his armed attacker the opportunity to stab him.

She stood, raised her arm and aimed the gun at the man in the white shirt. Time had run out.

She fired.

LEON, SURPRISED BY the shot, turned his head towards Eva as the man who had been choking him from behind fell back lifelessly to the floor. Then a look of confusion crossed his face because the other man had also fallen away and was screaming, blood pouring from his left

hand. The knife he had been holding tumbled noiselessly to the floor and, as it fell, Leon noticed the flash
of the blade. He looked from the blade to the gun in Eva's
hand. Had she shot them both? Eva stared at the situation in front of her, completely confused. Suddenly the
platinum-haired woman stepped fully into the cabin, an
industrial-sized knife in her left hand, wet with blood.

Without any warning she flew at the man who had
held her down on the floor only ten minutes earlier,
once again stabbing at him with the enormous knife. He
screamed like a child as the blade sliced into the tender
flesh of his thighs and he tried to throw her off, but she
dug long nails into his left arm and held on, stabbing out
with the knife in her right hand.

'Stop! What are you doing?' he cried out in shock as
she stabbed him again in the other thigh, the serrated
edge of the sharp knife cutting through the expensive
fabric of his suit like butter and tearing agonisingly at
the tissue and skin of his legs.

She screamed and she stabbed out again. 'You bas-
tard.' Another huge fountain of blood spurted up into
the air as she severed the femoral artery in his thigh.

Recovering from the shock of the attack, the man suddenly found the strength to punch her in the face and
the woman reeled back, stumbling as she fell out of one
of her vertiginously high heels. But she was back upon
him again in seconds, her bloodied face twisted into an
expression of utter hatred. 'You fucking worthless bas-
tard,' she spat, baring her teeth like a wolf and lunging
at him once again.

HE HELD HIS arms up to protect himself from the huge
blade she was wielding and she took the opportunity to

push the knife underneath his raised arms and stab him straight through the heart. Shocked at the strength of the tiny woman as the blade went right through him, the man stared at her unbelievingly before slumping back against the wall and sliding down onto the carpeted floor. He made a grab for the gun in the waistband of one of his fallen men, but his life was ebbing away.

He slid further down the wall of the aeroplane and the woman advanced towards him. She raised the foot on which she was still wearing her one remaining shoe and just before he fired the gun at her chest, she brought the spiked heel down hard, piercing him straight through the eye.

Suddenly the cabin was silent.

Eva and Leon stared, shocked at the bloody scene before them. Eva ran to the side of the dying woman but it was too late. She gently shut the woman's eyes and then pulled herself into a seat as her head was spinning. She closed her eyes; she could hear Leon checking the other corpses, using the huge knife to make sure no threat remained. She felt the bile rise in her throat.

For several minutes she sat in the darkness listening to the butchery. When she opened her eyes, Leon was gone. Eva looked around and noticed the curtain through to the front of the plane was drawn back. The door to the cockpit was open.

She looked at the silent figure leaning on the back of one of the two empty seats and looking out of the small cockpit window. 'Where's the pilot?' Leon indicated back into the cabin and Eva turned and suddenly noticed blue and gold epaulettes on the white shirt of one of the men lying in a pool of his own blood.

Vertigo suddenly engulfed Eva's brain. They were 40,000 feet in the air.

'The autopilot is flying the plane,' said Leon quietly.

'Can an autopilot land a plane?'

'Some can.'

'And this one?'

Leon turned and looked at her. 'I hope so.' Eva leaned against the wall of the plane as nausea threatened to overwhelm her once again.

'It depends on the Instrument Landing System equipment that this plane has and it depends on where we are going,' added Leon as if to try and provide some comfort.

'Do you know where we are going?'

'We are almost there.'

'Where?'

'Paraguay.'

TWENTY-NINE

THE CEO WATCHED as the small plane taxied to a halt on the private runway he had built in the tri-border region of South America. He had specifically chosen this strange, uncivilised area in between the land masses of Argentina, Paraguay and Brazil because it had a reputation for lawlessness, attracting smugglers, terrorists, drug traffickers, arms dealers, and organised crime figures from across the world. But it was also large enough to become lost in, which is exactly what he had done. A year ago he had sold March Properties, a company he had used as a cover in Paris, staying on as director for twelve months, meeting clients, going to the office to maintain his profile and monitor the company he had anonymously set up—Bioavancement S.a.r.l.. March Properties had rented to Bioavancement S.a.r.l. the Parisian land on which the company was based—making it a client of March Properties—so it was quite normal for him to be on the Bioavancement S.a.r.l. premises.

With the money from selling March Properties, he had found this plot of land just east of Ciudad del Este on the Argentinian side of the border, far enough away from any populated areas to discourage trespassers but close enough to take advantage of weak government and pervasive corruption in these South American states. He had paid a series of bribes to the authorities for the land and bought influence among leading legislators, police, criminals and judges to secure his privacy. Then he had built himself a low, highly fortified cattle ranch that went deep underground, positioning the buildings on the surface so that they were surrounded on all sides by thick green foliage, virtually invisible from the air. Inside, the ranch had the feel of a gentlemen's club and hunting lodge with a high tech specification, although the décor changed considerably the further down the levels one went. On the scorched dusty brown earth of his 'back garden' was his own runway, big enough for the two Global Express XRS long-range jets he had bought with the money he had accumulated during four years siphoning off from March Properties and which he used to ferry him to and from Europe. One of which he was now staring at with a creeping sense of unease.

He signalled to the head of security he employed, who had taken up a position near the small building that had functioned as an airport terminal for the arrival of the small, elite team of mercenaries and ex-agents the CEO had been instructed to purchase and train for situations such as this. The man nodded and, moments later, ten black-clad figures had taken up positions around the plane. The pilot had not responded for the past two hours. It could be that everyone on the plane was dead and the autopilot had made the landing; or it could be something else. Either way, something wasn't right. The CEO stared into the thick heat of the sultry air as the plane remained motionless. It was another pitch black Paraguayan night. In the distance they could hear the thundering from the Iguaçu falls, or Yguazú as the locals called them, 2.7 kilometres of 270-feet-high falls created when an angry god sliced the river in two after his lover ran off with a mortal, condemning the lovers to eternal falling. The CEO liked the swift and merciless justice of the story and admired the ruthlessness of the god. If only the exercise of power and revenge really was that simple.

On the runway, everything was still and they waited.

Finally, the stairway opened and a figure appeared at the top of the stairs, a woman wearing a tight, ripped dress.

He was about to request her identity from his security head when she suddenly seemed to raise a dark object that looked a lot like a gun and instantly one of the CEO's well-trained agents put a bullet between her eyes.

INSIDE THE PLANE, Eva jumped back as the woman's body slid and then landed heavily at their feet on the floor of the plane.

She looked at Leon. He had lashed the woman loosely to a hostess trolley they had found in the hospitality area and wheeled her to the open door to see what kind of opposition they faced. It had been a useful move but one that had sickened Eva. As if her body hadn't been abused enough.

Leon leaned carefully back into the cockpit and looked out of both sides of the angled windows, then returned and shook his head. 'They're clearly armed and uncompromising. I could see at least five armed men out of the cockpit and there must be more out front as well.'

'So what do we do?'

'We capitulate.'

'Are you serious? We don't even know who we're capitulating to.'

'If we go waving a white flag we have some chance of survival.' Eva stared at him.

'Think about it, Eva,' he said quietly, taking a step towards her and looking down into her dark eyes. 'They must have brought us here for a reason or they would just have killed us in London.'

Eva had already thought of that. 'Yes, but what for?'

'Obviously it's something to do with the information we had.'

'But neither of us has the information any more. It doesn't make sense.'

Leon shook his head. 'Look, we need to move. If they don't shoot us on sight—which I don't think they will— then we still have a chance. The longer we stay on here the more likely they are to come in and get us, at which point it becomes a fight.' Eva glanced to her left at the butchery they had created in the cabin. She'd had enough of all the corpses.

'Fine.'

'I'll go first.' Before she could argue, Leon had dropped his weapon and stepped into the open doorway of the aircraft with his hands in the air. He started down the steps to the ground and was immediately thrown to the floor on his front as men in black secured his wrists, hauled him to his feet and then trained their weapons on to Eva.

As she reached the last few steps she was lifted off them by an arm on either side and propelled down to the bottom where she was also thrown onto the ground with her hands behind her back. She gasped as the rough tarmac peeled the skin off the end of her nose. As her wrists were fastened behind her back, she heard the click of expensive shoes on the runway and looked up to see the figure of a man walking towards her. She was dragged to her feet and held fast between her captors on either side but she couldn't help the exhalation when the moonlight illuminated the face in front of her. 'You,' she breathed, looking up into a face she hadn't seen since her escape from the alleyway in Paris.

AS IT TURNED OUT, Legrand and Chard weren't the only ones to have noticed the link between the algae and the unexplained deaths that had been occurring in the UK. When they had arrived back at the station there had been a message about another death and a relative waiting for them. A man, the boyfriend of one Alana Srisai, a woman of Thai origin who lived in an area some thirteen miles west of London, in a frantic state of shock and grief. The man had received a distressed phone call from his girlfriend, left work and been forced to break down her door when she didn't answer it. He'd found her on her bed, her body twisted at an unnatural angle, an expression on her face that he described as 'terrified'. Shortly after that had come the death of Dan King, a tall lanky youth who had been found by his mother in his death throes and rushed to hospital. It hadn't taken much digging for Legrand and Chard to uncover that both the victims had been a part of a clean-up operation the previous day, that both had been sent home early feeling unwell and that neither had been wearing masks.

'This is terrible,' Chard said as they sat in his office waiting for a call back from the regional head of the Environment Agency that had organised the clean-up. 'That stuff is fatal.' Legrand nodded. 'But where has it come from?' The phone rang and Chard snatched the receiver, confirmed the caller as Don Porter and then flicked the phone onto speaker.

'Don, I've got with me here a colleague of mine, Inspector Legrand from the Préfecture de Police in Paris.'

'What's he got to do with this?' Porter sounded angry, exhausted and at the end of his tether.

Legrand ignored his aggressive tone. 'Mr Porter, I have had several murders in my jurisdiction which I think may be linked to events that are currently occurring in yours.'

'Oh?'

'Yes. It relates to the algae, I believe the algae may be highly toxic.'

'Have you told anyone?' A note of panic appeared in Porter's voice.

'No. We needed to speak to you first.'

'Why?'

'Where are the algae coming from?' asked Chard, butting in and ignoring Don Porter's question.

There was a hesitation on the other end of the line. Porter was reluctant to admit how long it had taken him to figure this one out and that inefficiency would become obvious if anyone asked him why they hadn't yet taken action against the company in question. 'It's an old waterworks in Sunbury, twelve miles west of London. Set up by a company called Bioavancement S.a.r.l.. No active clearances, no permits, nothing, they just appeared,' he exhaled crossly. 'We only broke in there in the last forty-eight hours,' he admitted, 'but we found huge pools—raceway pools I believe they're called—all filled with the stuff.'

'And you think this is the source of it?'

'Well, the source of it in my jurisdiction, yes.'

'What do you mean?' Legrand was impatient.

'This is not the only part of the country affected.'

'Do you know the algae could be toxic to humans?'

'Our tests haven't been conclusive about that so far.'

'What did you learn about the locations of the algae?'

'There are installations just like the one in Sunbury located in at least fifty other spots across the UK.' Silence. The two men looked at each other as the full extent of what was unfolding began to crystallise.

'You mean, this stuff is everywhere?' said Chard, 'I thought it was a localised London problem.'

'Oh no, Mr Chard, haven't you seen the news? The entire country is choked with it now.' After they finished the phone call Legrand and Chard spent several minutes just staring at each other.

'Why didn't you tell him about the virus?' Legrand asked, referring to the algae spores that seemed to be the cause of the deaths. A virus had seemed the most sensible label for what was being spread by the algal spores as the plants died.

'I got the sense he wouldn't handle it well. Besides we need to contact someone much higher up.' Legrand nodded. 'I'm going to call my ex-wife.' He reached for the phone.

THIRTY

EVA WATCHED A smile play around the edges of Daniel 'March' Marchment's lips as she was fastened into a chair next to Leon, inside one of the buildings that made up Daniel's ranch. She had not seen him since that night in Paris when he had dragged her into an alleyway and tried to rape her at knife-point. Seeing his face as she had looked up from the tarmac had been a complete shock. Here, suddenly, in the middle of this anonymous mess was a link both to her own life and to Jackson's. It made her wonder how much more there was about this situation that she had missed.

They were now deep underground and the 'olde worlde' shooting lodge atmosphere of the upper floors they had glimpsed when they arrived had been replaced by bare concrete with rough edges and functional furniture. Eva was strapped down to a metal chair bolted to the floor.

It had taken two of Daniel's men to get her into the chair but there were now four fighting to get Leon sedentary.

'Oh please,' said Daniel regarding the failing men scornfully. He walked over to a metal workbench, grabbed a small gun and shot it into the exposed skin at the nape of Leon's neck. Immediately Leon's body went slack.

Eva looked at Daniel.

'Relax, it's just a sedative. 'I'm sure we can find a more imaginative way to get rid of him.' He smiled.

Eva was unresponsive. She was trying to figure out what was going on and how—and why—Daniel had become involved in this.

'What is this, Daniel? I don't understand how you are caught up in this situation.'

'I'm not caught up, silly girl, I created this!'

'But why?'

'Well now that you're here, I may as well tell you all about it.' He seemed inappropriately, alarmingly jovial, which scared Eva much more than if he had been trying to threaten her.

The room was cleared apart from Daniel, the man who appeared to be his second-in-command, an unconscious Leon and two armed guards who stood absolutely still.

Daniel pulled a chair up in front of Eva, but just out of reach, and leaned in as if he were about to tell her a bedtime story.

'You might be wondering why you're here.'

'It was you who had Jackson killed, wasn't it?'

Daniel stared at her, his blue eyes cold. 'No,' he replied sharply, 'I did not.'

'I don't believe you.'

'Believe what you like.'

'After what you tried to do to me in Paris, I imagine you're capable of just about anything.' Daniel recoiled in mock horror. 'Oh come now, Eva, you were just in the wrong place at the wrong time. I needed you to leave, that was all—that seemed an effective enough way to encourage you to go crawling back home.' He stared at her, challenging her to talk about what he had tried to do that night, sensing her discomfort. She wouldn't give him the satisfaction of vocalising it.

'Fuck. You,' she hissed.

Unexpectedly, Daniel's face creased in anger and he stood quickly from the chair and threw it across the room. The crash when it landed made Eva jump violently.

Daniel stormed back across the room and he was looming large in her face.

'Your brother did this,' he spat, great drops of spittle landing on Eva's skin.

She stared at him, a cold hatred settling in the pit of her stomach.

'He did nothing to you.'

'He is responsible for the way all of this has nearly come toppling down on me, he is always trying to undermine me. If it wasn't for him and that woman Sophie then all of this would have been flawless.'

'All of what.'

'This…' He raised his hands and looked upwards towards the sky, which was of course the ceiling of the enormous bunker they were in.

'You're killing people for money, Daniel, that's all you're doing. It may not be the same as cutting their throats with a knife but by feeding them those supplements the result will be the same. There is nothing elevated or clever about this,' she mimicked his gesture, 'you're just a common criminal.' Daniel's face had turned a violent shade of pink. She sat and waited for a physical blow, a sharp retort or an explosion of words but he just stared at her as his expression gradually settled to a smile.

'Well then,' he said, almost laughing now, 'seeing as you have such a low opinion of me, that will certainly make this moment so much sweeter.' Eva stared at him, the satisfaction she had felt in insulting him seconds before disappearing as a deep sense of foreboding settled over her.

'What do you mean?' Daniel walked over to her, ripped off the right arm of her jumper and pointed at her bare skin. Eva craned her head and bent her right elbow out at a right angle so she could see what he was pointing at. Two angry red welts sat side by side on the flesh of her upper arm. She had felt her arm aching but assumed it was just the injected sedative.

'What's the second one?'

'What do you think it is?' Eva blanched.

'Is that how you killed Jackson too?'

'Oh stop going on about him, Eva,' said Daniel, angry again.

Eva looked again at her arm. 'If this is the same substance as in the syringes in Paris, why am I not dead?'

'It's slower acting, less potent. I need you infected but I need to time it with an engagement I have tomorrow morning at 5.' Eva stared at him, lost for words.

'You just don't get it do you?,' he said, laughing at her. Then, seeming to lose interest, he walked away from her and towards a large bench that contained three stacked monitors and several layers of computer equipment. He began tapping into the keyboard and then moving some of the equipment around. Finally, he produced a small hand-held camera on a tripod and positioned it in front of her.

Eva looked at the camera; she began to feel very nervous. She glanced over at Leon but he was still out cold.

Daniel left the equipment and walked back towards her.

'Don't worry, this is all for later.'

'Later…?'

He started to walk away again and then stopped as if something important had occurred to him. 'Would you like to know why all this is happening?' Eva said nothing.

'Well, I'll tell you anyway. I own a company called Bioavancement S.a.r.l.—heard of it?' He laughed. 'My company has signed a deal for supply and delivery of pools full of algae—lovely harmless algae—genetically engineered in our factory in the Sudan to produce a ground-breaking health supplement. With me so far?' Eva remained quiet. He was going over old ground and he knew it.

'Of course, what your little adventures have uncovered is that this supplement is part of a money-making scheme of mine that has involved collaborating with several rather well-known pharmaceutical giants to make a little extra profit and to exercise a little power. As you may or may not have seen, this supply and delivery has already taken place—rather earlier than agreed—and the UK's waterways are now well populated with our algae.'

'Presumably you didn't tell them about how quickly the algae would spread—these pharmaceutical companies. I can't imagine they would have signed up for the PR disaster you've created for them.'

'No,' said Daniel, 'we didn't tell them that. Neither did we tell them how it is resistant to every algaecide on the planet,' he continued helpfully, 'except of course the one we have here,' he said, indicating the room around him.

'But surely anyone can manufacture an algaecide?'

'Well, that's where this little plant is so clever because it is designed to hide its own genetic structure. Without knowing the genetic code, you'd never be able to make a guess at how to kill it, even a very well-educated one.' Eva suddenly remembered the document she'd read on the memory stick that confirmed what he was saying.

'The other very clever thing about the algae is that it has been programmed to be a carrier.'

'What for?'

'A virus, Eva.' He nodded at her arm. 'A virus we have developed, the virus that my Sudanese friends used on several victims in Paris and the virus that will eventually kill you. Now this, I don't believe was in the documents you have seen.'

'You can't put a virus into a plant.'

'No, that's quite right. But this algae is genetically engineered, Eva, and we have engineered it to hold the virus. At least until it dies.'

'But the algae is everywhere. You're going to infect hundreds of thousands of people.'

'Millions, I should think.'

'Why have you been injecting it into people—why try and inject it into me in Paris?'

'It seemed logical to use it as a weapon. A gunshot or a knife would attract so much attention but the virus, well that would take much longer for anyone to figure out the cause of death and attribute it to murder—if they ever did. Besides, when it comes to the crunch, the more people already dead or dying from the virus, the more desperate the need for the vaccine, and the more leverage I have.'

'Leverage?'

'Leverage.' He smiled at her and Eva felt convinced she saw a flicker of insanity dance across his eyes.

'I suppose you'll use the vaccine for the virus and the algaecide as a bartering chip.'

'Right. Although that's not the only leverage I'm looking for.'

'What do you mean?'

'There are…other interests involved in this. I can't take all the credit unfortunately.'

'Other interests.'

'Yes. I need the leverage that I have in mind with them to secure my future career.'

'You can't possibly have a future career after this. If what you're saying about the virus is true you've done much worse than profiteering.'

'It will blow over. Until it does I'll simply disappear— for a while. Change my identity. It would be easy to get lost in one of the three countries bordering this lawless region and there are some excellent plastic surgeons here who specialise in giving people like me a new lease of life.' His eyes flashed. 'All you need is money these days, Eva, and you can do anything.'

THIRTY-ONE

ALONE IN THE holding cell with an unconscious Leon, Eva thought about what Daniel had said. People were so fragile and so complicated. How had someone she had known with grazed knees and a conker collection turned into such a monster. Eva pulled her ripped jumper further around her as she stood leaning against the wall. Daniel had locked them into a windowless cell with only a metal cot and a toilet furnishing the bare, concrete room.

IN THE CORNER, Leon began to stir on the metal bed. Eva glanced over at his huge form as the sedative began to wear off. He murmured quietly in his state of drugged semi-consciousness and Eva noticed his fists were clenched. Suddenly he sat up, swung his legs over the bed and took two enormous steps across the room. He paused for a second and then lunged at Eva; picking her up by her neck, he flung her against the wall.

'Leon!' He stared blankly at her and continued to tighten his grip on her neck.

'Leon!' Eva clawed at the fist clamped around her throat with her left hand but he continued to squeeze his fingers around her airway, his eyes unseeing. Suddenly, Eva realised he wasn't even awake. She raised her free hand and slapped him hard around the face, with as much force as she could muster.

Immediately, his eyes focused. He looked confused.

Then he released Eva's neck and she shoved him away from her.

He looked at her, uncertain.

'I'm sorry.'

'Jesus, you nearly strangled me,' she said rubbing her throat.

'Eva, I'm really sorry.' He took a step towards her.

She held up the palm of her hand, indicating that he should keep his distance.

Leon retreated back several steps and sat down on the edge of the metal cot he had been lying on minutes before. He rubbed his face with his hands and then looked up at Eva.

'Why don't I know how we got in here?'

'Daniel shot you with something—another tranquilliser, I imagine.'

Leon frowned. 'What else have I missed?' Eva sighed, walked over to Leon and sat down on the metal bed next to him. She rubbed her neck and glared at him.

'Eva, I'm s...'

'Yes, I know.' Eva didn't enjoy the fact that, as a woman, she was genetically programmed to be physically weaker than Leon. She didn't want to be reminded of it.

'I still can't really figure out why Daniel is involved in this,' she said after several minutes of silence.

'How do you know him?'

'He was a friend of Jackson's from school. I...well, I met up with him when I first arrived in Paris, when I was looking for information. He wasn't very helpful.' She willed him not to ask her anything else about that encounter.

'What happened to your arm?' Eva followed his gaze

to where Daniel had torn off her sleeve. 'Daniel also developed the algae to carry a virus,' she said quietly, still looking at her arm. 'It was the same thing that I injected into the man in the park in Paris—that they tried to inject into us. That was what killed him in that awful way.' Leon continued to stare at her and she watched his face as the realisation dawned on him. Eva looked at the floor. She didn't want sympathy. 'Check your arm,' she said, suddenly looking up. He put one hand up the sleeve of his jumper and felt the area at the top of his arm. He gazed back at her. 'Only one mark.' Eva dropped her gaze to the floor again. Why only her? Slowly, she raised her eyes and looked at Leon. He was flexing his arms, trying to bring full sensation back to his muscular body after the effects of the sedative.

'Leon, who are you?' He looked at her surprised.

'I mean really, who are you?' He didn't reply.

'Every time I ask you a personal question you dodge it and I still don't know what you do or how you came into my life,' she continued. 'I want to know why you have been helping me—what's in it for you?' Silence filled the inhospitable room.

'I don't think you have anything to lose now,' Eva said, indicating the mark left on her arm where the virus had been injected.

Leon gazed at her for a second then shook his head and sighed. He rubbed at his wrists where the plastic bonds had been.

'I'm a mercenary,' he said finally.

'A…what?'

'A gun for hire, a contract killer, a thug.' Eva wasn't surprised that he didn't work as a bank clerk or a gardener. But neither had she been expecting that.

'I don't understand—what does that actually mean?'

He looked at her, as if to try and understand if she was joking. When he realised she wasn't he continued. 'People hire me to do things for them—things which aren't necessarily within the law—kidnapping, warnings, tailing, occasionally termination if the money's good enough.'

'Did you kill Jackson?'

'No.' He seemed affronted. 'We were kindred spirits, I would never have done that.' Eva got up and walked over to the other side of the room, running her fingers through her long hair.

'How long have you done this for?'

'Ten years. I used to have an intelligence job but I have…episodes. They have made it difficult to hold down a career like that.'

'Episodes.'

'Times when I need to lose myself. That's how I met your brother—in rehab. We both seemed to suffer from the same need to escape.'

'Into drugs and drink.'

'Yes.' He looked at her defiantly. She stared back. Once she might have judged Leon for this obvious weakness, but not anymore. It was frightening that someone would just allow that to be their life on an ongoing basis—normal life with periods of self annihilation—but who hadn't done it to some degree or other?

'Look, I'm sorry…' she began.

'It's the life I've chosen,' he interrupted, 'I'm good at what I do and I earn a lot of money. Don't be sorry.' They looked steadily at each other for several seconds. It was time to talk about something else.

'OK, Valerie,' said Eva suddenly. 'I overheard the conversation you had with her at her flat that day. You knew her.' Leon shook his head and sighed and then dropped his head into his hands again. He clearly didn't enjoy being put on the spot.

'We worked together,' he said meeting her gaze once again.

'You mean she was the same as you?'

'I don't know.' He looked up. His eyes were huge and dark, his pupils massively dilated from the chemicals in his system.

'I mean, obviously I recognised her immediately when Jackson introduced me to her. We had worked together and she got several of our team killed by changing the agreed plan on one of the jobs to protect her own interests. In fact, I never really found out if she wasn't working for two parties at the same time. Her behaviour then triggered the episode after which I met Jackson.'

'So you knew what she was?'

'Look, Eva, I had a vague idea but people change you know. Jackson seemed so happy with her and at first I couldn't figure out whether she was still that person. She even told me that she had left all that behind her—all the deceit. Of course, she hadn't.'

'What do you mean?'

'About three months after Jackson introduced me to her, I think she became scared that I would tell Jackson what I knew about her. She asked me to meet her in a hotel one night to talk about the old times, to set it all behind us. She offered me a "pick me up", we drank, I should have seen it coming.' Leon looked genuinely pained at this point. 'She got me so high I was out of my mind and then we slept together. The next day I got a message telling me she had recorded the whole thing and, if I ever mentioned it, she would tell Jackson I tried to seduce her. She sent me this edited version of what she had and it really did look like that was what I had tried to do!' He laughed bitterly. 'Clever bitch. After that there was nothing I could do other than watch. Those photos I showed you—I took those during one of my "surveillance" missions. I couldn't talk to Jackson about it but as soon as she made that tape I knew there was something wrong with the situation so I started keeping tabs on her. I don't know if she knew I was on her case but she didn't step out of line, not even once—it was confusing, I couldn't decide one way or the other. But when Jackson disappeared…I knew she had to be right at the heart of it.'

'Do you think she killed him?'

'I still don't know. I thought she might have, until she was attacked by the men who took you. Why do that?'

'A cover? They were working for Daniel.'

'And for Joseph Smith also. Valerie's the only loose end…'

'I should have done more you know,' said Leon, interrupting her. 'I could have done more.' His head was in his hands again.

'I don't know, Leon.'

He looked up suddenly. 'I could,' he said aggressively.

'So why didn't you.'

'Jackson changed a lot, Eva. In the last few months before he disappeared he was like a different person. I thought he was using again.'

'What happened?' Leon dropped his gaze from hers and stared at the floor.

'The signs were all there as far as I was concerned. He was going on about all these crazy theories—he said he couldn't tell me the details as it was confidential, but that there was danger, so much danger—and some kind of murder plot. He told the same stories as when I met him in rehab—different details but the same kind of tales of being pursued by killers and being almost like a spy. I just felt like he was fantasising about his being in danger because he was using drugs again—it seemed to feed a really dark side of his imagination.' Eva remembered what Irene Hunt had told her about Jackson's recruitment. Leon was much closer to the truth than he realised.

'What did you do?' Another pause.

'Nothing.'

'But don't you think he needed your help?'

'Eva, you have to understand, I was so angry with him. We had made a pact to stay clean—other than Valerie's interference I had been free of it all since rehab—and it was a promise to each other I thought we'd never break. I needed him not to break it. When it seemed that he'd done just that I…I just couldn't bear to be around him anymore.' Eva tried to be sympathetic but such sentimental weakness from a man like Leon….it was hard to believe there wasn't more involved. And she found it interesting that he took no responsibility for that night with Valerie, that whatever he had taken was not his fault.

'So did you find out if he was using?'

'Yes.'

'And was he?'

'No. But by the time I knew it was too late.' Eva looked wearily at Leon. Could he have saved Jackson?

'I had my own demons, Eva. I had to stay away from him. I didn't want to get sucked back in.' Eva nodded slowly. What was the point of going over it now anyway, it was all just far too late.

But Leon didn't stop talking. It was almost as if he felt the need to confess. 'The night before he disappeared he called me and he left a message saying he had to see me, a matter of life or death. He sounded distraught, frantic.'

'What did you do?'

'I met him like he asked and that's when he started talking about protecting Valerie and Sophie. He left me this list of instructions and contacts for Sophie—at the time I didn't even know who she was so it seemed crazy. He was nervous, sweating, too hyper.'

'And that convinced you that he was using again.'

Leon nodded. 'It seemed so ridiculous—I mean, the things he was saying sounded ridiculous. Even though I knew what I knew about Valerie, the details of what he was claiming—which we now know are true—were so fantastical and the details he gave me were so disjointed. At the time, it didn't seem possible that the threat I thought he was imagining could be real.' Eva said nothing.

Speaking seemed to take all Leon's energy out of him. He stood up and walked to the other side of the cell, where he sank down to the floor with his back against the wall and just stared into space. Eva didn't ask any more questions. She felt torn between sympathy for him and anger that he might have saved her brother's life. But she was weary; and he was only a flawed human being just like everyone else. The conversation had at least been informative. Now she understood his connection to Valerie, his violent, erratic behaviour and the strange, unstable air that surrounded him. Perhaps he'd had an 'episode' in the time she had known him—it would fit with the way he swung so quickly from crazy to sane.

But that didn't change anything for her right now.

She laid her head against the cold metal of the bed and shut her eyes. She thought of the virus that occupied her body. She felt like clawing her skin off to try and get to the poison. She was living on borrowed time and she had no idea how much.

THIRTY-TWO

'WAKEY, WAKEY, RISE and shine!' Suddenly Daniel was at the door to their cell and it was being unlocked by one of his men. 'Time for your starring role, Eva,' he said, laughter dancing in his cold, blue eyes.

Leon jumped up straight away, but maintained his distance when Daniel produced another tranquilliser gun.

'Bind her hands again,' Daniel said to the man nearest to him who proceeded to carry out the orders, leaving Eva once again immobilised.

'And him.' Daniel pointed to Leon and then kept the tranquilliser aimed at him until he was completely tied up. Then they were taken into another grey room with rough-edged walls, high ceilings and an enormous skylight, under which a large screen had been set up, as well as a table supporting several computers. In the middle of the room was a single chair with the video camera in front of it.

'If you'd like to take a seat there,' Daniel said to Eva, indicating the chair as if she had a choice. Eva's heart began to sink. Slowly she sat down on the chair in front of the camera and tried to compose herself. She wondered how she should be feeling in this situation. She felt oddly calm.

Daniel gave an instruction and the screen in front of them flipped to life revealing four conservatively dressed men, three white, one of African origin. All were in the grip of middle age, but they were well-preserved, expensively suited and two had recent tans. They were sitting around a curved conference table and all four wore the same acorn pin that Eva had seen on Daniel's jacket in Paris. Two of them flinched when they saw the set-up.

'This was meant to be a private discussion,' said the man sitting on the far right, a standard white male of average height with brown hair and a large pale face. 'We've warned you before about this.'

'Are you talking about her?' Daniel laughed. 'Oh don't worry about her, she won't be a threat to you. Have you seen the news?'

'Yes.' This time one of the tanned men in the centre answered. 'Congratulations. Four years of development have certainly paid off.'

'But we have seen no evidence of the virus,' said the first man again. 'You know that was the main purpose of this exercise.' Exercise? Eva was trying to work out who these people were and what they were talking about. She couldn't place them and now she couldn't understand how they were involved or what the aims of an 'exercise' might be.

'Who are they?' she asked, figuring she had little to lose by speaking up.

He spun around to face her. 'Be quiet,' he hissed right in her face. 'This is my moment.' The four on the screen stared implacably at the camera, waiting for him to continue. They seemed to view Daniel in the same way as one might a petulant grandson with a science experiment.

Eva felt incredibly confused.

'Ah yes, the virus, the final piece of the puzzle—the pièce de résistance, if you like,' Daniel said theatrically.

'Will you tell them about it or shall I?' Daniel was looking at Eva as he spoke. She stared back at him.

'Oh very well then,' he said holding up a syringe.

Eva gave a start. She looked quickly down at the two
marks in her arm. If she had already been injected with
the virus then what was in that syringe?

'This, my friends, is the virus we have developed at
your request. It delivers a blow to the body that none
have yet survived—a combination of two diseases of
old age, one of which weakens every muscle in the body,
including heart and diaphragm, until they just give up.
And the other which rapidly fills the lungs with fibrosis, or bodily tissue, until there is no longer any space in
the victim's lungs for her to breathe.' He turned to Eva,
jabbed the needle into her arm and drove the plunger of
the syringe down to the hilt. She closed her eyes as she
felt the liquid disperse under her skin.

'Eva here has already been injected with a fatal dose
of this clever little virus, but until two seconds ago she
had, oh around,' he checked his watch, 'four hours to
live.' Eva met Daniel's gaze. He was almost salivat-
ing with anticipation. 'Now, however, with this additional shot of concentrated PX 3—and this is just for
your benefit, gentlemen—she has around four minutes.'
He dropped his hand to his side and smiled down at
Eva in satisfaction. 'I've never seen this live before,' he
whispered, 'I'm looking forward to the show.' Then he
winked at her.

Eva was overcome by nausea. She opened and closed
her bound fists. Four minutes… 'This virus you are
about to see in action is being carried by the algae that
is currently populating the UK's water systems. As soon
as the plant dies, it releases spores and once the spore is

inhaled, the victim begins their journey towards death. It can take an hour, it can take several days, depending on the number of spores inhaled. There are just a few cases in the UK at the moment but we anticipate a flood by tomorrow night.'

'And clearly you overcame the issue of plant virus transfer to humans.'

'This isn't a plant virus, it's a human virus. The plant spores have simply been genetically engineered to be the carrier.'

'Impressive.' Daniel walked around to the other side of the table and pulled out a small case with an acorn symbol on the side.

'Now there is an antidote to this virus, my friends— as you requested—and I have that right here,' he said, flipping the side of the case open to reveal around 20 syringes. 'And this is where I have deviated slightly from the plan.' Eva watched the faces on the screen.

'I've never understood why ACORN wanted to stop this epidemic when it was just getting going and…well I'm not really minded to help you do it. I know you wanted this,' he held up the case, 'as a bargaining chip for yourselves, but first of all it's going to be mine. In order to get your hands on it you're going to have to give me what I want.' There was a pause. The faces of the four men gave nothing away; in fact they didn't look shocked at all, almost as if they had been expecting this. Seconds later, the man with the pale face spoke once again. 'What is it that you want?'

'I want your oil interests,' said Daniel triumphantly. 'All of them.' The four men exchanged glances.

'I have a list here of the oil fields I'm interested in,' he waved a document at the screen, 'and this is being emailed to you now. The transfer will be all legal and above board. The prices are not quite market value but you're really not in a position to argue. Everything is prepared, all you have to do is sign on the dotted line. You have until she dies to think about it,' he said, indicating the chair Eva was strapped into.

Eva could feel her eyelids becoming uncontrollably heavy.

'Shouldn't take too long,' continued Daniel, 'probably just under two minutes now,' he said, looking at his watch. 'So gentlemen, what do you say?' Eva could feel changes in her body exactly along the lines that Daniel had described. A sudden tightness gripped her chest. She tried to draw in a breath and began to choke. The muscles in her throat seemed so relaxed that she was unable to speak. Then she realised she could no longer hold her head upright. Her body began to slump forward.

Somewhere in the distance Eva heard one of the men speak.

'And you're certain this is the direction that you want to take, Daniel?'

'One hundred per cent.'

'You have no interest in being part of our ongoing organisation?'

'No, I don't have the patience to play the long game—not for Kolychak or the rest—I want out.'

'We thought you might say that.' Suddenly a brief burst of gunfire echoed around the enormous concrete room. All Eva could see through her half-shut eyelids was her own legs and she was shocked when a scuffle broke out next to her that resulted in her being toppled in her chair and landing face down on the floor. She determinedly instructed her legs to kick out but, try as she might to move her lifeless body, she couldn't. She could no longer even shout, she just stared mutely at the ground in front of her face, struggling for air as her lungs filled up with scar tissue. Suddenly there was a sharp jab in her right thigh. Had she been shot? Eva felt her eyes roll upwards. Her entire body was numb but her brain was alert and in panic overdrive. She was trapped in a corpse.

Then unexpectedly some feeling began to flow back into her limbs. A hotness burned around her mouth and ears, travelling around the back of her skull and down her body to her toes. She was flipped over, released from the chair and she was on the move in Leon's arms.

He deposited her behind a metal desk at the side of the room that had been pushed over to create a cover and pulled out a gun.

'What the hell is going on, Leon?' Eva said croakily.

'I just saved your life,' he said, indicating the box of antidote vaccines, from which one was missing.

THIRTY-THREE

FROM BEHIND THE metal desk Eva had a clear view of the man she knew as Joseph Smith—the man who had injected her at John Mansfield's flat—holding a gun to Daniel's head in front of the large video monitors. Around the room all of Daniel's men lay dead or dying and others—presumably Smith's men—had taken their places. Tremors of shock travelled through her as she looked uncomprehendingly at the scene. She waited to see what would happen but for several seconds nothing did. Had Joseph Smith not been working for Daniel? How had he got here from London?

Eva sat up and rocked forward on her haunches, forcing the feeling to flow back into her body.

Suddenly Leon pulled her around to face him. He began to speak quietly, urgently, his words tumbling over each other.

'Eva, listen to me. Everything I've told you is the truth. I am who you think I am. Remember, I just saved your life.' He shoved something into the pocket of her jeans and Eva realised it was her phone.

'What?' Eva didn't understand what he was saying and started to back away from him but he grabbed the front of her jumper and pulled her to her feet.

'She's here,' he said and started dragging her out from behind the table and towards Joseph Smith.

'Leon, what are you doing!' She kicked out at him and he slapped her hard around the face.

'Don't struggle, you will only make this worse.' He pulled her across the room with him until she was standing next to Daniel. She looked over at him; he was deathly pale, sweating and shaking almost uncontrollably. Suddenly his eyes widened as without warning Joseph Smith fired the gun into the top of his head.

Eva stopped breathing. She was covered with Daniel's blood. She screamed and fell backwards; Leon caught her and she pushed him away, stumbling and trying to right herself. Her breathing accelerated, hyperventilating.

'Why is she still alive?' She heard one of the men on the screen muttering. 'Take care of her—not there. Take her to the Falls. This station must be destroyed. Get that vaccine distributed—and the algaecide. That fool has nearly ruined everything.' Eva was confused and utterly terrified. One side of her brain tried to make sense of who was doing what, why they were doing it and why no one seemed to be on the side that they should be. She caught a nod between Leon and Joseph Smith and the two men began pulling her back out of the room once again. Smith was also dragging Daniel's corpse, a bright red smear marking the floor behind them. Eva looked the other way. She tried to make eye contact with Leon but he refused to meet her gaze.

She was confused by what he had said to her behind the table—was he going to try and help her? He's a mercenary, she reminded herself. He told you that himself. He is his number one priority and he will always side with the winning team. Eva stopped struggling.

She allowed the two men to carry her back to the surface and followed them mutely to a huge jeep, an open-roofed vehicle with sleek, black slides. The night had become cool, there was virtually no sound other than the thud of boots on the dusty ground. Eva could smell sewage. She wasn't sure whether the air was permeated with it or whether Daniel had soiled himself before he died. Leon took Daniel's body from Smith and began strapping it into one of the back seats. Smith pushed her flat against the side of the car and bound her hands. Then he dragged her around to the other side of the car and shoved her into the front passenger seat. He pulled a metal bar across her that fastened like a fairground ride, pinning her to the seat. She pushed against it with her arms but it didn't budge. Smith's dancing black eyes smiled back at her. 'I think this time your luck has run out.' Eva didn't respond. What could she say? It felt like he was right.

In the front seat, Leon climbed in, tucked a huge rifle in beside him and started the car. Smith climbed into the back seat beside Daniel's body and the car took off at speed.

ONCE THEY WERE out of the barbed wire surrounds of the ranch, the landscape was flat and heavily wooded and Eva looked around at what she imagined might be her last moments. In the distance the sun was beginning to rise and spectacular streams of pink and orange were spreading across the sky.

Eva kept her gaze focused on the rising sun. Then she shut her eyes and listened to the sound of the wind, the sound of her breath and the sound of her heartbeat. It was steady and slow.

When she opened her eyes again the sun was now

rising at speed and awe-inspiring countryside was flying past them on either side of the car. Suddenly they
pulled into a skid. She looked over at Leon. He was shaking hands with Joseph Smith who had jumped out of the
car when it stopped and run around to Leon's window.
'Seventeen minutes,' the other man said before turning
away. By the side of the road on which they had stopped
was a sign that said Iguaçu Falls. Eva vaguely recognised the name as somewhere in South America. She
watched as Smith crossed the empty road and climbed
into a waiting vehicle.

Slowly, Leon drove their car down the track to the
Falls, before turning off onto a maintenance road which
was strewn with rocks and rubble. Eva could see what
looked like a sheer drop on the other side of a row of
trees and a flimsy barbed wire fence. They were not
right at the edge of the Falls, but from the noise they
could not be far away.

At the end of the road they came to a halt. To their
right, Eva could see in the distance one of the Iguaçu
waterfalls car parks. In front of them a rocky slope that
led down to the water below, with a sheer drop at the end.
The thundering noise from the nearest part of the Falls
was loud now and the water was fast moving. Strapped
into her seat like this the drop did not look survivable.

EVA TURNED AND stared at Leon, her eyes burning a hole
in the side of his head. She said nothing; she wasn't going
to beg or plead with him. But inside she felt robbed of
her judgement—had she trusted this man? She had never
really known him but now it seemed that the real Leon
was even further from who she thought he was. But had
she really ever known he was trustworthy? Eva realised

that no, she hadn't known that, she'd never been in a position to do anything other than go along with him, whether she trusted him or not. But she certainly hadn't seen this coming.

She laughed softly to herself and Leon glanced up, surprised. He quickly looked away.

She watched as he parked the car at the front of the ramp then took the keys from the ignition and threw them out of the window.

THAT WAS WHEN she struck. Eva had managed to flip her body sideways in her seat as Leon threw the keys and now lashed out suddenly, kicking him in the side of the face with her left leg and then kicking down hard on the handbrake release and then the brake itself with her right so that the car began to roll down the hill with both of them in it. Leon recovered quickly and tried to fight her off but she had entangled his seatbelt in her legs and he couldn't free himself and reach past her for the handbrake at the same time.

'Move your foot from the handbrake, EVA!' He screamed at her, but she continued blocking him, the handbrake fast down as the car began to pick up speed.

'EVA, MOVE YOUR FUCKING FOOT,' he sounded utterly terrified.

'EVA!'

'Unlock this bar, Leon,' she shouted back, indicating the device keeping her in her seat. He looked at her.

'Unlock this bar or I swear we both go over that fucking cliff.' Without a second thought Leon reached forward and pressed a button on the dashboard and the bar sprung from Eva's chest. The car was metres from the edge of the drop, when Eva released her door handle and threw herself out. At the same instant she felt the car jerk slightly as Leon pulled up the handbrake but the forward momentum continued. She landed hard and continued rolling down the slope until she managed to pull herself to a halt.

Ahead of her the car had reached the edge of the incline just as the handbrake finally brought it to a skidding stop. Slowly the car turned so that it was side on to the drop. It teetered for several seconds on the brink. Eva looked for Leon but she could no longer see the driver's side of the car as it was so far over the cliff. Thick foliage held the vehicle suspended for several seconds before the weight of the machine drove it over the side of the drop.

THIRTY-FOUR

IRENE HUNT TOOK a short sip of her tea. They were sitting in the plush surroundings of The Wolseley on Piccadilly in London. Eva had finished her plate of scrambled eggs and was two-thirds of the way through her second coffee.

SHE HAD RECAPPED for Irene how she had run from the scene of the crash back to the car park and hidden until the first tourist bus had arrived. Through those three hours she had looked continuously for Leon but he had not appeared, even though she had kept a careful watch on the path he would have to have taken if he had made it from the car before it fell. She had approached one of the tour operators as soon as their passengers were off the bus, claiming to have been kidnapped and mugged. Without her passport and with her obvious injuries there was great concern and, as the bus-load of German tourists returned from viewing the Falls, it was decided that they should take her to the tour company's headquarters in Iguaçu. There she had contacted the British Embassy in Lima who had flown a representative to meet her and to whom she had told a carefully patched-together story about where she had been held and by whom. They had found Daniel's ranch with enough evidence of smuggling and murder to make her story believable but the place was empty of anyone with a heartbeat and ransacked by the time they got there. Then Eva had put in her call to Irene Hunt leaving only two words in her message: 'Joseph Smith'.

As it turned out, two policemen—one of whom happened to be Hunt's first husband—had identified one of Joseph Smith's fingerprints from the flat in Paris where Eva had found the dead red-haired Englishman, and had provided that, along with evidence they had apparently already uncovered about Daniel's algae, virus and all, to Irene.

And then the algaecide had appeared and an antidote was delivered, the name of the donor organisation—the Association for the Control Of Regenerative Networking—known only to those who could be relied upon to keep their mouths shut.

'The government paid a fortune for it,' Irene Hunt had told her. 'That company forced them to pay an enormous premium. I've never heard of such large figures going through unofficial channels.'

'Who were they?'

'Of course there was no time to check them out properly. Some faceless front no doubt.'

'Was that all they wanted then—money?'

'It would seem that way, yes.' Eva thought of the four men she had seen on the screen deep underground in Paraguay. Daniel's reference to their organisation's 'long game' made her feel convinced that there was more to it than simple financial blackmail. What had their 'exercise' been and was that the end of it? She had mentioned these questions in her debrief but there was no apparent enthusiasm to pursue them. 'You don't seem particularly shocked by this.'

'Little shocks me anymore,' said Irene.

The waiters came to clear the plates and Eva finished off a glass of water and then her coffee.

'I want to know the truth about Jackson,' she said when the table was empty.

Irene looked up at the unexpected question. 'I told you, we still don't know what happened to him.'

'Not that.'

'Then what?'

'I don't think you told me the truth about why he came to you. I still don't believe he would ever have left our family like that without a good reason—my father's affair wouldn't have been enough for him to abandon me and my mother. It's not his style.' Irene Hunt looked down at her tea—lemon, no milk—and then finished it.

'Eva, you would be best advised to let this drop now.'

'Why, because the powers that be want me to, or because you do?' The other woman looked at her hard and for a moment there was a screen of hostility between them.

Finally, Irene sighed. 'Because I do.'

'Why?' When Irene responded, she spoke quickly, as if she felt ashamed. But her face wore an expression of great relief.

'After the affair with your father things were very difficult for me, Eva. Granted it was a situation of my own making, but nevertheless it was not easy. You saw how badly it affected Henry. He was a new relationship, my first since my last husband, and we were held together by a very fragile thread. If I hadn't been pregnant at the time I wouldn't have seen him for dust. I still sometimes feel he has yet to forgive me.'

'Why did you do it?'

Now Irene was uneasy. 'I don't know, Eva, why do

we make any of the mistakes that we do in life—never consciously. At the time, I was in an environment where I was struggling. The Lebanon was not an easy place to be, especially for a western woman. I needed comfort and that came in the form of your father.'

'But it went on for such a long time.' Irene pushed her cup away. 'It was intense. When we returned it felt like no-one else really understood what had happened—that can push you closer to someone and create an artificial need for them like you wouldn't believe.' Eva didn't say anything. For once she felt some sympathy for the situation Irene had been in, particularly after the way things had unfolded with Leon.

'When Jackson came to me, I helped him—because he helped me. I doubt you know this but he was already running from Daniel Marchment. Just a week before the affair was exposed your brother witnessed Daniel take a crystal decanter to a woman's head on a boat in St Tropez. It was a rape gone wrong—apparently Daniel had a habit of taking what he wanted but this time the girl had resisted. When her body washed up on Pampelonne beach Jackson confronted Daniel and that was when his father weighed in and threatened Jackson. Daniel's father is someone we had been watching for some time—although we have never been able to catch him, we know that he has long been associated with criminal networks, and most recently with the Russian gangs taking over the French Riviera. When our microphones picked up your brother telling that man that what his son had done shouldn't go unpunished—followed by Marchment's death threats—we unofficially recruited Jackson in return for offering protection. I helped him fake his own death and he began as a semi-official employee, a disposable asset to be used in volatile situations.' Eva frowned.

'I had agreed with Jackson to contact your father,' continued Irene, 'and tell him the truth but then the affair blew up and I was so angry about the effect it had on my marriage I never did. And then when you turned up at my house…I just wanted you to go away. I couldn't bear for all that to be resurrected once again. Guilt is such a very powerful emotion.' She paused.

'I'm aware that I made an enormous mistake allowing who you were to stop me taking the information you had about the algae. I have let my emotions cloud my professional position. I'm not sure my career will survive it.' Eva noticed Hunt didn't actually apologise.

'But what about Jackson, why didn't you listen to him?'

'By that point he had become discredited. His information was coming from someone we thought we knew to be a false source and he was behaving incredibly erratically. His file is full of his escapades into narcotics and it seemed fairly clear that this was the road he had once again gone down. In the end we cut him loose. It's not particularly admirable but as far as the powers that be were concerned he was entirely disposable.'

EVA LEFT IRENE Hunt at The Wolseley and took a walk through Green Park. It was a bright morning, cold air but blue skies, her favourite kind of December day. She had time to kill and thinking to do after the conversation with Hunt.

She decided to go and get a coffee.

Seating herself in the window of a chain coffee shop across from the park, Eva ignored the looks from passers-by staring at the injuries on her face and gazed out at the street. It was mid-morning and all around people were rushing to their everyday lives. Tourists were taking pictures and paying overinflated prices for bus trips, lovers were kissing, sharp-suited business people were taxiing to meetings. Everything around her was normal. Nice and normal. She smiled to herself and sipped her strong coffee. A newspaper lay on the next table so she picked it up and began to read. The headlines trumpeted the defeat of the mystery algae, giving full credit to the government for developing the algaecide, and naming John Mansfield as the government representative responsible for the disastrous Bioavancement S.a.r.l. deal. The article said he had been found dead in his home, apparently from a heart attack. But there was no mention of the virus. Instead the algae story had been pushed to the second page by a scaremongering article on a new strain of bird flu—something no-one could be blamed for specifically. Everyone was to be vaccinated and the article listed vaccination muster centres and help-lines for those infected. My God, Eva thought to herself, are we never to be told the truth?

AS SHE WAS sipping her coffee and making her way through the rest of the day's news she felt a gentle vibration in her bag. She opened it, pulled out her phone that Leon had returned to her in Paraguay and held it in her hands. Her eyes came to rest on the lit screen. Suddenly her body was alive with adrenaline. She stared at the phone, eyes wide in disbelief as the letters of the display flashed up again and again.

'Jackson calling.'

* * * * *